# Praise for the Secrets Series

Immediately absorbing and brimming with intrigue. With plots that keep the reader breathless and richly detailed settings in ancient Egypt, these books truly captivate. A must-read series for upper middle-grade adventure lovers.

— Michelle Kadarusman, author of *Music for Tigers* and *Girl of the Southern Sea*

A satisfying adventure for ancient Egypt's many fans.

— *Kirkus Reviews*

A thrilling story from start to finish. Sesha is a great character in a thrilling mystery.

— Kevin Sylvester, author of the Neil Flambé series

A magical series of ancient mystery and heroism that will endear readers.

— B.R. Myers, author of *Rogue Princess* and the Nefertari Hughes Mystery series

Readers will love this impossible-to-put-down adventure!

— Alice Kuipers, author of *Me and Me*

Sesha reminds me of Katniss Everdeen in her bravery and keen mind — she's a protagonist kids will be talking about long after they finish.

— Angela Misri, author of the Portia Adams Adventure series

The lure of ancient Egypt, a plucky heroine and an exciting quest combine in an irresistible, fast-paced adventure that will draw readers in and keep them entranced until the very last page.

— Joyce Grant, author of *Sliding Home*

Sesha's adventures will sweep readers across deserts and into the duplicitous world of Egyptian royalty.

— Colleen Nelson, author of Governor General's Award–nominated *Harvey Holds His Own*

The heroine is smart, brave, resourceful, and persistent, the stakes grow ever higher, while palace intrigue and wild romps through catacombs supply all that an adventure-loving reader could desire.

— Pam Withers, award-winning author of *Stowaway* and *First Descent*

A fantastic adventure series that appeals to both children and adults, Alisha Sevigny's Secrets of the Sands transports the reader to ancient Egypt with impeccable research … Will keep you racing through the pages.

— Lee Matthew Goldberg, author of the Runaway Train series

Woven with mystery and intrigue, this middle grade tale will create a new generation of Egyptology fans!

— Melanie McFarlane, author of *There Once Were Stars*

# THE ORACLE OF AVARIS

**Secrets of the Sands**

*The Lost Scroll of the Physician*
*The Desert Prince*
*The Oracle of Avaris*

SECRETS OF THE SANDS

# THE ORACLE OF AVARIS



ALISHA SEVIGNY

All characters in this work are fictitious. Any resemblance to real persons, living or dead, is purely coincidental.

Publisher and acquiring editor: Scott Fraser | Editor: Jess Shulman
Cover designer: Laura Boyle
Cover illustration: Queenie Chan
Printer: Marquis Book Printing Inc.

**Library and Archives Canada Cataloguing in Publication**

Title: The oracle of Avaris / Alisha Sevigny.
Names: Sevigny, Alisha, author.
Series: Sevigny, Alisha. Secrets of the sands ; 3.
Description: Series statement: Secrets of the sands ; 3
Identifiers: Canadiana (print) 20210300264 | Canadiana (ebook) 20210300280 | ISBN 9781459744356 (softcover) | ISBN 9781459744363 (PDF) | ISBN 9781459744370 (EPUB)
Subjects: LCGFT: Novels.
Classification: LCC PS8637.E897 O73 2022 | DDC jC813/.6—dc23

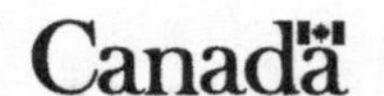

Canada Council for the Arts Conseil des arts du Canada

We acknowledge the support of the Canada Council for the Arts and the Ontario Arts Council for our publishing program. We also acknowledge the financial support of the Government of Ontario, through the Ontario Book Publishing Tax Credit and Ontario Creates, and the Government of Canada.



Printed and bound in Canada.

Dundurn Press
1382 Queen Street East
Toronto, Ontario, Canada M4L 1C9
dundurn.com, @dundurnpress

Wherever the art of Medicine is loved,
there is also a love of Humanity.
— Hippocrates

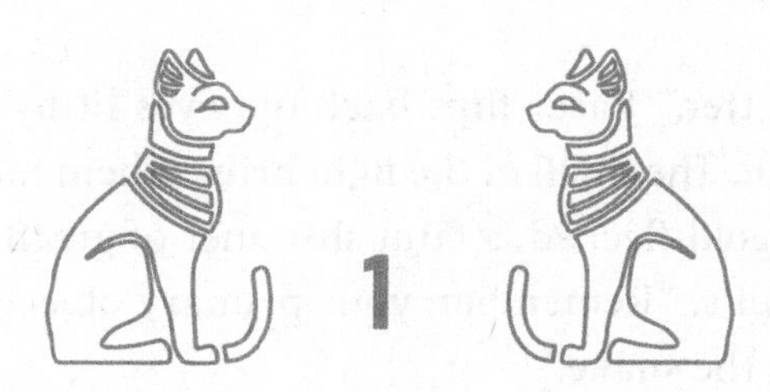

# 1

THE KNIFE WHIZZES through the air, missing my face by a cubit.

"Disarm him!" Reb hollers, the ship's massive sail billowing behind him.

I duck, then dodge again, as the dagger slashes at my torso in an X attack.

"Light on those toes, Sesha." Paser circles me, pointing the obsidian blade at my feet. "Envision yourself a temple dancer."

"Your health seems much improved, Paser," I pant, backing up toward the boat's stern, eyeing the weapon in his hand.

"I had a great doctor." He grins, then lunges again. I sidestep his arm, whirl to grip his elbow, then administer a couple swift jabs to break it — were I applying actual force — followed by a blow to the chest, sending him mock-sprawling to the freshly scrubbed deck.

"Better." Paser flips back up, eyes lit by the setting sun. The thrill of the fight brings them into sharp focus; gold-flecked, a faint shimmer of green ringing the pupils. "Remember, your primary objective is to defang the snake."

Hands on my hips and breathing hard, I lift a questioning brow, blood thrumming. "Defang the snake?"

"You must disable the hand with the weapon." Paser demonstrates, brandishing the blade. There is strength there, as well as grace, a hand that wields a soldier's tools as easily as a scribe's. "If you are unarmed, your sole task is to make your opponent drop their knife."

"Or you can run away," Reb chimes in as he hoists himself up onto the ship's ledge, feet dangling. Paser is helping us with our combat skills, though Reb is already quite proficient with the Hyksos's excellent bow.

"True, but when you're in an enclosed space, such as this" — Paser gestures at the impressive vessel we're on, then hands me back my father's blade — "you may have no choice but to defend yourself."

I sheathe the dagger. "Speaking of defence, how do you think the people at the oasis are faring?"

"Min is there, and Pentu and Zina," Paser names the healer, the beekeeper, and Reb's friend who stayed behind to care for the recovering villagers. "They are in capable hands."

"I am thinking more of the spy who escaped," I say, guilt flaring. Pepi and I had not noticed the pair who'd followed us from Thebes when we went to get the scroll. "What if he leads Pharaoh to the oasis?"

"He won't," Paser reassures me. "Pepi said the chances of the spy making it back through the desert were slim."

"I am more worried for us." Reb lifts a hand to shield his eyes from the sunlight reflecting off the river's surface. "The last time we were on a boat it did not go well." He peers out at the water, as if conjuring his near drowning, the vessel's sinking, and our being stalked by crocodiles.

"At least we have not been shot at with arrows," Paser says, grinning.

"There's still time," Reb mutters.

"This boat is a lot more stable than the fisherman's craft we, um ..." I begin.

"Stole?" Reb scratches his beaky nose.

"Borrowed?" I suggest.

"Sank," Paser offers. "But don't let any of these sailors hear that." Laden with dazzling treasures, the ship that's transporting us has come from the rich Kingdom of Kush and is bound for the Hyksos capital. Having reached the delta at last, we're entering the final leg of our journey; Avaris lies north on the most eastern branch of the Nile.

"I can't believe we're almost there." Apprehension and excitement swirl in my stomach, tied as tight as any sailor's knot.

"My apologies for the delay." Paser's eyes crinkle.

"You could not help getting sick," I say. He was one of the hardest hit by the illness that struck the oasis. It is always of note to see whom the demons let be and whom they come for; I did not let them take my friend. "I'm just glad you're better."

"Thanks to you," he says, voice soft.

"And the scroll," I remind him. While tending Paser, I discovered it held a mysterious incantation that proved extremely beneficial to his health.

"You were the one to summon *Heka*, the universal magic, and send it into my body to wipe out the sickness," he counters.

"You, Reb, and Min saved most of the villagers." I wave a dismissive hand. But dealing with the illness did put us several days behind power-hungry Yanassi. The chieftain had left for the Hyksos capital to claim the crown from his dying father, taking Princess Merat, his betrothed and our friend, with him.

"Yes, yes, we are all wonderful healers." Reb makes a face at us. "I just hope the horses are well cared for." After racing across the sands to the port at Cusae, we were unable to bring the creatures on the ship, so we left them in the care of local officials. There, Pepi had made negotiations for us to board one of the many vessels departing for the Hyksos city.

"It is for the best." Paser nods at poor Nefer, Pepi's beloved donkey. She alone was permitted to come with us, and only because Pepi paid handsomely for our passage. Curled up at one end of the ship, she is lying next to a pile of barley straw, which she has not spared a glance for since our departure. Pepi believes the sturdy creature, born to land, is not fond of boats.

My eyes go to him now. He is speaking to the captain, who appears most honoured to be bringing the esteemed king's nephew home. From the sailor's respectful demeanour, it is clear that Pepi is held in high regard, whether due to his family connections or his own merits, likely both. Along with Yanassi, Pepi has been summoned by the Hyksos king, his uncle Khyan, who wishes to announce his successor. It is one of the reasons we sail for Avaris.

"Do you think you'll be able to heal Akin?" Paser nods at the scroll in my robes, citing the other reason.

"I do not know," I admit, recalling the soldier's grave injuries after his fall from a horse. Yanassi's second-in-command is also husband to my friend Amara, and we are all praying the papyrus holds the key to his recovery. "His leg is likely on the mend. His spine, however, is another matter …" I exhale deeply, wishing my breath could fill the sail to make us go faster. "The scroll is his best chance, but the longer he goes without treatment, the higher his risk." I am nervous about performing the surgery on my own, without Min as originally planned, but the oasis physician assured me I am up for the task. I myself have doubts.

"You truly believe the scroll has power of life over death?" Reb holds his hand out for the surgical papyrus. I take it from my robes, reluctant to pass it over, but I do. He knows as well as I to be careful, and he gently extracts the delicate document from its casing, inspecting the ancient scripts and the potent incantation I'd discovered when healing Paser.

"If what Pepi said is true, then it also lies at the centre of a pair of prophecies," Paser says, contemplating the enigmatic scroll. "What were the oracle's words again?" Pepi was reluctant to reveal the prophecies at first, insisting that we focus on dealing with the sickness and those who fell ill from it. It wasn't until the night before we left the oasis, with the majority of its inhabitants on the mend, that he finally agreed it was time. That moment he uttered their sacred words will forever be imprinted on my heart.

*"Years ago," Pepi says, his expression solemn, "there was a prophecy made by the famed Oracle of Avaris. One that is well known among the powers who rule the*

*lands." A wind rustles the palm fronds, causing shadows to dance across his face. I become aware of holding my breath, knowing I am about to hear something that will change the course of my life. Again. Taking a deep breath, Pepi casts his eyes skyward, as if commending his soul to the gods, then begins to recite.*

*At last.*

*We lean forward to catch his every word.*

New Kingdoms, Old Kingdoms
Kingdoms in Between
For Those Who Wish to Rule Their People
The Scroll Is the Key
The One Who Holds the Healer's Papyrus
Is the One Who Wields this Power
Of Life over Death
When the Gods Come to Devour

"Anyone else worried about the devouring gods part?" Reb says now, gingerly handing me back the papyrus, as if afraid it might bite him.

"I am more worried about why Yanassi wants the scroll," I say, rolling it back up. "He said it was to heal Akin, but what if he wants it to cement his right to rule and justify an attack on Thebes?" I tuck the document back into my dust-stained robes. "Even now, he may be garnering support from the powers at Avaris and the surrounding villages for his military plans." I look out at the water, the sky glowing crimson. "A war between the kingdoms could rip the lands apart." I shiver, thinking of the Hyksos's lethal weapons, their horses. Back in Thebes, I'd warned Pharaoh of their impressive technology, but only the gods know whether he was listening. "If Yanassi assumes the throne, this great river will run red with blood."

"There is a chance the king could name Pepi as his successor," Reb reasons. "After all, he *is* Khyan's nephew."

*He is more than that*, I want to say. *He is Khyan's son*. But I bite my tongue. I swore to Pepi I would not reveal his secret. Yanassi cannot find out. If the chieftain perceives Pepi to be a legitimate threat to his successorship, it could put his life in serious danger.

"But Pepi does not believe he is meant to rule the land." Paser crosses his arms and gives me a levelling gaze. "He thinks Sesha is."

I shake my head in protest at Paser's still-incomprehensible statement, my heart quickening again. "I cannot be meant to rule a kingdom, nor do I want to."

"What *you* want may not matter," Reb remarks. "Pepi is certain that the other prophecy refers to you."

While we were still reeling from Pepi's revelation of the first prophecy surrounding the scroll, he stunned us further with a second one. His mother, Kalali, had revealed it as she lay dying in his arms, a tragic ending to a mission gone wrong.

*"She said there is another prophecy concerning 'one from the line of the physician,'" Pepi tells us, "who will rule the lands in peace for forty years." His mouth twists. "I suppose it was phrased quite prettily now that I think upon it. Perhaps it was only the blood bubbling from her mouth that spoiled the effect."*

*"What was the wording of it?" Paser asks, soft but insistent.*

*Pepi looks at me and recites:*

When the Healer's Papyrus
Is Held Firmly in Hand
One from the Line of the Physician
Will Rule the Land
For Forty Years
Light and Learning Will Reign
And Peace and Prosperity
Will Thus Be Maintained

*"Who else knows of these prophecies?" Reb asks Pepi.*

*"The entire court at Avaris and beyond knows about the first," Pepi responds. "I am not sure who knows of*

*the second, nor when my mother learned of it, though I have a notion from whom."*

*"'One from the line of the physician,'" Paser repeats slowly, looking from the Hyksos to me and back to Pepi again. "You believe Sesha is destined to rule the lands." It is not a question.*

*"Yes."*

Now, I try to brush off his assertion. "The woman had an arrow through her throat at the time," I protest. "He may have misunderstood, as things were understandably … fraught." Paser and Reb remain silent. "But you are right, Reb." I lower my tone, voicing what's been brewing at the back of my mind for some time. "What if we can convince Khyan to name Pepi as his successor? He would make a worthy king."

"He is a spy," Reb points out.

"Precisely. He can get people to give him the information he needs and do what he wants, then make them think it's their own idea." I tuck a stray piece of hair the winds blow behind my ear. "He's also brave and honourable. Basic attributes, yes, but not ones all leaders possess. He cares about his own people but helped us, Thebans. He speaks of other cultures with respect, as he does of learning and the desire to educate his people." My gaze falls on my mentor, now eating amiably with the captain, as we sail into the descending coral sun. "And, most importantly, he desires peace."

"Others would follow him," Paser admits. "He could keep the tribes united and let Thebes be."

"Yanassi will not give up the Kingship without a fight," Reb warns as the fiery orb slips below the horizon.

I feel the outline of the obsidian blade, strapped to my leg once again. "Then we may be obliged to give him one."

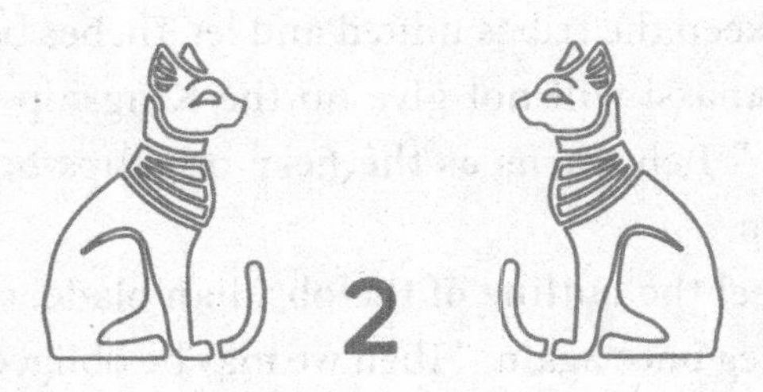

# 2

I WAKE WITH A START, chilled from the cool night air and dreams of Pepi's mother. Sitting up, I take a drink from my waterskin, shaking off the unsettling vision of Kalali passing from this world to the next, the second earth-shaking prophecy on her lips. One Pepi staunchly believes is about me. I would have laughed at the stunned expressions on my friends' faces when he first spoke the words out loud, were I not so shocked myself.

*"You think Sesha is meant to rule, and that Avaris will accept her in Yanassi's place?" Reb's mouth hangs open. "A young girl instead of the son of their king? A Theban girl?"*

*"Avaris is more accepting of people from different backgrounds than your city," Pepi says, dismissing Reb's incredulity. "There is a chance the king there, should he*

*still be alive" — I hear the slight catch in his voice — "can be convinced. Khyan puts complete faith in the oracle. But we must hurry, before he can no longer be reasoned with."*

*"Why do you think this is Sesha?" Paser demands, still pale from the oasis illness that only recently held him in its grip. "There are many physicians who have children."*

*"There are," Pepi agrees. "But her father was considered the finest among them."*

*"What about Ky?" To say I am shaken is like saying the Sphinx is a minor topographical feature.*

*"It might be Ky," Pepi concedes. "Remember I said it concerns you and your brother. But both prophecies refer to the healer's papyrus." He nods at the document bound to my body. "Which is currently in your possession and continually makes its way into your grasp, like it is meant to be there."*

*"Let me see if I understand." Reb puts up his palms, as if to slow the onslaught of Pepi's revelations. "Yanassi and others, including your king, think the scroll is the key to ruling an empire and that it has some special healing ability?"*

*Pepi nods toward Paser. "Seeing your friend walking around after the condition he was in has me inclined to believe it."*

*"And you truly feel that Sesha is destined to reign over the Hyksos in a period of prosperity and learning?" Paser echoes.*

*"I do." Pepi crosses his arms.*

*I squirm under his unflinching gaze. "Do I not have a say in the matter?"*

*"It is a great destiny." Pepi's expression is intent. "You'd save thousands of lives, more than you could as a healer. From our conversations I assumed we want the same thing, Sesha. Peace."*

*It feels like I am stuck in quicksand and sinking fast. "This is madness." I massage my temples with my fingertips. "I need time to think."*

*"There will be time for that on the way," Pepi says. "Meet me at the horses at sundown." He turns and strides away, leaving us gaping after him.*

*"Who says I'm coming?" I shout at his back.*

But it was an empty threat. For here I am on my way to Avaris to heal Akin, to find Merat once again, and to prevent the war and bloodshed that will follow if Yanassi assumes the throne.

"Hathor, help me," I whisper to the night. Knowing I will not go back to sleep before sunrise, I get up quietly and walk to the end of the ship. Looking up at the glittering sky, and at Khonsu, half-full, I think of the princess, as I so often do. Will the chieftain marry her before we can get there?

The hairs at the back of my neck ripple like the waters below, and I turn to see the outline of a man leaning back against a golden statue of Set. It is the

Nubian, a fellow passenger. Sharpening his curved *khopesh* sword on a stone, he stares silently from under his linen headcover, keeping a vigilant watch over the treasures on board.

I nod in wary greeting.

He does not respond, only whets his hooked blade back and forth on the stone. *Scritch, scratch.* The curved weapon is the length of my arm, making the obsidian dagger strapped to my leg seem … insignificant.

My friends and I have felt his hostile gaze on us more than once this voyage. We mentioned our unease to Pepi who told us to be cautious but seemed confident no harm would befall the king's nephew and his companions.

"The Nubian is a mercenary," he said. "Believe me, he does not make a habit of working for free. So long as no one is paying him to bring about our untimely demise, we are safe enough."

I swallow, turning my back on the mercenary to face the dark waters. There is a presence at my side.

"Can't sleep?" Pepi murmurs.

"Bad dream," I say, accustomed to his silent materializations.

"I have those," he says, his smile wry. "I will keep you company."

"You should rest, yourself."

"I do not require much sleep," he says.

"I noticed." Pepi always seems to be awake, up before Ra and to bed long after the god departs for the underworld. I realize with a start that I, too, have become accustomed to little sleep. "Has it always been that way for you?"

Another brief smile crosses his shadowed face. "My mother used to call me her little giraffe," he says, seeming to feel her near, as well. "And not in honour of this handsome neck." One of his hands comes up to stroke the column, ruffling the stubble along and below his jaw. "Which has found itself on the chopping block more than a few times."

"Giraffes do not need much sleep, then?" I ask, not having personally observed the napping patterns of the gangly, spotted animals.

"Almost none at all. They doze here and there, maybe an hour or two, standing and sometimes even with one eye open." He smiles. "I need a little more than that," he says, "but not much."

"I wonder why they sleep so little."

"For similar reasons, I suppose." Pepi's smile fades. "Resting too long is dangerous."

We are quiet for a few moments after that.

"This oracle at Avaris, is it —"

"She," Pepi interjects.

"She," I amend. "Is she always right?"

"She foretold Khyan's own rule." Pepi looks up at

the cosmic ocean sparkling above. "The oracle does not always make prophecies, but the ones she has made have all come to pass. We will need her to verify my mother's words to the king and the court."

"Who *is* she, exactly?" I say, curious.

"A revered priestess, who acts as an intermediary between the people and the gods. Kings and servants alike can petition her for answers to their questions."

"And you think she was the one to disclose the second prophecy concerning the scroll to your mother?" If the oracle knew Kalali, she might also be able to prove Pepi's paternity, which would greatly assist with *our* plan of setting him on the throne over Yanassi.

"I believe so." His voice is soft. "My mother must have learned of it sometime before her death."

Wanting to spare him any further disturbing images, I change the subject. "Why do you not support Yanassi's aggression against Thebes?"

"Though part of me loves my 'cousin'" — another wry smile touches his face — "we think differently on many matters. Especially political ones." He looks out at the lightening horizon, seeing something or someone I cannot. "My mother was an agent for peace. She wanted it for her children, just as I want it for mine. She gave her life trying to bring it about; I will honour her memory and dying wishes by doing the same."

"Most would say you are a better choice than me to rule Avaris."

He rubs a hand over his bristly scalp. "It is not my destiny."

"Some might say we make our own destiny."

Another fleeting smile. "Perhaps."

"The mission, with your mother, when was it?"

He gives me an acknowledging look. "Just before you found me in a pit."

"It was you," I murmur. "You turned yourself in to Pharaoh's soldiers."

"I allowed myself to be captured," he corrects.

"Why would you do that?"

"To give my sister time to get away."

"Your sister?" Reb yawns, coming up behind us with Paser.

"As Thebans inherit the roles of their fathers and mothers, it is common for us, as well," Pepi says, turning to face them. "Ours was a family operation."

"Where is your sister now?" Paser asks.

"I know nothing of her fate." Pepi's voice is soft. "None have seen or heard of her since. She is likely in the Field of Reeds with my mother, where I was headed, as well, after a few days in that filthy hole. I swore on their spirits, and to the gods, that if I got out of there, I would complete our mission to find the scroll, see the prophecies fulfilled, and peace between our nations maintained." His eyes, already intense in their expression, narrow further. "And by the gods, I will."

"When did it occur to you that Sesha might be the one from the prophecy?" Paser emphasizes the word *might*.

"I wondered at first, when I learned who her father was," Pepi admits. "But it was only after she mentioned the healer's papyrus, after Akin's accident, that I became certain."

"Is this why you agreed to train her as a spy?" Paser's voice holds a whiff of accusation. "You've had your own motivations the entire time."

"Who among us does not have their own motivations?" Pepi reasons, and I think of Reb, Paser's, and my freshly hatched plan to set him upon the throne. "I am sorry for the deception," he adds, with a brief nod of his shorn head. "But, as Sesha knows, keeping information secret is the only way we accomplish our missions. And stay alive. You should prepare your things." Pepi tilts his head subtly at the Nubian, his meaning clear. We are out of his hearing, but still must be careful. "We'll be arriving in the capital soon. By the gods, let us hope we are not too late."

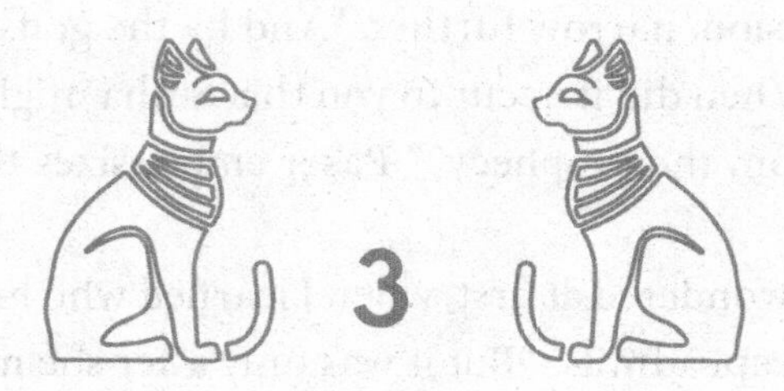

# 3

THE SIGHTS AND SOUNDS of the port city invade the senses. We stand, fascinated, at the prow, watching ships of all shapes and sizes come and go from the large bay, exuberant sails flapping in the brisk wind. Deft oars manoeuvre the variety of crafts through tight quarters with practised ease. Birds screech overhead and white splotches spatter the deck like scattered raindrops. One errant drop lands directly on Reb's head. He lets out a cry and puts a hand to his hair, pulling it back to inspect the white-green glob in disgust.

"A blessing from the gods!" A crew member cackles as he scurries by, tossing ropes down to outstretched hands who nimbly secure the vessel to the dock.

"How fortunate," Reb mutters. He spits on his hand and wipes it on his grubby linens. Equally as raucous as the seabirds above are the people below, swarming over the docks like Pentu's industrious bees.

Captains, queens of the harbour, order their workers to load and unload their wares, hollering here, shouting there, pointing and gesticulating wildly. Labouring crews wipe sweat from their brows, calling to one another in strange and varied tongues in greeting or to pass on instructions to their crew members. Officials and merchants wave their arms, inspecting and directing the cargo this way and that. Vast amounts of timber, metals, and charcoal change hands, are lifted, carried, and heaved using ropes, pulleys, and brute strength. Everyone seems to know what they are doing and where they are going, in what appears to be highly efficient chaos.

I step off the ship and onto the dock, grabbing for Paser, who goes first, the motion of the boat making me sway. He holds out a hand to steady me as Reb lands solidly on the boards beside us. They dip, along with my stomach. Reb inhales, bird poop forgotten in the thrill of arriving in the Hyksos capital at last. "The air is different here."

The breeze is cool on my face and I take a deep breath, inhaling the pungent scents of brine, decay, and fish.

"The wind carries with it fresh salts from the *Uat-Ur*, the Green Sea," Pepi calls down. "It is somewhat more invigorating than sand." He grins over his shoulder, tugging at Nefer's lead. After assisting the crew with mooring the craft, he's turned his attentions to the donkey, waving straw under her nose to coax her down the creaky plank. She steps one tentative hoof at a time, letting out a frantic bray as Pepi tugs the braided rope around her neck. Nefer seems to like water about as much as sandstorms.

"You'd think she'd be eager to leave the ship," Paser remarks. "She was wretched the entire journey."

"What is known often appears safer than the unknown for many creatures, even if they are unsatisfied with their current conditions." Pepi clicks his tongue at the stubborn donkey. "That is why many prefer to stay where they are, instead of moving forward."

The Nubian walks by and slaps Nefer unceremoniously on the rump. Her eyes roll back in her head as she staggers the remaining steps, landing as ungracefully as I did upon the dock, knees wobbling. Pepi offers her the barley, then ruffles her wiry black mane, putting his nose to her face as she chews resentfully. "Well done, beloved one. We are home."

We take in Pepi's vibrant domain, surveying the sights, sounds, and smells of a thriving city, wholly new to us. Once fully under Egyptian power, today Avaris is presided over by the Hyksos rulers who settled here years ago and proceeded to grow in numbers and strength through trade, marriage, and a steady stream of immigration. Gradually, they assumed full control of the region, holding it competently in their grasp for decades.

People take no notice of us, bustling around as we walk to the end of the dock and over to an official. "What is your business in Avaris?" the man says, without bothering to look up.

"Come now, Daba. You do not recognize me with my new hair?"

The scribe looks up in surprise and squints at Pepi. He blinks a few times, recognition crossing his sharp features.

"What hair?" His thick brows rise. "You are even uglier than the last time I saw you." Paser, Reb, and I exchange a look. This is not how Thebans would speak to a member of a royal family. Not if they want to avoid the pits, that is.

But Pepi laughs, one hand rubbing at his head, fuzzy as a stone fruit. "You are just jealous. It is much cooler like this."

Daba snorts. "You look like one of those pompous, obnoxious Theba—"

"Allow me to introduce my betrothed," Pepi interrupts, with a graceful gesture to encompass us, his other hand still holding Nefer's lead. "This is Sesha and her brothers, Reb and Paser." It was agreed we'd keep to our original story, this being safest for everyone involved. “From Thebes,” he adds pleasantly, and the scribe blinks again but stands a little straighter.

“It is a privilege.” He nods, then gives Pepi a curious look. “I had not heard of your own engagement.”

Meaning he *has* heard of Yanassi’s. Which implies they are safely arrived in the city. I feel boneless, like the fish we ate for last night’s supper. Merat is close. And Amara and Akin. The scroll presses against my body, under my grimy robe. I do not know how much time Yanassi’s man has, or if the wounded soldier even still lives.

“We are keeping our happy news quiet so as not to overshadow my cousin and his intended,” Pepi says smoothly. “The chieftain has announced his upcoming ceremony, I assume?”

“It’s been the talk of the city since he and his bride-to-be arrived. The people can speak of nothing else.” The scribe puts down his lovely reed — my fingers itch to hold it — and clears his throat. “It seems the news even revived the king, who you’ve come to see?” The dark brow lifts again.

“My uncle.” Pepi seizes upon this information, all teasing aside. “How does he fare?”

“It is rumoured he’d almost left for the underworld when the arrival of his son and new daughter significantly revived his spirits.” The man looks at me, expression interested, and I self-consciously pull my wind-mussed hair to one side, most of it having escaped its plait. "May it be that your own happy news brings him back from the Land of the Dead permanently."

"Let us hope so," Pepi says fervently. "This is a most welcome update, praise Hadad. Come," he says, turning to us. "We will go and see the king."

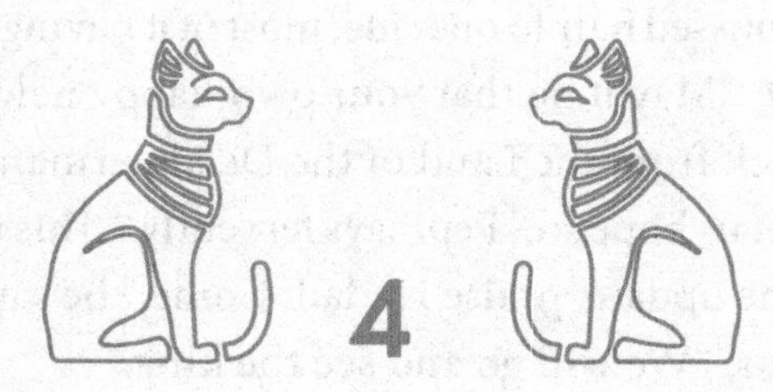

# 4

WE FOLLOW PEPI THROUGH the crowds of traders, sailors, and fishermen, heads swivelling like owls. There is an energetic pulse to the capital, a rhythm Pepi tunes in to at once, as he increases his pace, and we strive to follow. He appears most eager to see Khyan, and it strikes me again that the man *is* his father, whether the ruler knows it or not, and that Pepi cares for him deeply.

The king must have quite the force of personality to rule such an important international city. For someone to hold the respect of so many on his own merits, and not only because the gods deign it so, is impressive. Avaris is the key port for goods coming into the entire region and its wealth is obvious just by looking at the well-kept structures and diverse peoples lining the streets, captivating to watch as they go about their day. The citizens are clad in colourful robes and look well fed and happy, in contrast to the pinched and anxious faces that line the market in Thebes.

"The Egyptian quarter is that way," Pepi says, pointing in the distance. Paser and Reb exchange an eager glance. I know they're thinking of Paser's uncle. We once envisioned finding his estranged relative and convincing him to take us to another land, far from those who seek to ensnare us in their sticky webs. Though that plan appears temporarily on hold, I do not blame Paser for wanting to meet his only living blood relation.

"Thebans also dwell among us, as do members of other regions, from the near east to the far west, and even more north still." Pepi inhales as we pass by delicious-smelling food cooking over a fire. "Avaris is similar to that pot, with different ingredients mixing together to make the stew more flavourful. For the most part, people live in harmony with others and respect their neighbours' customs, which they are free to honour, so long as they cause no harm to another."

Pepi's posture is different in Avaris. The cagey spy I knew, always confident, now walks with a quiet dignity. It is clear he is proud of his birthplace; he draws himself up taller, shoulders back, his chin raised high.

"What will you tell Yanassi about the scroll?" Paser asks. "He'll want to know if we have it."

My chest tightens at the image of handing over the priceless papyrus to the chieftain.

"I will present it as a gift to the king," Pepi says. There is a *shaduf* bucket's worth of satisfaction in his voice at the thought of impressing Khyan.

"What if he gives it to the chieftain?" Reb dodges sparks from a Kerman metalworker who pounds away at a piece of bronze, shaping it into a long dagger. Other blades hang from the walls of his stall, gleaming and sharp to the touch.

"We cannot keep the scroll from Yanassi," Pepi says, as we pass more busy stalls. There seems to be an excess of craftsmen in Avaris, producing and creating with the raw materials that come into the area from the sea and nearby lands. "If my cousin wishes to examine the document, then it will be so."

"He will get the scroll?" My heart sinks.

"You need it for Akin's surgery," Pepi reminds me. "We will tell him you must study it beforehand. He cares for his soldier, and I believe he'll allow this."

"And then?" Reb asks. "Once he has the scroll, what is to stop him from immediately declaring war on Thebes?"

"As long as the old king lives, Yanassi will need his endorsement. The king will want the approval of his council before letting his son lead them into war. There are many divided interests," Pepi says. "I also doubt the princess will want him attacking her family and city; it might be that Merat holds some sway over Yanassi."

"He desires her, that is clear," Paser says to Pepi. "There are many who do. The real question is, does he love her? And if so, will it be enough to turn his mind from war?"

I sigh. "It would be nice to know the answers to these things."

"Where is an oracle when one is needed?" Reb quips.

Ahead, the Hyksos palace complex comes into view, large and sprawling. Built upon a flat hill, one building connects to the next, and second levels joined by walkways create a whole other realm upon rooftops. To the south and east lie blooming gardens. Adding to the fragrance of the herbs and flowers are orchards and vineyards, where grapes are presently being harvested. People crush them underfoot in vats wide enough for four men.

"The vineyards are substantial." Reb swallows thirstily.

Pepi smiles. "Some say that when the pharaohs sipped their first taste of Levantine wine, they liked it so much they imported the vines and those qualified to curate them." One man, dancing enthusiastically, slips with a whoop, his feet flying up in the air. Laughing, his friends bend down to pick him up and brush him off as the group resumes their merry grape crushing. "Come," Pepi beckons, "the main entrance is to the north."

We follow him to a large area covered by an enormous overhang supported by massive wooden columns. Painted golden ochre, it provides shade and is a formidable deterrent for anyone seeking entrance. Soldiers line the portico, clad in linen *shendyts* and armed with deadly looking spears. The head guard, a giant of a man, stands in front of the massive doorway, spear gripped tightly across his broad chest.

"Will they recognize you?" Paser whispers. So far no one has paid us any attention. In Avaris, people seem free to come and go where they please.

"Let us hope not," Pepi murmurs. Before I can ask what he means, there is a menacing shout and the spy flinches.

"You, there!"

Guards rush over and I automatically reach for my blade, but Pepi holds up a warning hand. "Do not draw your dagger, Sesha."

My friends and I form a small circle, our backs together. In moments we are surrounded by twenty or thirty men, some with spears.

"Can you not tell them who you are?" I say, desperately.

"They know." Pepi keeps an eye on the giant soldier. "That is the problem."

"Yanassi bid us keep watch for you!" The giant's voice is deep and rough. He leans forward, grabbing Pepi by the arm, and my breath stops. "Welcome home!" The giant captain enfolds Pepi in his hulking embrace and my jaw drops as Pepi laughs, both men thumping each other on the back. My shoulders relax, and Paser and Reb lower their hands as it sinks in that we are in no danger of being slaughtered where we stand.

"How were your travels?" The soldier holds Pepi back and examines his changed appearance, eyes blazing with joy. He sniffs at Pepi. "You stink of Thebes." The other men jeer and hoot at the city's mention. "Let us give you a bath!"

Alarm mixes with resignation on Pepi's face as a few men, led by the giant, pick him up and lift him high into the air, despite his loud protestations. They carry him to one of the large vats and we follow, looking wide-eyed at one another. Pepi is shouting and laughing, uttering threats, but the men pay him no heed. The giant counts down as the enthusiastic soldiers swing him back and forth, then launch him into the vat, where he lands with a *splat*, face-first. Good-natured taunts and shouts ring out, as the vintners elbow one another and call to Pepi in hilarity, asking how this season's crop is.

Reb, Paser, and I rush forward to see if Pepi is all right. He is sitting up and laughing, wiping the mess off his face and his arms, splashing red-purple juice at the men who come closer to tease.

"That is better!" The giant soldier strokes his beard with his left hand. "Now you will smell like our sweet wine instead of Theban arrogance." He offers Pepi a meaty hand. The spy accepts it sportingly and the captain hauls him to his feet. He puts his forehead to Pepi's, clasping his hands behind the spy's shaved head. I catch the words spoken softly. "Welcome home, King's Nephew."

"It is good to be home, old friend," Pepi says. "Thank you for keeping it safe."

The large man scoffs, "Save your thanks. It is my honour to serve our king and his family." The pair face the gathering people, whose excitement is contagious. "The king's nephew is home, safe and well!" he shouts. "Unharmed, except for this hideous haircut, the gods be praised."

The crowd cheers and takes up the chanting of the spy's name. Pepi lifts a hand, humbly acknowledging their exclamations, dripping in sticky grape pulp. People rush forward, eager to hail the returning royal. Reb, Paser, and I stand back from the crowd, which is growing exponentially, watching the people of Avaris welcome home one of its sons.

"They have a most unusual custom of greeting royalty," Reb sniffs.

Paser grins, unexpectedly causing my heart to flip over in my chest. "I like it."

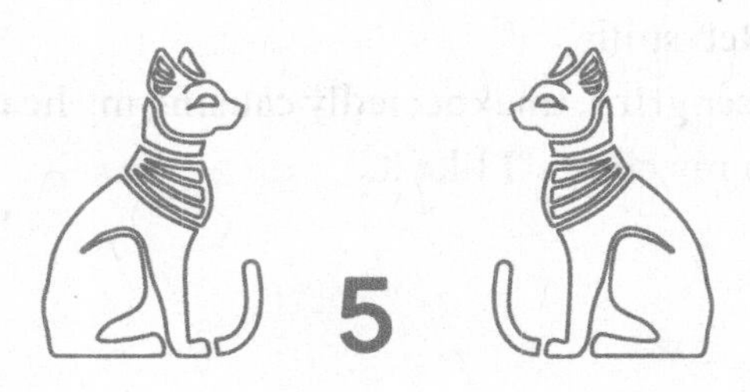

# 5

"YOU HAVE SOMETHING, just there." I point at Pepi's ear.

He wipes at the grape skin dangling from his lobe. "Many thanks, Sesha." The large captain, whose name we learn is Abisha, escorts us into the palace.

"Your uncle will be most pleased to see you," Abisha says, arms as thick as palm trunks swinging at his sides, one hand again gripping his spear.

"I had hoped to be a little more presentable." Pepi flicks a squished grape off his arm.

"He is used to your ways." Abisha smiles.

"My ways?" Pepi says archly, but lets the comment go. "His health has improved, then?"

Abisha nods. "The healers and priests have been working around the water clock, praying and offering a variety of enchantments."

"Daba mentioned that Yanassi and his new bride's arrival bolstered the king's spirits."

Abisha's broad shoulders stiffen. "He is most pleased to have his son home, safe and well."

"And what has my cousin been doing since his return?" Pepi inquires mildly.

"Mainly meeting with council and sending out messengers at all hours," Abisha says. Panic wrenches my insides. Is the chieftain already drumming up support for his war? The grim look on Pepi's face says he's thinking this, as well. "At the moment he is showing his new bride the sights of our fair city."

"They are married, then?" My heart plummets. We are too late.

But Abisha shakes his head. "The princess was most insistent on waiting for your arrival. She said she would not marry without her friends at her side."

I barely keep in my exclamation of relief.

"Yanassi was agreeable to this?" The skepticism is evident in Pepi's voice as we walk past an inner courtyard with a beautiful pool, surrounded by towering columns and palms.

"It would seem so." The doubt in Abisha's voice mirrors Pepi's.

"How is Akin?" I ask eagerly.

"Breathing." Abisha gives me a sidelong glance, obviously wondering what my interest is in Yanassi's best man. We reach an enormous door set in stone, and Abisha turns to Pepi. "Do not be alarmed at your uncle's appearance," he says quietly. "The demons have been at him for some time." Pepi nods, face tight, and we follow the giant guard through the door.

Large potted ferns and other leafy plants fill the lavish room, bringing to mind the lushness of the oasis. Blue and green lines border its smooth walls and the scents of herbs and medicines linger in the air. A large bed in the middle of the room is encircled by gauzy linens, which drape over the sides of the mattress. Currently tied back, the sheer curtains frame an elderly man propped up on pillows that must be stuffed with ibis feathers, because Reb sneezes three times in quick succession as we approach.

"May you keep your soul," the old man rasps to Reb, who looks to Pepi in alarm.

"This is our customary response to the involuntary expelling of nasal fluids," Pepi murmurs.

The king assesses Pepi's grape-stained appearance. "Been sampling my wine, Nephew?"

"Yes, Uncle." Pepi clears his throat and steps forward. "It promises to be an excellent vintage this year."

The king feebly motions Pepi over to his bedside. "Stop babbling about wine and come closer, Apepi, my child."

It might be a greeting a king would say to any family member, but I see that Pepi cannot quite suppress the surge of emotion at the endearment and formal use of his name; it creeps up his neck and stains his cheeks as he rushes forward into the outstretched arms of the man he holds above all others. Their joy is contagious and my eyes water as the genuine affection between the two envelops those in the room.

Pepi pulls back from the Hyksos king and looks over at us. "Uncle, this is Sesha. My betrothed. Her father was Ay, the Great Royal Physician to the pharaoh and his family. She, too, is a gifted healer and a scribe. I am proud to call her my intended wife."

Beside me, Paser starts at the word *wife*. Uncertainly, I step forward. I know we planned to abide by this ruse, but for Pepi to introduce me so boldly, and so immediately, makes me feel like I am back on that swaying dock.

"I know Ay." The king's unexpected comment puts me even more off balance. "He removed a peculiar growth from my toe." He wiggles his foot under the linen sheet in emphasis.

I incline my head with respect. "I'm sure it was his honour, My King."

The king snorts. "Any common healer could've done it. I put it to him as a test. To see how proud the man was." He smiles at me, eye wrinkles creasing like a folded papyrus fan. "Not bad, for a Theban. He was a good physician."

"Thank —" The doors burst open and Yanassi barrels in, his burly strength and frantic energy immediately filling the space.

"Cousin!" he pants, as if he has run the length of the palace. "You are returned!" Throwing his arms around Pepi, he pounds him on the back, as Abisha did. My eyes are already searching for Merat when she steps delicately through the doors after the chieftain, looking even more beautiful than I remember, shining braids swinging, eyes as rich and dark as dates, a light flush high in her cheekbones.

She runs over and the three of us embrace her, hugging in a tight circle, exclaiming and interrupting one another with interjections and questions. There is a loud banging on the ground behind us and we turn guiltily to face the King of Avaris who, in our excited reunion, we just turned our backs on. Abisha stands at his bedside, hulking, sternly holding the spear he rapped to get our attention. The princess gives us a final look, squeezes both my hands, then goes to stand beside the chieftain.

"Do you have the scroll?" Yanassi demands.

Pepi nods, expression calm. "We do."

"What scroll?" the king says sharply.

I look at Pepi in surprise. Did Yanassi not mention our quest? I wonder what he let Khyan think as to why

Pepi did not come at once to see the ruler off to the underworld and hear the naming of his successor. At the king's urgent summons, no less.

"The one we have long searched for, Uncle." Pepi motions for me to come forward. "The elusive healer's papyrus."

The king blinks. "Extraordinary." He sounds breathless from either the effects of his illness or suppressed emotion. "Can it really be the document?"

In response, I bring the scroll out from under my robes, fingers clutched tightly around its cylindrical shape. Stomach clenching, I give it to Pepi, who kneels and holds it aloft, presenting it to his uncle.

Khyan lifts a trembling hand. "Wherever did you come by it?" He seems almost hesitant to touch the papyrus but eventually takes it from Pepi's grasp and brings it to his nose, inhaling deeply. A puzzled expression crosses his face. "How can this be? The text is rumoured to be a thousand years old, yet the ink and paper smell fresh."

"It is an authentic copy," Pepi says. "Sesha and her father made it. It was she who led us to it."

"It is not the original?" Yanassi's fists clench at his sides, as if to keep himself from snatching the document out of his father's hands.

"I can assure you the transcription is of the highest quality," Paser says, stepping forward. "Sesha was the best scribe at temple, and her father's reputation as royal physician remains untarnished."

"Really?" Yanassi scoffs and moves closer to the king's bedside. "I hear the man was a heretic." His words strike me hard and fast, like the sting of a scorpion. They poison my blood, making it run hot under my skin.

"My father was a great man," I say, gripping my temper with both hands.

Merat glides forward. "Sesha's father served my family without equal." Her manner is poised. "The Pharaoh of the Black Land has only the best attend his needs. All people know that Ay was the most gifted healer to come out of Thebes in decades."

Yanassi snorts. "That is like saying he is the most fragrant piece of waste in the trash heap."

"He came to this city to train your own healers, right here in Avaris." My chin tilts up to keep my gaze level with the intimidating chieftain. "Which would make them equally as fragrant." The tension in the air thickens, like a storm about to break. Abisha, spear still folded across his enormous chest, looks amused by the family dramatics.

The king clears his throat. "Yanassi, do not disrespect the father of your cousin's betrothed. She is family now."

"She is more than that," Pepi says. All at once I know what is coming and take a step forward, as if to keep him from speaking, but it is too late to stop the words leaving his mouth, or their consequences. "The oracle has proclaimed Sesha our future ruler."

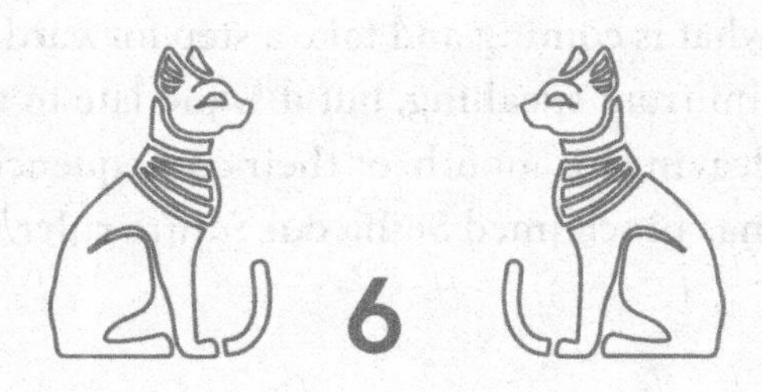

# 6

THE ROOM IS SILENT as twin waves of shock and disbelief crash down on its occupants. It feels like I am about to undergo the mummification process. Live.

"What is this nonsense you spout, Cousin?" Yanassi finds his voice first, all welcoming joviality gone from his demeanour. "Is this some kind of prank?"

"It is not a joke," Pepi responds. "The Oracle of Avaris shared the prophecy with my mother, who relayed it with her last gasps of air."

Like Kalali, I am finding it increasingly difficult to breathe.

"Is this true?" the king demands.

"As a priestess bound by her vows, she would not lie." Pepi motions to the papyrus the king is examining.

"She died in my arms, in search of that very scroll you have in your hands."

My friends and I look at one another, eyes wide. Pepi's mother was a priestess?

"Tell me this prophecy, word for word." Khyan lies very still. To his credit, he is handling the outrageous revelations admirably. I suppose one does not last long as ruler without the ability to deal calmly with whatever comes at them. A trait Yanassi does not seem to have inherited.

Pepi recites the script as commanded:

WHEN THE HEALER'S PAPYRUS
IS HELD FIRMLY IN HAND
ONE FROM THE LINE OF THE PHYSICIAN
WILL RULE THE LAND
FOR FORTY YEARS
LIGHT AND LEARNING WILL REIGN
AND PEACE AND PROSPERITY
WILL THUS BE MAINTAINED

"One from the line of the physician?" Yanassi splutters. "This is nonsense." His eyes narrow at Pepi. "I knew you were jealous of my right to kingship. For you to stoop so low with false prophecies only proves I was a fool to trust you."

Pepi gives his cousin an apologetic look. "I

am aware that this must come as a deep shock, Cousin."

"Shock? It is preposterous. You think I am just going to roll over and let this inexperienced young *Theban* rule our land?" Yanassi laughs. "On your word?"

"Not mine. The oracle's." Pepi looks at the king. "I know you put great stock in what she says."

Khyan is silent. "When was the prophecy made?"

"I am not certain," Pepi admits. "My mother might have learned of it at a temple ceremony. Uncle, you know my motives. I have no wish to rule —"

"Now we know why you wish to marry *her*," Yanassi sneers. "Anything to secure the throne for yourself."

Pepi flushes. "I have never wanted that burden —"

"You are not man enough to bear that burden!" Yanassi roars. Abisha steps forward, no longer entertained by the family dramatics.

"Enough," he barks at Yanassi. "Your father is ill; I will not have you snarling at his bedside like rival lions."

"I am the one to rule this kingdom," Yanassi says coldly. "Not him." He gives me a withering glare. "And certainly not this sandblasted scrap of a Theban!"

"Yanassi." Khyan's voice rings out, still with authority. "I am not dead yet. Our people have always listened to the oracle. That is how we got where we are today."

"I hope you are not fool enough to believe every schemer coming to you with stories of a prophecy,

Father." Yanassi folds his arms angrily across his large chest. Probably to keep from wrapping them around someone's neck.

"Solstice is almost upon us, let us summon the oracle at once to settle matters," Pepi confidently implores the king. "I know she will support my claims."

Khyan closes his eyes, appearing weary and deflated. "The oracle is missing."

"Missing?" Pepi repeats, like he does not understand the word.

The king opens his eyes. "We are keeping her absence quiet for now, but for the first time ever, she is late."

"Late for what?" I ask.

Pepi answers for Khyan, face pale. "Twice a year, before solstice, the oracle comes to Avaris for people to address her with their concerns."

"She was due several days ago," the king says. "The alignment is in seven days, and we have heard nothing."

I wonder if I am as pale as Pepi. Without the oracle, the second prophecy's authenticity may be cast in doubt, especially if Yanassi has his way. And despite Pepi asserting that I am the one to rule, my "brothers," as well, might be considered potential contenders. It occurs to me that the easiest way for Yanassi to resolve his problems would be a swift knife in all our backs.

While we process the king's revelation, Pepi recovers admirably, gesturing at me and my friends. "We will go to find the oracle," he declares.

"No." The command in Khyan's voice is clear. "You are needed at my side." The king studies Paser, Reb, and me. Perhaps a similar thought about Yanassi and knives occurs to him because he looks at Pepi and says, "You will tell them what they need to know; they can go on their own."

"As you wish, Uncle." Pepi bows his head, deferring to the Hyksos ruler's orders.

"This is absurd." Seething, Yanassi spins on his heel and leaves the room. Merat, who has remained quiet, casts a pleading look our way, then follows him. It jolts me to see her go after the chieftain.

"Now, if you will excuse me, I need to rest before dinner." The king closes his eyes again. "And you need to wash."

"Of course, Uncle." Pepi takes his hand. "I am sorry for the upheaval our arrival has caused."

"Do not be sorry. It does my spirit good to see you." Khyan squeezes his hand. "I am just glad you made it … in time."

"Me, too," Pepi murmurs. He takes his leave of the king and we exit the royal chambers.

The minute we are in the hallway, I burst out at Pepi, "Why in this realm did you tell them the oracle proclaimed *me* as ruler? We do not know this for sure!"

"I do. And you heard Abisha," Pepi says in a low voice, looking over his shoulder. "Yanassi is already sending out messengers, potentially to raise support for an attack on Thebes under the guise of preparing for his marriage! It is good if we give him something else to think about for the moment."

"You put a big target on Sesha's back." Paser is angry. "On all our backs." So, that has occurred to him, as well.

"I was unaware of the oracle's absence." We follow Pepi down the corridor, unsure of where we are going but having no other choice; our surroundings are unfamiliar. "It is why I was so quick to suggest we leave in search of her; that way you are beyond Yanassi's reach. And the chieftain will likely not try anything while his father still lives."

"You would think planning a wedding would be enough to occupy his time," Reb says, his tone is as salty as the sea. "How are we to find this oracle?"

"I may have some idea of her whereabouts." We walk by servants and other occupants of the palace, all of whom give Pepi respectful nods and carry on their way.

"And where is that?" I demand.

"I will tell you," he says. We hurry to match his quick stride. "But first I must meet with the courtiers and nobles whose interests are aligned with ours." The spy's face is determined. "Or at least they were before I left. And before doing that, I need to bathe. As do you three."

"What about Akin?" I exclaim. Yanassi had been so furious he hadn't even mentioned his soldier.

"I will leave it to you, Sesha. If you think his surgery can be done in the next day or two, that is fine. Otherwise, you will have to wait until you are back."

Reb throws his hands up. "What if we don't make it back?"

Pepi stops walking and turns to face us. "You three are ready for this. If anyone can find the oracle and return her to Avaris, you can." His expression is intent. "The fate of both our kingdoms rests upon it."

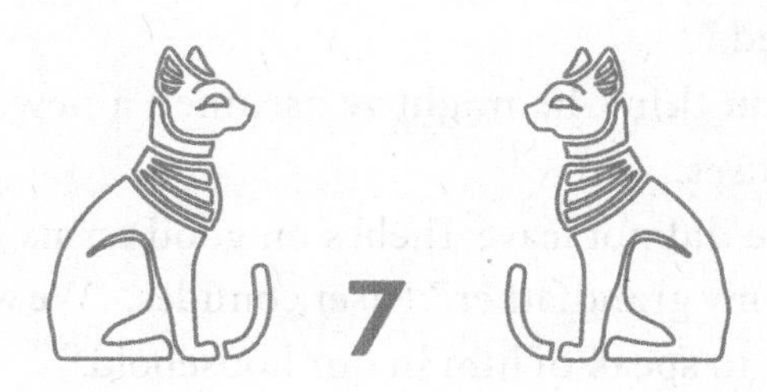

# 7

"I FEAR YOUR ASSOCIATION with me puts you both in grave danger. Again." I speak in a hushed whisper. Servants usher us past polished shrines toward separate baths.

"We've become accustomed to it," Reb says, resigned.

"And would expect nothing less." Paser drapes his linen towel round his neck.

"It's not too late for you," I say, knowing they may balk at my next words, but unable to resist all the same. "You can keep to our original plan and find Paser's uncle. Perhaps he can help you flee or —"

"I know you do not really believe we would abandon you." Paser shakes his head, and I allow a small smile. "Besides, finding my uncle might not be so easy. I have only his name to go on, one he may have changed."

"You think he might've assumed a new name?" Reb muses.

"He did not leave Thebes on good terms with his father, my grandfather," Paser confides. "We were forbidden to speak of him in our household."

"What happened between them?" We keep our voices low, but the chattering servants ahead pay us no attention.

"Like Pepi and Yanassi, they disagreed strongly on many matters, particularly politics," Paser says. "Based on the few things my mother *did* say, I gather my uncle had no desire to be a soldier like his father and his father's father before him. My grandfather was a proud man and would have been furious, humiliated even, at my uncle's refusal to uphold the family's great legacy."

We nod; in Thebes, the rejection of a father's occupation is typically looked upon with scorn.

"From what I understand, my grandfather said if my uncle would not pick up a sword for the kingdom, then he must leave his home. There was a terrible fight. My uncle told his sister he was leaving for Avaris, where men were free to make their own destinies. He asked her to visit him one day." Paser's tone is rueful. "Of course, she never did. She married my father, who was a scribe, and stayed in Thebes, where they lived and died." Like many people from our city, Paser's family perished in a sickness that swept the land years ago, one that made the oasis illness seem a minor trial in comparison.

"That is why your grandfather trained you." I think of Paser's impressive skills in fighting and weapons. His grandfather cared for and raised him after his parents died and likely sought to replace the son he lost.

"It is strange to think, but this man, who I've never met, is the only remaining member of my family." I hear the longing in his voice.

"Not the only one." I put a hand on his shoulder. "A family is something we are born into, but also something we can choose for ourselves, should we wish it."

"We may be orphans," Reb adds, "but we have one another."

I look at my friends, who have accompanied me through trials that would cover numerous temple walls and who are about to do so again. "I am lucky to have you both."

"We know." Reb grins.

The king declares a feast to celebrate Pepi's homecoming. That evening we find ourselves seated at low tables while food and drinks are brought around by servants. Dish after dish of sumptuous, mouth-watering delicacies are served, along with copious amounts of beer and wine. Caught up in all that has transpired, I cannot eat a single bite. I sit watching everyone else eat, folding and refolding my linen napkin.

Despite the festivities, the mood around the table remains tense. Yanassi is brooding, looking daggers in our direction. Merat sits beside him, both on the king's right. Pepi and I are on Khyan's left and Paser and Reb sit next to me. Yanassi's glares aren't the only thing making me fidget. In all the excitement of oracles and prophecies, I have not yet had a chance to see my patient and am most anxious to do so.

"How is Akin?" I venture to the chieftain during the first course, reminding him that he still needs me to heal his man.

Yanassi, who is puffed up like an antagonized rooster, bristles a little at my inquiry. "Not well. I hoped you'd be here with the scroll sooner." His voice is accusatory. "I gather you were busy plotting your overthrow."

"The messenger brought a sickness to the oasis," Pepi says, watching his cousin carefully. "Delaying our departure significantly."

"A sickness?" Yanassi's surprise is obvious. "What kind of sickness?"

"A vicious purge of the bowels and stomach," Pepi says. "We thought he carried it from Avaris, but I see with my own eyes everyone here is well enough." He motions with his half-empty goblet at the people around us, laughing and eating. The tension at our table does not seem to affect them — there is a celebratory feeling in the air.

"He did not bring it from here." The king shakes his head. "Perhaps he picked it up elsewhere, before arriving at the oasis."

"How are the people?" Yanassi demands, putting his cup down. "Are they well?"

"They are. With a thousand thanks to these three." Pepi gestures to us. "Although he is a gifted physician, Min could not have brought them through it alone."

The king's gaze rests on me. "It appears whatever made your father a great healer also lies in you."

"She inherited his gift," Pepi says. "I witnessed her save her brother's life with my very eyes." For a moment I think he refers to Ky, but his eyes cut to Paser, who nods in confirmation. Something otherworldly did pass between us that night I laid my hands on him.

"You truly believe you can heal Akin?" Yanassi eyes me, suspicious. He, apparently, does not. "Min was meant to do the surgery."

I take a deep breath. "I will do my best."

"She will need the scroll for now." Pepi keeps his voice casual. The document is still with the king as far as I know. "To study, in preparation for the procedure."

Yanassi makes an irritated sound, and Merat puts a graceful hand on his arm. "You have waited this long, my love, can you not hold out a few days more, for Akin's sake?"

I blink. *My love?*

The endearment has a startling effect on Yanassi's demeanour. He straightens, putting a large hand on top of hers. "You are right, my flower. A few days is a small thing to see my best man healed. I, too, would like those closest to me by my side when we marry."

Paser and Reb are gaping at the pair. Has the princess tamed the lion?

I become aware that Yanassi is speaking to me. "… how much time will you need to prepare?"

"I do not know," I admit. Though distracted by the new — genuine? — depth in Merat and Yanassi's relationship, my healer's instincts can no longer be suppressed. "I should check on Akin as soon as possible."

Yanassi picks up a chicken leg and rips into it with his teeth, chewing then swallowing, as he surveys me. Tossing the drumstick aside, he stands abruptly. "I will take you to him. Now."

I hesitate, torn between wanting to assess the injured soldier at last and apprehensive of my first time alone with the chieftain. Pepi indicates with a quick nod that I will be fine. Standing, I follow Yanassi, leaving behind the din of the room in addition to my friends and relative safety. With a last look over my shoulder, I see Merat leaning forward, speaking animatedly to Paser. Accustomed to being followed without question, Yanassi walks ahead without checking to see if I'm coming.

"What is Akin's condition like?" I say to the chieftain's muscular back, after a few moments of trailing him in silence.

"He is strong, but his spirit is being greatly tested." He still does not look behind him.

"And his wife and child?" Despite the chieftain's hostility, I wish to know how my friend Amara fares. Helping a woman bring a babe into this world is a sacred experience, one that links two people — three, if you count the child.

"Fine." Yanassi's voice remains short as we enter the courtyard. Vivid purple and blues flash between the pillared columns, glimpses of the sacred lotuses dotting the pool's surface. We walk in terse silence through the palace grounds, to the west, where additional buildings sit.

"Believe what you want, but I do not wish to rule the lands," I say, at last. "It is my hope that the oracle will be able to clarify the prophecy. There must be a mistake."

"Mistake?" Yanassi snorts. "The very idea that you are the one from the prophecy is an outrageous affront to the gods."

"Why did you leave your cousin in a pit?" The question comes from out of nowhere.

Yanassi stops abruptly and I almost walk into his battle-scarred back. He turns to finally acknowledge me, a snake who's spotted its next meal. His voice is deadly quiet. "I wonder why you feel it is your right to ask such questions?"

"Some would say I earned it." I try not to appear intimidated. Men like Yanassi only hunt harder when they smell blood. "By risking my life to retrieve the scroll at your command."

"You were not pleased with your end of the trade, the scroll for weddings in Avaris?" Yanassi's voice is mocking. "Though I admit it seems a frivolous reason to traverse a desert."

"There were other dangers on the journey besides crossing a desert," I say quietly.

"Ah, yes. Pepi mentioned something of your … conflict with Queen Anat. I recall my own dealings with her, during negotiations for the princess." I note the posture of his body, the dark expression on his face.

"You despise her."

"I'm sure the feeling is mutual." The venom in his voice is as toxic as a viper's. "She thinks I am boorish Hyksos scum."

"She gave you the princess," I point out.

"A tactical move," he scoffs. "She thought it would turn my mind from attacking her fair city."

"And has it?" Sometimes the best probing instrument is a blunt one.

"I am planning for a wedding, am I not?" he reasons, resuming his walking.

"You have no intention of waging war on Thebes, then?" I hurry after him, not bothering to hide the disbelief in my voice. Ignoring me, he turns down another corridor, striding toward a room at the end of the hall. I follow him in. The light is dim, and it takes a few seconds for my vision to adjust. Someone calls my name.

"Sesha!" A dark shape rushes over and embraces me in a tight hug. Unexpected tears of relief come to my eyes. Amara pulls back to examine me and picks up a frazzled strand of my hair, her smile full of gratitude and hope. "You need another application of henna."

"It is wonderful to see you." I smile back, praying ferociously that Akin's condition is treatable. "Apologies for our delay. There was a sickness at the oasis we had to contend with. We only arrived in the city this day."

She grips my hand in alarm. "Are the people well?"

"Recovering, by the gods' good graces. It was not as bad as it could have been."

Her shoulders slump in relief. "And the scroll? Were you able to obtain it?"

"We have it." I give her another reassuring smile. "Where is Akin?"

"Here," a quiet voice says.

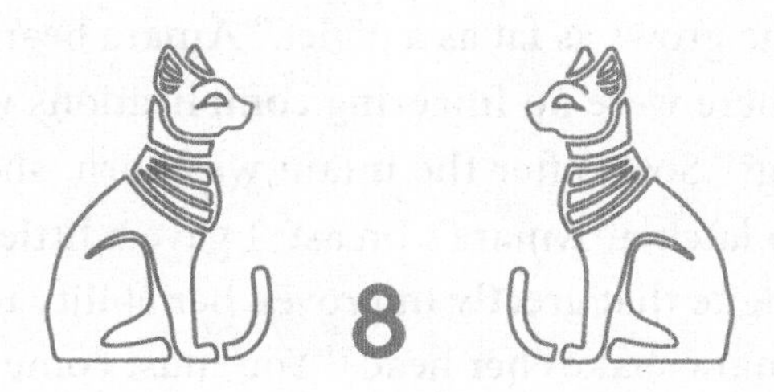

# 8

YANASSI IS ALREADY MOVING to the man far back in the corner, propped up against the wall on a woven reed mat. I keep the shock from my face upon seeing Akin's condition.

"You need to keep your strength up," I say instead, with a nod at the uneaten food beside him.

The soldier waves a listless hand. "Amara brings me food all day."

"That doesn't mean you eat any of it," she chastens him.

Sensing that this might be a frequent argument for the pair, I search for another topic. "Where is my namesake?" I refer to their babe.

"With my sister," Amara says. "My family is here in the city."

"She is well, then?" A warm glow infuses my heart.

"She grows as fat as a piglet." Amara beams.

"There were no lingering complications with her feeding?" Soon after the infant was born, she struggled to latch at Amara's breast; I gave a little snip to her tongue that greatly improved her ability to nurse.

Amara shakes her head. "You must come and see her for yourself."

"I would like that." I kneel at Akin's side to better inspect Yanassi's second-in-command. Thankfully, there is no scent of putrefaction. To the contrary, the smell of the fresh uneaten olives makes my own stomach grumble. Seeing Amara, and my patient alive, restores my appetite.

Amara laughs. "I will bring you something." She leaves the room, and I am alone with Akin and Yanassi, who keeps silent during my examination.

I check Akin carefully for any of the sores or open wounds that often come from remaining reclined at all times. They are usually found on the lower back or the heels, wherever the pressure is greatest. But it appears Amara has been doing an admirable job of keeping Akin clean and rotating him to rest on different sides. Aside from his startling thinness and the blinding despair in his eyes, he does not look as bad as I first thought. What *is* considerably diminished is his life force, and perhaps this is what first struck me.

Akin's spirits lie heavy and low, like an impenetrable fog on the Nile. When Amara exits the room, what little strength the fallen soldier clings to leaves with her.

"This has gone on too long." Akin closes his eyes. "Daughter of Ay. You must release me from my misery, I beg you."

"Is the pain so bad?" Very carefully, I palpate his leg, which seems to be healing well.

"There is no pain at all in my legs, nor can I move them. What is less bearable is the wasted pile of uselessness I have become." Looking down at his body he lets out a bitter sound that is not quite laughter. "My wife needs to bathe and change diapers for both her daughter *and* her husband."

"It can be difficult being rendered suddenly helpless," I say, voice soft. "Especially for a brave warrior such as yourself; one who is used to the wind in his hair and a horse beneath him." An idea strikes and I turn to Yanassi, who stands behind me, watching.

"You could put him back on his horse," I say to the chieftain.

Akin makes a choked noise. "Are you insane? I cannot ride."

Ignoring the soldier's sputtering, I direct my remarks to Yanassi. "You could sit behind him, supporting him. Find a strong and steady creature, one with a calm temperament."

The chieftain looks skeptical. "What if it damages his body further?"

I lift a brow at Yanassi. "He was moved here, across a desert, was he not? Besides" — I turn back to my patient and direct my next words to him, gently — "the health of your spirit is of equal importance to that of your physical body. You asking me to end your life is an indication it is not doing that well."

"The palace healers have been bringing medicines and chanting their prayers." A defensive note creeps into Yanassi's voice. "They see adequately to his needs."

"*Adequate* is not a word I want to describe my husband's care." Amara returns with a tray brimming with olives, bread, creamy dips, and fresh vegetables. "Sesha will now assume his treatment." Her brisk tone leaves little room for argument. "She will be the one to perform the surgery."

"What about the healers here?" I say as Akin closes his eyes, not seeming to care either way. "Will they not object to having a Theban doctor attend their patient?"

"He was your patient first." Amara sets the tray firmly down on the table. She is right, of course. I am familiar with the soldier's body and spirit, having already worked with his *Ka*. Nobody wants Amara's husband healed more than I. Except, of course, the Hyksos woman herself, and his chieftain.

"You believe that you and the scroll are enough?" Yanassi crosses his arms, apparently quite adept at reading the doubt on my face.

I am not positive. But if Akin is to remain my patient, I do not want to put fear in the soldier's or his wife's thoughts, as those have tangible effects on both spirit *and* body. Instead, I raise my voice to fill the space, a declaration that echoes through the chamber. "This is an ailment with which I will contend." May the gods be on my side.

I am back to sharing a room with Merat. I keep glancing around and picking up items here and there, to assure myself it is not a dream. The princess and I finally have a chance to catch each other up on all that has happened since we last saw one another, ending with an extensive analysis of the dual prophecies.

"… and Pepi thinks you are the one from the line of the physician?" Merat says for the dozenth time, biting her lower lip. "What about Ky? Or a child of another physician?"

"I said that, as well." My shoulder lifts helplessly. "But Imhotep's scroll features in both prophecies, and Pepi believes the document and I are connected."

"I agree with him there," Merat admits, studying me. "What you have done so far has been nothing short of amazing. The gods seem to be at your back, Sesha. Perhaps there *is* truth to what this oracle says."

"I cannot fathom how I am meant to rule anything." I suppose I will have the chance to clear things up when we find the oracle. If we find her. The pressure in my head increases. "May we speak no more of it for now?"

"Very well then." Merat flops down upon a pile of cushions and changes the topic. "Can you believe my sister and your brother are to be married?" she says, with an incredulous laugh.

"When they are of age," I remind her, picking up a vial of perfume and uncorking it. I sniff the spicy sweet fragrance. "They are still ch … ch … children." I sneeze and, eyes watering, put the stopper back in the bottle.

"Not for long." She takes the perfume from my hands and applies a few drops to her wrists, her inner elbows. I see the question in her eyes she keeps from asking.

"What is it?" I say, though I intuit what she wants to know. Her mother's murderous inclinations, however, are a sore point between us and likely prevent her from inquiring after her parents. Tilting her head to the side, she dabs the fragrance on her long, graceful neck, the base of her throat, behind her earlobes. I take pity on her — besides, my nose will not stand for continued perfume application. "Your parents looked well." I saw the pharaoh and queen when I was in Thebes retrieving the scroll — a charged encounter to say the least, but at least I can bring news of them to Merat.

"Oh?" She feigns mild interest, putting the vial down. "Did they … did they inquire after my well-being?"

"They miss you," I say. "Your father especially, I think. Though your mother seems to feel your absence, as well." When the queen spoke the words *my daughter*, her voice caught like linen snagging on a splinter.

"I've been deliberating matters." Merat bites her lower lip again. "I do believe they are doing their best for their people." I remain silent, recalling the queen's comment about famine being a handy way "to rid the land of excess." No doubt she means to protect her immediate family, but by her own admission, she views the common people as expendable. "I have decided to go through with my wedding, without any further silly schemes on our part."

"Do not lose your fire, Merat," I urge her. "We will figure something out. You do not have to marry Yana—"

"That is enough, Sesha!" Her tone is as sharp as my father's blade. "I have been a fool, holding out for the merest chance that the person I desire will miraculously wake up to realize they return my affections."

I know she refers to Paser. I get the next words out past the lump in my throat. "There is still a chance —"

"Not when *you* walk around in the moonlight, kissing him under the stars and asking him to wait for you to return from your adventures," she snaps, and I see that Merat has not lost any of her fire after all; it has only been redirected. At me. I flush at the heat of her words and at my actions the night before leaving the oasis to get the scroll.

"I was doing my best to keep you both safe." Conflicting emotions cause my voice to climb high, up beyond the clouds. "Your feelings for Paser were obvious to anyone who cared to look. The chieftain would have cast him out into the desert should he have competed for your affections," I say. "Or worse."

A jagged laugh trills out of Merat, and the faint echo of Queen Anat in it chills my blood. "Compete for my attentions? His gaze falls only on you. And believe me, Sesha, you cast a lengthy shadow on everything else around."

"I do not wish to quarrel with you." I strive to bring my voice and emotions back down to this earth. "I apologize if I caused you pain, but please, I beg you, do not resign yourself to this marriage."

"My mind is set on this course." Merat's eyes flash dangerously, daring me to defy her. "There was much time to think on my journey to the capital. I *will* marry Yanassi. And perhaps if the chieftain comes to love me, I can keep him from waging war on my city." She walks to the window and looks out, up at the stars overhead. "You are not the only one who can be brave, Sesha."

A thousand sentiments stampede through my mind. I pick the truest one from the chaotic herd trampling my heart. "You will make a fine queen," I say, turning to leave her.

"We shall see," she calls after me. "Though, if the prophecy is correct, and you are to rule, then I suppose you will take that from me, as well." The hot bitterness in her voice sears my soul as I leave the room.

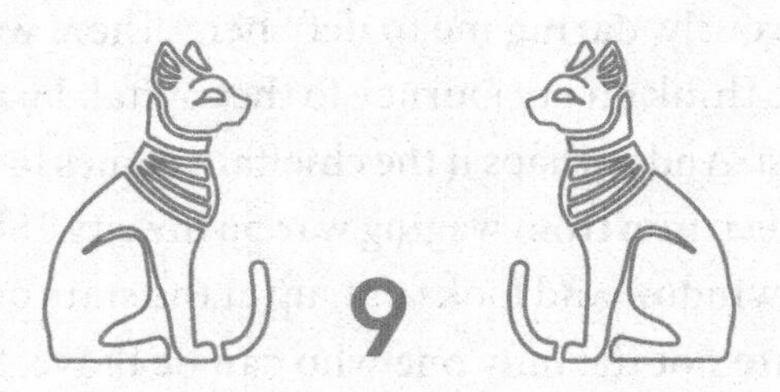

# 9

I FIND MYSELF UP on the rooftop, needing air and space to breathe, stalking its length like a penned-in cheetah. Night is coming. Both moon and sun share the dusky blue sky before Ra finally gives way to Khonsu's milky luminosity, descending in a blazing ball of flames. The silvery paleness of the waxing moon subdues the fire under my own skin. Such duality, on a consistent, permanent basis, steadies me. My breathing slows as I contemplate this dance between the two gods, this yielding and taking of territory. If humans could be as graceful about it as the deities are, life might be more peaceful.

*Peace is where you make it*, my mother's voice whispers at my ear. I take another deep breath, feeling her presence shimmer over me, as soothing as the moon.

"May the gods help me; I love them both," I whisper to the voice.

*Love, any pure love, is never a thing to regret. What you do with that love is what matters.*

"And what *am* I to do?" I say, more loudly this time. The affairs of my heart are trivial compared to all we must do to prevent the land from erupting in chaos.

"You are not considering jumping, I hope?" A voice startles me, and I whirl to spot a frail shape behind me, reclined on a mat and pillows. It is the king. The outline of Abisha's towering form is a few steps off to the side, spear at the ready.

"I am sorry." I duck my head, embarrassed to be caught conversing with myself. "I did not know anyone was up here."

"I find it peaceful at this hour," the king says, looking out over the rooftops that stretch into the night. The odd candle is lit in houses where people have retired for the evening, beacons in the dark. "Though I am excited to witness the sights of the next realm, I will miss the ones here." There is regret in his voice as he takes in his flourishing kingdom. His home.

"The sights will be much the same, don't you think?"

"How so?" The king gives me a curious look.

"My father said our monuments are a direct reflection of the heavens." I point. "The three great pyramids line up with the trio of stars in Osiris's crown." I move my hand, tracing the shapes and patterns. "The Sphinx represents the lion in the sky, and the Nile itself mirrors the winding white river of stars above." It occurs to me that the monuments I refer to were not built by his people. In fact, though Khyan's city is robust and bustling, the Hyksos appear more restrained when it comes to investing their time and resources into grandiose structures. Perhaps that is why they currently prosper over Thebes.

"Well, I am relieved to hear that you are merely contemplating the heavens and not leaping to your death," Khyan says politely.

I exhale. "Might I speak with you?"

He is amused. "Is that not what we are doing now?" The Hyksos king seems to have a sense of humour, always a useful thing.

I tilt my head at Abisha. "Privately?"

The guard doesn't move, but his eyes cut to the king, who nods. "Forgive my asking, but I'd appreciate the removal of any weapons on your person before our doing so." Surprise must show on my face because the king gives a small smile. "I have not lived this long without being overly cautious. And I do not make the habit of underestimating young women on a mission."

"There are many who do." I bend down and unstrap the obsidian dagger from my leg. "To their own detriment, of course." I stand. "But what makes you think I'm on a mission?"

"You are going in search of the oracle, are you not?"

"It seems I have little choice." I place the sharp blade in the bodyguard's outstretched hand. Abisha gives me an ironic bow before moving off to allow us privacy.

"One always has a choice. And you have that same look my nephew gets when he is up to his eyebrows in plots and schemes." The king appears to know something of Pepi's clandestine activities. Approving of them may be another matter. "Pepi's mother, another formidable woman, looked much the same way when she was planning on changing the world."

I clear my throat. "Pepi tells me you knew Kalali quite well."

The king raises a bushy eyebrow. "She was sister to Yanassi's mother, and part of our family. Of course I knew her well."

"Well enough that there is a chance Pepi is your son?"

The king blinks at me in astonishment. "By the gods, you are a bold creature."

"Pepi should be the one to rule. Not Yanassi. And definitely not me." My voice is urgent. "You know Yanassi hungers for Thebes to bow to him. He will incite a war, while Pepi would govern your kingdom well." I hold my breath, gauging his reaction.

The king is silent a moment. "Does Pepi know you come to me with such a significant matter? I cannot imagine this bid for kingship comes from him."

"Why?"

"Because I have hinted as much over the years, and my nephew never expressed any interest in assuming the throne. He is more concerned with his freedom and his adventures. You are not the only one it has occurred to that he would make a good king." Khyan pauses. "Even if he is *not* my son."

I take another breath. "He thinks he is."

"And why would he think that?"

"His mother told him so."

The king sighs. "In addition to being a priestess, Kalali was a spy, a brilliant one, and not above inventing stories as a way to achieve her means."

I feel the sting of his words on Pepi's behalf. "Can you rule out the possibility entirely?"

"It does not matter what I think. There are those who love him, but others would require strong evidence to accept him in Yanassi's place." My heart sinks. I had counted on the king as an ally. He continues, "It has been assumed that Yanassi is the rightful heir for some time now; I do not want my kingdom torn apart."

It sounds as if Khyan has made his decision. I let loose my one final shot. "What about the oracle? If she is as great as you claim, she should have no difficulty in divining the question of Pepi's true lineage. If we return with her, perhaps she can prove to you *and* the kingdom that he *is* your son and worthy of ruling Avaris."

"Blood alone does not make someone worthy or unworthy," the king wheezes, sounding fatigued. Abisha hears it, as well, and takes a step forward.

I press on, "You said yourself you trusted the oracle's prophecies in the past, that they played a large part in your own fate."

Khyan takes a minute, as if deciding how much he should say. "Prophecies from the oracle are special occurrences. Typically, they are made in threes — though there may be years between them — and align with significant astrological events." The king looks up at the sky. "As it happens, this coming solstice coincides with a rare lunar eclipse." He looks back at me as if debating again how much to reveal. "So far there have been two prophecies surrounding the healer's papyrus. It would not be surprising if a third and final foretelling were to come on that night. And if the first two are any indication, it will likely have critical implications for the land and its peoples, both yours and mine. I believe it is imperative you find the oracle before then."

A third prophecy about the scroll! I force myself to remain calm. "Does Pepi know this?"

"As his mother was a priestess, I'd imagine he is aware that prophecies often come in threes, and he likely is aware of the coming eclipse. Whether he has connected these ideas, I cannot say." We contemplate each other, both familiar enough with Pepi to know that he has.

"Do you have any idea where the oracle might be?"

"The best place to look would be at the priestesses' temple, but its whereabouts are very carefully guarded," the king says. "Aside from the oracle, only one person knew of its precise location ..." He closes his eyes. "And she recently died with an arrow through her throat, I am told."

"I have some experience with finding things," I say softly.

"I wish you luck." Khyan's voice is sincere. "My best men have been unable to turn up a trace."

"You said you do not underestimate young women on a mission," I remind him.

He studies me, purple thumbprints under his ancient eyes. "So I did."

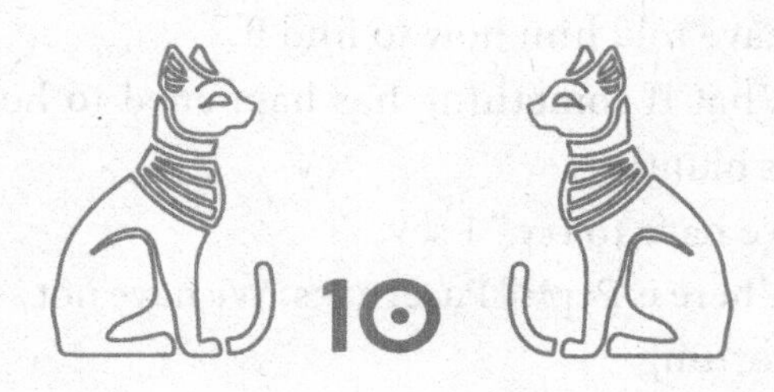

# 10

"YOU ARE HEALING AKIN today?" Paser asks the next morning over breakfast.

"I'm going to try." I swallow my bread. "I will need your help for the surgery. We leave tomorrow to find the oracle."

"You really think we can find her before the eclipse?" Reb says, before biting into a piece of juicy melon. They had taken the news of the third prophecy in stride.

"Together we have done extraordinary things," I say.

"How does one go about looking for an oracle?" Paser pops a date in his mouth.

"One starts at the priestesses' hidden temple. The king said only Kalali knew of its whereabouts. As Pepi said he had an idea of the oracle's location, his mother must have told him how to find it."

"What if something has happened to her?" Reb asks us bluntly.

"We have to try," I say.

"Where *is* Pepi?" Paser asks. We have not seen him this morning.

"In his script sanctuary," Merat says, coming in. She meets my gaze; last evening's temper has faded.

"Script sanctuary?" I echo.

"Yes, he has a whole collection, gathered from kingdoms far and wide." Merat waves a hand. "He calls it his 'Sanctum of Scrolls.' Yanassi showed me when we first arrived."

I salivate at the thought of the priceless information contained in such an assortment of documents: spells, incantations, prescriptions, and herbal potions ... a unique trove of treasures.

"Merat offered us one of the guards as an escort this morning, to help look for 'our' uncle," Paser says. "What time will Akin's surgery be?"

I understand Paser's compulsion to find his relative. "This afternoon, after I've had a chance to review the scroll."

With a promise to meet me back in time for the operation, the trio leaves. Eager to see this scriptorium — likely where my own scroll is being stored — I ask for directions from the servants and at last find the room in a far-off wing at the end of the palace. Poking my head in, I see Pepi at a table, surrounded by several papyri and what looks to be a map or two.

"Merat said I would find you here," I say softly, so as not to disturb his sanctuary. He is not startled, no doubt having heard my approach.

"Come in, Sesha." His voice is warm. "You, of all people, will appreciate this particular room, or rather its contents, I should say."

I walk in, unable to tear my eyes from the marvellous assortment of writings. Not since the chamber under the temple in Thebes, where Paser and I found the original scroll, have I seen so many documents in one place. Light shines in through a high window, gilding many of them in gold. Most of the writing is hieratic script, but there are other forms, intricate and unfamiliar.

"This is incredible." My voice is hushed. The gods feel close in this room, their sacred words together in one place. "Where did you find them all?"

"My *uncle*" — his lips twist wryly — "mother, and I have been collecting them for some time. We share a passion and respect for the written word." He looks up and around. "Do you feel it? There is much power concentrated in this room."

I do feel it, along with an immense rush of gratitude that I am able to read and write so many of these words. It is an extraordinary gift my father gave me.

"Some of them are quite old." He motions to documents that look like they will crumble into dust if one so much as breathes on them. "Perhaps you would consent to transcribe copies of the rarer ones, as you did with Imhotep's scroll, to preserve them for future generations?"

"It would be a great honour." I feel light-headed at the thought of having the ancient papyri at my fingertips.

"You can study your scroll here," he says, nodding at the long cedar table, and I touch the smooth wood. Examining the scroll in this sanctuary will be a welcome change from swirling sands and boisterous sailors.

"I will see to it that you have all the equipment you need," Pepi says. "How are you feeling about undertaking Akin's procedure?"

"Scared," I admit. "What if I cannot heal him? Or worse —" I swallow "— if he dies at my hand?"

"It does not sound like he is doing all that well."

"At least he lives," I say softly.

"There is something to be said about the quality of one's life." Pepi's tone is gentle.

"There is some truth to that," I admit. To allow one to suffer when there is no chance of recovery is awful and cruel. "But Akin is not dying, nor by his own admission, in pain. His condition is stable. He could make a different life if he wanted."

"Like many, the solider is a proud man," Pepi says. "Convincing him he might find joy, without full use of his once-formidable body, may be a difficult, if not impossible, task."

I make a frustrated sound. "If only we could consult the oracle about the outcome of the surgery. Or whether I should even perform it or not!"

"There are many things she could resolve," Pepi agrees, expression serious. "Which is why you need to find her as quickly as possible."

I take a deep breath. "The king thinks there might be a third prophecy."

"I agree with him," he says calmly.

"He also said the best place to begin looking for the oracle is at her temple, but that Kalali was the only person to know of its whereabouts."

"Not the only one." Pepi taps one of the maps with a finger. "As you know, my mother belonged to that sect of priestesses. They guard the oracle who is produced from their midst every generation. A few nights before she died, my mother told me of their location, a highly protected secret." He looks down at the map, murmuring under his breath. "Almost as if she knew ..."

Distracted by the papyri, I only now notice the small pile of glittering green gems by Pepi's hand. He'd lent us the mystical stones to aid in Paser's healing; they were a powerful complement to the scroll.

"You think the priestesses will assist us?"

"I hope so; they might know where she is, or what became of her." A shadow crosses his face. "It was my fault my mother died. It should not have happened the way it did."

"As you stand here well and whole before me, I think she would feel her sacrifice worth it."

"Or she'd be angry with me for failing to protect Tany." He swallows, a small muscle in his cheek moving involuntarily. "She was my only sister. I was to look out for her."

Ky, my sweet brother, now a member of the royal family, materializes in my mind. Will I ever see him again? Or is he starting to forget me, our family? My heart aches. "I know what it is like to love and lose those closest to you."

"I had a small hope she might be here, in the city." His face is bleak. "But no one has seen or heard from her."

"Perhaps that is another question for the oracle."

Pepi takes a reed and begins to mark one of the maps. "I would go with you, but my uncle is right, I need to be at his side should his condition worsen, or to receive any instructions he might pass on to me. I must also watch Yanassi. He says he is planning a wedding, but I do not fully trust him. The hand-off of power is a precarious time filled with hidden opportunities and threats from all sides."

"Do not worry, Pepi. You trained me well." I tap the map. "Now, tell me how to find the priestesses."

"I will." He stops drawing to pick up the glittering gems beside him and puts them in my hand. "When you find the sect, show them these — priestess stones. They were my mother's."

After learning what I need to know from Pepi, I spend the rest of the morning poring over the scroll and cases pertaining to Akin's surgery. To my growing dismay, I cannot find a single promising treatment for an injury like his across the entire papyrus. I tell myself I must be missing something. I was certain that the great medical document, with its impressive history, would contain the answer. Taking the scroll with me, I study it while walking to Akin's room and feel a rekindled glimmer of hope as I spot the ancient incantation that had such remarkable results for Paser. Surely it will have some power over Akin's affliction, as well.

Angry shouts outside his chamber make me look up from the scroll in alarm.

"How dare you?" An anguished voice hastens my footsteps. I enter expecting to see my patient, but aside from Yanassi, Amara, and the baby wrapped snugly against her belly, the room is empty.

"Where is Akin?" Panic grips my chest.

"Gone." Amara's distraught face sends my heart to my stomach.

"He is on his way to his surgery," Yanassi informs me.

"By whose hand?" I demand, indignation sweeping through my body.

"Kazir, the best healer Avaris has on offer," Yanassi sneers. "One with several more years of experience than a scribe barely out of temple."

"You did not consult me." Amara is furious. The baby, as if picking up on her mother's mood, lets out a distressed cry.

"I did not need to," Yanassi says coldly. "Akin is my second; I will decide what is best for him."

"He is my husband!" Amara snaps, one hand patting the child's back to calm her. "Sesha was supposed to perform the procedure."

"What happened to needing the scroll?" I interrupt, bewildered, holding up the document. Yanassi's eyes flicker to the papyrus.

"Give that to me," he demands. "I will bring it to the healer."

My hand tightens around the document. "I will deliver it myself. Amara, take me to Akin."

"You will not interfere!" Yanassi shouts, slamming a meaty fist into his palm.

Ignoring him, we hurry from the room. I follow Amara with a quick look over my shoulder, but Yanassi does not follow. I hope we are not too late.

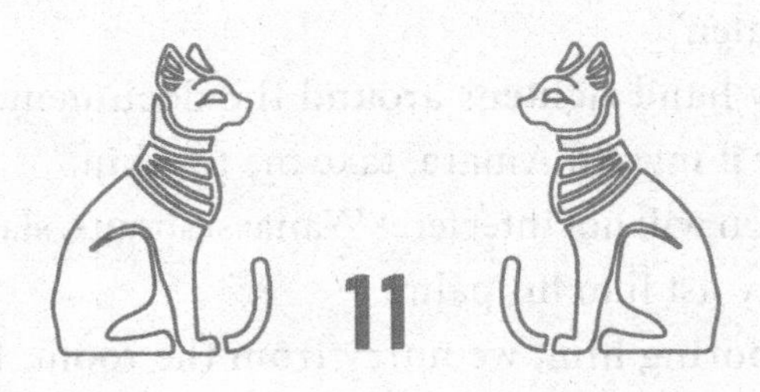

# 11

MY THOUGHTS WHIR along with my feet as we fly through the halls like birds startled from their perch. After all this time, why couldn't the chieftain wait?

"This way," Amara calls, one hand still on her baby, who settles, lulled by the motion. Turning left, we dash past several startled servants, causing one to almost drop the tray she is carrying. We reach the medical wing at last, breath coming in gasps, and burst into the room.

The healer-priest, Kazir, stands beside the still form of Akin, hands hovering above the injured soldier. He looks up, startled at the interruption. "What is happening?"

"That man is my patient," I gasp, pointing at Akin with the scroll.

"She will be the one to perform the surgery." Breathless, Amara walks up to her husband and inserts herself between his inert form and the tall priest.

Bafflement crosses Kazir's homely face as he takes me in. "How many successful surgeries have you performed with this type of ailment?" he questions.

"None." I grip the scroll tighter, doubt creeping along my veins. "But I have studied intensively and trained under the very best healers in Thebes."

"Though your training has no doubt been comprehensive, young physician, I myself have performed hundreds of surgeries over the past twenty years, many of which were highly successful." His eyes flicker from us to the dozing soldier. Kazir must have given him a tincture to ease him into unconsciousness. "Part of that success is owed to a thorough diagnostic assessment of my patients. After making a full examination of Akin, I have determined that this is an ailment I will *not* treat." He pauses, allowing his words to sink in. Then he walks over to me and puts a hand on my shoulder. "And — in my humblest of opinions — neither should you, Daughter of Ay."

Already taken aback by his announcement, I almost fall over. He knows who I am?

"She has the great scroll of Imhotep," Amara protests. "The document is filled with old magic, *Heka*." I can almost see the hope slipping, like sand through her fingers. "There must be something in it that can help."

"There is a powerful incantation," I say, avoiding admitting what I discovered earlier — that it's the *only* thing the scroll seems to contain that might help Akin. "It worked wonders on my friend. And another healer used a procedure from this very scroll to cure my brother of his illness. It saved his life!"

"By all means, recite the incantation, if you wish." The healer gestures at Akin. "But it is my belief that operating may severely worsen his condition, or even kill him. It is out of our hands and in the hands of the gods now. I will inform the chieftain of this myself."

I look over at my friend, helpless, wanting to deny what Kazir has said. But I realize that the healer has the mettle to voice what I already feared deep down, from the moment I laid my hands on the soldier: Akin's injury may simply be too grave for us to contend with. Even the great Imhotep has not given us such a miraculous procedure. Amara, whose desolate expression must match mine, lets out a sob, seeming to fold around her baby. I put my arms out to support her, the child warm between us.

"I do not mind that he is lame," she weeps into my shoulder. "But what am I to do about his heart? It will be more broken than his body by this news."

"Akin is strong," I say with a gentle squeeze. "And so are you. You will find a way through this, together."

Akin's eyelids flutter open. "Is it over?" His voice is hoarse, his dilated pupils full of cautious optimism.

Amara squares her shoulders and swallows her own grief to confront her husband's, brave as any soldier striding into battle. The healer, Kazir, looks at me and we step forward to join her — and the child held tightly to her chest — in letting Akin know he has much left to live for.

Afterward, Kazir and I leave the room to allow Akin and Amara some privacy.

"Is that really the legendary scroll of the great Imhotep?" The healer eyes the document with respect.

"It is only a copy." I offer it to him, allowing him to examine it. "Transcribed by my father and me."

"Incredible," he murmurs, studying the papyrus carefully. "Your father was an extraordinary physician. How fitting that he was the one to perform the transcription."

"You knew him?" I say, my heart beating faster.

"We trained together," he says, confirming what my gut tells me. "He was a brilliant healer and showed me a most effective treatment for binding the bowels."

I shake my head. "You are not the first person to tell me he studied and trained here in Avaris, but it seems unreal. It is strange to think he had a whole other life before me and my brother, before he met my mother."

"He must have been as excellent a father as he was a physician for you to feel like you were his entire world," Kazir remarks.

I blink back the tears forming in the corners of my eyes. "He was."

The healer nods and hands me back the scroll. "I will go and deal with the chieftain."

"He will not be pleased," I warn. "Yanassi expects nothing less than his second to be restored to his former strength and abilities."

"I am aware," the healer says dryly. "But one does not argue with the gods."

"You have my thanks."

He tilts his head, examining me. "For what?"

"For showing me something."

"What was that?"

"That sometimes it takes as much courage to accept what is, as it does to challenge it." I look down, at a loss. "Now if only I knew when to do which."

"That will come with time." Kazir gives me a faint smile. "Then again, it may not. But a good healer always does what they can, and that is all they can do."

His words have a tinge of prophecy-speak, and as he leaves me standing there, my thoughts return to the impossible task my friends and I are about to perform: leave for the unknown to find a lost oracle, in hopes of setting Pepi on the throne and securing peace for an entire kingdom. A peace that will last a lifetime for many. The gods feel near just then, perhaps due to my earlier immersion in their words. I whisper my vow out loud, in case they are listening.

"We will do all that we can, and that is all we can do."

And then we will pray that it is enough.

I find Paser and Reb later that afternoon in the courtyard. They are hot and dusty from inquiring about the city after anyone fitting Paser's uncle's description, to no avail. I tell them about Akin and they assure me I am not wrong to respect another healer's opinion, particularly one with years of experience.

"A part of me feels like I am failing Amara and her husband," I say. We sit beside the lotus pond watching small frogs jump from pad to pad.

"That is only your pride talking, Sesha," Reb says, not unkindly. "You'd think you'd have learned to recognize it by now."

I look at my friends. "You do not think I am a terrible coward?"

"It is not cowardly to know what one can contend with and what one cannot," Paser reasons. "It is good sense."

I sigh. "I must have missed that lesson in temple."

"You did start late." Reb grins.

"Still. I would like to try something." I can't forget Akin's devastated expression, Amara's anguish, and Kazir's advice. *A good healer does what they can, and that is all they can do.* "Maybe I cannot operate, but it will not hurt to perform the incantation for Akin."

"The one from the scroll?" Reb asks.

"That is an idea," Paser says, thoughtful. "When you used it in my healing, there was something … I cannot quite explain."

I look at him in curiosity. "Try."

He shrugs, looking helpless. "It was as if … as if the words themselves infiltrated my skin, dissolving the sickness eating at my blood and bones. But it was more than the incantation alone. It was you, too, Sesha." Paser looks at me. "When you put your hands on me, an incredible warmth flowed into my body." He closes his eyes, in memory. "It was electrifying and soothing, all at the same time." Reb snorts and Paser open his eyes but ignores him. "You are a gifted healer, and the scroll is more than a medical document." He echoes Merat's sentiment. "Maybe there *is* something to these prophecies Pepi speaks of." We are silent amidst the chirping frogs.

"When do you propose to perform the rite?" Reb gets back to the matter at hand. "We're supposed to leave tomorrow."

"Tonight, when all are asleep." I look at my friends. "May I count on your assistance?"

"Always," Paser says.

We look at Reb, who sighs. "I'll bring the candles."

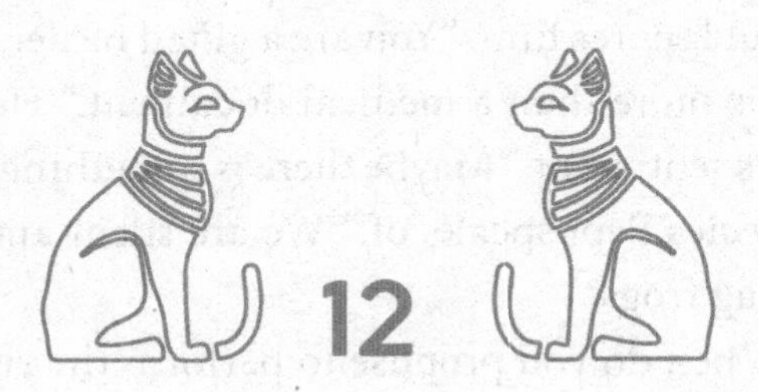

# 12

TORCHES FLICKER AT the entrance to the dining hall. They illuminate Merat standing with the chieftain, who tosses his customary disgusted look our way. She touches his arm and whispers something in his ear. He gives a brief, tight nod and goes inside while she turns to greet us. Merat's charms seem to be working; Queen Anat and her courtiers instructed the princess well in wielding her influence.

"Did you learn anything at all in your search this morning?" I refer to the brief hunt for Paser's uncle, including Merat in the question.

"Avaris holds many people," Paser admits, sounding uncharacteristically dejected.

"It was like looking for a needle in a sandhill," Reb says. "Good practice for traipsing off in search of a lost or hiding oracle who may or may not want to be found."

I stop short. "What makes you think she does not want to be found?" If the oracle is deliberately in hiding, our task may be even more difficult than we imagine.

"Would you want people pestering you with questions on everything from when it's the right time to plough a field, to who should preside over kingdoms?" Reb shakes his head. "Everyone, from farmers to pharaohs, demanding answers? What if you say something someone does not want to hear? Or what of the consequences if you are wrong? If it were me, I'd run and hide, too."

"We do not know for sure that the oracle is hiding," Merat reminds him as we enter the great hall. "And Pepi says she has never been wrong."

I shiver. Is Reb right? If we bring the oracle back to the capital with the intention of setting Pepi on the throne and effectively usurping Yanassi, are we also putting her, in addition to ourselves, in danger?

"Regarding your uncle," Merat says with a meaningful look at us, "I will keep up the search while you three are away and offer a reward if he identifies himself to the throne, or for any information on his whereabouts."

"You have our eternal thanks, Princess." Paser gives her a grateful smile, and she beams it back at him, sunlight reflecting off gold.

"It is the least I can do for my friends," she says as we proceed through the room together, tossing her hair in acknowledgement of the court's admiring stares. We approach the king, who has rallied for another dinner with his esteemed councillors and subjects.

"I hear Akin's surgery will not be happening," Khyan says gravely, after greeting us. His colour is slightly better this evening, though he is still an ashy grey.

"The chieftain's healer felt it would cause more harm than good." I take my seat next to Pepi as Yanassi takes his, glowering, beside the king. The chieftain's accusatory glare makes me thankful it was not I who advised cancelling the soldier's procedure.

"Kazir is a respected diagnostician," Pepi echoes. "If he felt it was safer to let Akin be, we can be assured it is the wisest course." He is dressed finely this evening. An ornately carved toggle pins his linens at his shoulder, and they drape elegantly down his lithe body. Merat is not the only one receiving admiring glances. As the king's nephew, he is a choice catch himself. With a jolt, I remember *I* am the one who has supposedly caught him. In the spirit of our charade, I imitate Merat and flutter my eyelashes at Pepi for the benefit of those watching.

"Is there something in your eye, Sesha?" Reb whispers.

The king is agreeing with Pepi's previous statement. "While our hearts grieve for our friend Akin, this means you and your brothers can leave at once to retrieve the oracle." He looks at Pepi. "You have told her what she needs to know, Nephew?"

"Yes, Uncle. Preparations are being made for their departure at first light tomorrow."

"Very good," the king says and takes a small sip of his wine, signalling the rest of us to begin our meal. As we eat and drink, I look around at the numerous high-ranking officials who dine with us again, in celebration of our homecoming and prospective weddings. I wonder which ones align themselves with Pepi, which ones with Yanassi, and which are undecided.

"You will need someone to take Akin's place," the king is saying to the sullen chieftain.

"No one can take his place," Yanassi retorts, ripping off a piece of his bread.

"You need a second, Yanassi." The king's voice is gentle. "It is wise to choose one quickly, before it causes infighting among your men."

"Perhaps you should take your own advice, Father." Standing, Yanassi shoves the bread into his mouth, then takes a large sip of wine to wash it down. "Excuse me, my appetite seems to have wandered off." He leans over Reb to grab a chunk of meat, then does the same.

"I wonder how he eats when he's actually hungry," Reb murmurs. We watch him stride over to confer with his entourage. It hits me that the loss of Akin is not only a deeply personal one for Yanassi, but a professional one, as well. His friend is his trusted confidant and enforcer, commander of his troops, and his finest horseman. Without Akin at his side, Yanassi is vulnerable, in more ways than one. Though Akin's condition fills me with sorrow, it aids our own cause, creating a temporary distraction for the chieftain. Yet with the scroll and some luck, I am about to try and remedy that situation later tonight.

Pepi clears his throat and lifts his glass high. "Let us think of Akin, brave warrior, loyal companion, beloved husband and father." His voice carries across the room, and Yanassi's shoulders stiffen. The courtiers lift their own goblets, and one of them passes Yanassi a full cup. "May he heal and be comforted with the knowledge that he served his chief well." Pepi locks eyes with Yanassi and takes a drink, as others do the same.

My gaze falls upon a familiar, albeit unfriendly, face in the corner of the room. It is the Nubian mercenary from the ship. I elbow Paser sharply and nod in the fierce-looking man's direction. "What do you think he is doing here?" I lean over to whisper to him and Reb. Pepi would've mentioned if he invited him to the palace; his presence here must be at someone else's request.

"He appears to be eating," Reb whispers back.

The Nubian feels our eyes and returns our stare. I picture him sharpening his long blade on the boat. He does not have it in the open tonight, but I'd wager it's within arm's reach. The chieftain walks over to the Nubian and begins to speak with him. The two appear to know each other well, which does not strike me as a good thing. Yanassi says something and the Nubian's eyes flicker over us again, as a slow, wicked smile spreads across his face. Unlike the chieftain's, my appetite deserts me for real. It is replaced by a feeling that whatever the pair are discussing, it does not bode well for me and my friends.

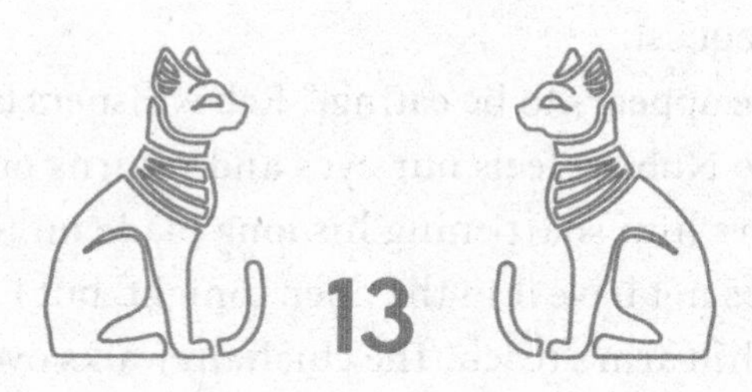

# 13

AFTER DINNER, MERAT takes me to a shrine at my request. I leave an offering for my parents and the gods there, praying they will be at Akin's side with me later this evening. The gleaming monument is an exact replica of one you would find in Thebes. Beside it is a large platform, where one typically consults the oracle on the solstice. The people will be wondering at her whereabouts soon.

"It must give you comfort that many things here are similar to home," I say to Merat.

"Yes, the Hyksos adopted many Theban cultures and traditions." That is what Pepi said. "They do keep some of their own, however." Merat looks over at the burial ground. "While we bury our dead in tombs, they keep theirs close, interned within their settlements." Her nose wrinkles. "They also have the oddest custom of being buried with their horses."

I think of Pepi's affection for Nefer, who's currently in the palace stables, no doubt enjoying her reprieve from desert and river crossings. "When you consider the assortment of goods our people are buried with, it is not all that strange a Hyksos warrior would want their equine partner accompanying them to the underworld." Merat makes an agreeable noise and puts her arm through mine. We begin our walk back to the palace. One of Yanassi's men escorts us, trailing at a respectful distance.

"There is something I must tell you, Sesha," Merat says after a few seconds of this bliss, voice low.

"Yes?" My breath catches in anticipation.

"Did you see that man Yanassi was speaking to earlier at dinner? The Nubian?"

"Yes." The unease is back. "Pepi said he is a mercenary."

Her worried expression intensifies as she glances over her shoulder at the escort, presumably estimating whether he is within earshot. "Yanassi has hired him," she whispers.

"To do what?"

"I am not sure," she admits. "I can try to find out, but as you are leaving in the morning, there may not be enough time to discover his purpose without arousing suspicions."

"What makes you so sure the Nubian is in Yanassi's pocket?" I ask, though I do not doubt it.

"I saw him give the man silver. Lots of it."

"You are quite the spy yourself," I say lightly, trying not to let worry ruin our last moments together.

She takes a deep breath. "When you come back, there is a good chance I may be married."

"I know." I swallow. "I do not want to lose you."

"You will never lose me. I am your friend always." She smiles. "Who else can put up with my jealous fits?"

"You have no reason to be jealous," I remind her. "You are a princess, soon to be a queen. Everything you want for is yours, should you ask for it."

"Not everything," she sighs. "But you are right. I have much to be thankful for. Not the least of all, you. Your loyalty and bravery are valued, never forget that." She squeezes my hand. "I do not feel so alone when you are around. Take care on your mission and promise you will come back to me, unharmed."

"I will," I promise.

"I believe you," she says, pensive, and gives her head a little shake. "I just cannot dispel this feeling that something looms on the horizon. Something that might change our lives forever."

"Have they not already?" I force a laugh. "Besides, I am certain every young woman feels that way before she is wed."

She waves a delicate hand, wristlets chiming lightly. "I can handle Yanassi. This is bigger than that."

Her foreboding statement lifts the hairs on my arms. "Do you think it is related to the prophecies?"

Merat shrugs. "I do not know. Perhaps when you bring the oracle back, we will finally have some answers."

"What if, like Reb says, the answers are not something we wish to hear?"

"Then we will get through it as best we can," she says simply. "Just come back."

"I have come for you two times already," I remind her as she stops to unclasp a gold bracelet, an exquisite protective amulet, one I have never seen her go without.

She smiles, but there is worry at the back of her beautiful eyes as she clasps it around my wrist. "Take this charm and make it a third."

"Move the torch this way," I whisper to Paser. He obliges, and I pull Kalali's stones from my robes. Like Paser's eyes, the gold-green gems glint in the torch's light. Crouching by Akin, I place the gems close to my basket and lay out the items beside my patient. Carefully, I take the scroll from its protective casing, inhaling the sweet smell of the papyrus. My father's writing, so fine and precise, jumps off the page, etching itself into my heart. Seeing his script still feels unreal, as do the small additions here and there, written by my own hand.

I read it a final time, making sure of the words, then roll it back up and slide it into its casing. Selecting a bundle of incense, I light it with one of the candles Reb provides. It catches at once, smoke curling up into the dark and dazzling sky. Amara has arranged for Akin to be brought to the rooftops, and we are tucked away in an alcove where he's fallen back into a restless sleep. Inhaling several deep breaths of the pungent-smelling herbs, I raise my hands and the sinuous smoke to the heavens.

"Gods and goddesses of the Black Land and beyond," I whisper, "lend your strength to my healing. I call especially upon Sekhmet, lion-headed goddess of healing. Aid me in my work this night, grant your grace to save this life." My fingertips tingle as I feel her strength flow down my arms and into my body. Then, waving the cleansing smoke over the soldier, I work my way from the top of Akin's head to the tips of his toes, and back again.

Putting the herbs down, I take the glittering crystals Pepi gave me and place them on and around Akin's body: one at the top of his head, another in the centre of his forehead, a third at the base of his throat, and a fourth on his heart. I place a stone in each of his palms and his hands curl around them. I put another on his abdomen and just below, and one under each foot so he is encircled, protected.

Breathing in another lungful of the burning incense, I begin to intone the ancient incantation. My tongue trips over the strange words at first but gradually gains confidence and speed as I find my rhythm. The sacred script soon comes smoothly, and I murmur it with increasing fervour. Holding my hands above Akin's face, I breathe in more of the intoxicating incense and summon *Heka*, the invisible life force of the universe. I feel it flow through me, passing out of my hands and into Amara's husband.

Lightly, I place my hands on him, cupping them over his eyes, reciting the incantation aloud and without cease, a prayer to the gods. Positioning my hands at the sides of his head, I focus completely on sending healing energy into Akin's mind, body, and spirit. Following the path of the crystals, I move my hands down to his chest, his abdomen, then concentrate on his lower body and legs. Over and over, I murmur the spell, directing *Heka* from the universe down into Akin. All else fades away and there is nothing but me and him, the words of the scroll, and the unfathomable magic of the gods.

I do not know how long I do this, but after some time sense I'm reaching the limits of my endurance. And then Paser and Reb are beside me, our hands on Akin, speaking the incantation together. We repeat it several more times in unison, voices blending together in the night, rising up to the stars. At last, without premeditation, we say it a final time. My fingertips, still crackling, feel separate from my body as they trace the protective symbols over Akin, the Eye of Horus over his brow, the ankh over his chest. Picking up one of Min's sachets, I throw it on the fire, and sparks fly as an aromatic scent fills the air.

"It is done." I sit back on my heels, spent, watching the soldier's face. He's still sleeping from the draught Amara procured from Kazir, which, along with the incense, has sedative properties. I collect the sparkling green-gold gems then turn to my friends, feeling drained. "It is time for us all to rest now." Tomorrow is a big day.

"You did well, Sesha," Paser murmurs, patting my leg. "Even if we cannot do much for Akin physically, perhaps the incantation will help his spirit."

"The mind and body are connected in mysterious ways," Reb agrees, the smoke of the incense burning low beside us.

Amara comes forward with a blanket; she'd stayed back, letting us work our magic. "I will sleep with him here, under the stars," she whispers, shooing us to our own beds. "You did all that you could, Sesha. The rest will have to be up to Akin."

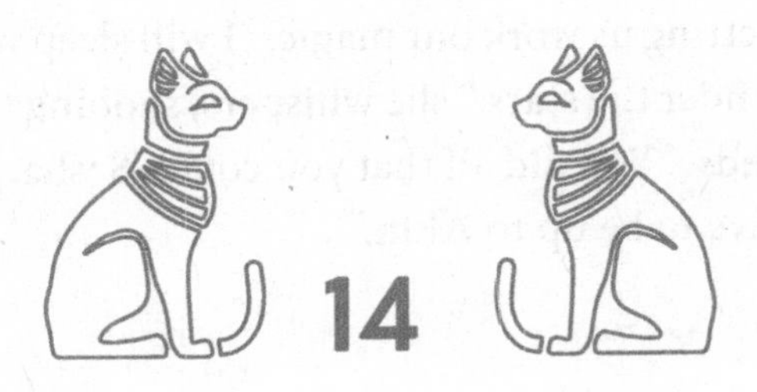

# 14

THE NEXT MORNING Pepi imparts his final instructions, carefully going over his map that leads to the hidden priestess sect's temple.

"With luck the oracle is with the priestesses, or they will know where she is." Pepi considers Paser, Reb, and me. "It is unlikely you will make it back before the solstice." My friends and I look at one another. The eclipse is in four days. "If you are with the oracle during the eclipse, you might be able to witness the third and final prophecy, if indeed she makes one." Pepi's tone is urgent. "The people can wait to have their questions answered, a prophecy is much more valuable. After that, bring the oracle to Avaris as soon as you can."

"I wish you were coming," I say as he hands us the map. Paser takes it, being the best at navigation.

"As do I." Pepi's eyes are shadowed. "But the king does not have much time left, and I need to rally support here in case Yanassi makes any sudden moves."

"I will keep him distracted." Merat came to see us off. She brushes her hair back over a bronze shoulder. "Planning a wedding feast to rival the ages should occupy some of his time."

"Take care of the king." I put a reassuring hand on Pepi's arm. "It is good you are spending these final days with him." In my readings of the scroll, I found a reference to an illness that seemed similar to the king's. Other than the cauterization of tumours, it also states there is no treatment.

"Thank you, Sesha," Pepi says, his gaze unflinching. "I would not remain behind if I did not think you more than up to this task; it is another step in your destiny." Nefer noses Pepi's hand as if aware of her master's restrained emotions and her own impending departure. The donkey's vacation was short-lived. Pepi has loaned her for our journey, along with two of his horses, much to Reb's delight.

The chieftain comes around the bend. A cutting figure beside him leads another massive horse, as heavily laden with supplies as our own. The Nubian. He chews something and spits it on the ground as the pair draw closer.

"What is that man up to?" Paser says.

"Which one?" Reb murmurs.

"I may have some idea." Pepi's eyes go back and forth between the chieftain and the mercenary. "Good morning, Cousin. Have you come to see our young questers off?"

"It appears my betrothed has beat me to it." Yanassi scowls like he's breakfasted on a salad of bitter herbs.

"Really, my love, they are my subjects and friends," Merat sweetly chides as she walks over to him. "Surely you cannot begrudge me such a small thing? Sesha has done much for us," she reminds him.

*More than he deserves.* Though it was for Akin, Amara, and their babe's sake that I retrieved and used the scroll, not the chieftain's. *And it may not do much anyway.* I feel an echoing pang at not being able to surgically fix the soldier's injuries.

Yanassi casts me a dark look. "I am sending my own quester in pursuit of the oracle," he announces, thumping the mercenary on the back. The malice emanating from the Nubian is unmistakable, his *khopesh* sword hanging ominously at his side.

Reb's mouth drops. "That man is to accompany us?"

Merat and I exchange a glance. We now know what the silver was for. Pepi's comment regarding the mercenary comes back with a sharp twinge of unease. *So long as no one is paying him to bring about our untimely demise, we are safe enough.*

It appears the Nubian is now being paid.

"Sesha and her friends do not need accompaniment." Pepi folds his arms across his chest.

Yanassi waves an indifferent hand. "Very well, then, may the best search party win." Merat looks at me, then begins chattering to the chieftain, giving us a moment to get some final direction from Pepi, who affects to look casual.

"Be careful," he says quietly. To Paser and Reb: "You are both skilled with the bow and Paser is an extremely capable fighter, but this man is a trained killer. Stay away from him."

"No doubt he will try to follow us." Paser's hand goes to the knife at his side. Pepi supplied them with bronze daggers, in addition to their bows for hunting. I have my father's blade.

Pepi makes a show of checking that our bags are properly secured to the horses, his voice a forceful whisper. "Then you must find a way to lose him and get to the oracle first. Come back safely." He nods at the map. "Yanassi may have some idea of where the sect is located, but you are at an advantage with the only map in your possession."

Finishing our preparations, Reb makes his way over to the Nubian's horse, admiring the fine animal given to him by the chieftain. "You are a beauty, aren't you?" he remarks.

The Nubian views Reb with marked dislike and turns his back on the scribe. Reb's arm shoots out and there is a flash of forged bronze in the sun. Water begins to seep from the fresh slit in the Nubian's canteens.

"Ah, we should be leaving now." Hurriedly, I climb onto Nefer as Paser jumps on his own horse. Reb joins us, features arranged in innocence.

"I have the utmost faith in you all." Pepi's hand covers his mouth to hide his smile. He'd seen Reb's knife, as well. Fortunately for us, the Nubian and Yanassi did not. "May Shai, god of luck, be with you. Consult the priestesses, find the oracle, witness the prophecy, and bring she who divines it back to Avaris."

"We will," I say. Pepi gives Nefer a last farewell pat, as Paser and Reb nudge their horses and set off. Merat turns and waves them goodbye, eyes cutting to Paser as inconspicuously as Reb's dagger. She is becoming more skilled at hiding her emotions. My hand rotates her bracelet encircling my wrist.

Pepi brings his nose to Nefer's. "Bring them back safely, friend," he whispers, then clicks his tongue and gives her flanks an encouraging slap. Letting out a resigned *hawww*, she turns to follow Paser and Reb, who trot ahead admirably, despite their limited time on horseback. Thought not quite as elegant as the horses, Nefer's steady gait catches us up to the boys.

"I told you we would have another adventure," I

call to Paser as Nefer pulls alongside their horses.

"Life's been one adventure after another since you walked into temple," Paser grins, holding on to the reins Pepi fashioned to direct the animals. Paser has gained back the weight he lost during his illness and his arms, always well sculpted, are more defined, his shoulders broad. "Nice bladework with the Nubian's canteens, Reb," he says to his friend with a laugh. "That should keep him busy for some time."

Reb grins back. "It will allow us to get a lead at least."

"He will find us eventually." I have no doubt the Nubian is an expert tracker.

"We will not make it easy for him." Paser perches forward on his horse, in anticipation of the upcoming journey.

There is a shout behind us and some colourful exclamations from Yanassi. Unless Merat is talking about wedding costs, the leak in the canteen has been spotted. I glance over my shoulder, to where Pepi circles the mercenary's horse, feigning a puzzled look as he crouches to examine the dripping canteens alongside the other men. Catching my eye, he smiles and holds a hand up in farewell.

I wave back and, despite the enormity of our mission, my heart is as light as Ma'at's feather of truth at travelling with my friends, and them alone, our backs warm in the rising sun.

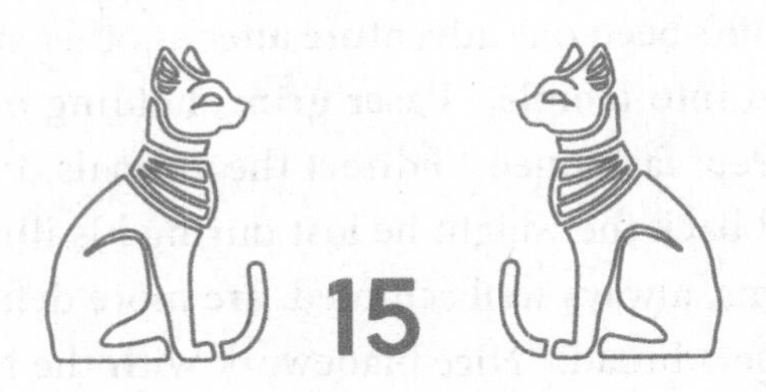

# 15

"WHERE ARE WE?" Reb asks, shielding his eyes from the bright rays. I am already missing Avaris's channel breezes.

"It is difficult to say, exactly." Paser squints at the map in his hands. It is midday, two days since we left the capital — and Yanassi's deadly mercenary — behind.

"On the bright side of the river, we've lost the Nubian," I say, trying to keep the mood positive. As far as journeys go, this one has been fairly uneventful. It is a welcome change.

"Can I look at the map?" Reb asks Paser.

He shrugs and leans over his horse to pass it to his friend. "Much luck."

"We were supposed to travel to the west and slightly north," I say. Pepi thought it would take three days to reach the priestesses, depending how hard we push the animals and how often we stop to eat and rest. If our good luck continues, we should arrive later this evening.

Reb taps the papyrus map. "I think we've veered slightly off course. It should only set us back a few hours."

"Next time less beer at lunch," I tease Paser. Our last stop was in a town well known for its breweries, and we replenished our canteens with the nutritious drink by trading an hour of our time attending to minor ailments of the villagers.

"Very funny, Sesha." He grins. It is wonderful to see him out here, happy and free, the breeze ruffling his hair, which is scandalously long for a scribe.

A *ffffffff* exhalation comes from his direction.

"Don't take leading us astray so hard," I say, as Paser's horse noses the ground to investigate something in the grass. "It —"

A piercing whinny rends the air and Paser's animal rears up, forelegs striking out in panic. Paser tumbles off its back, landing hard on the ground, breath knocked out right along with mine as Akin's injuries flash before my eyes.

"Paser," I cry, about to get off Nefer when there is another, louder *ffffffff* rattle. This time I recognize it for what it is, having traced the hieroglyph representing that sound countless times. A deadly horned viper slithers through the grass straight for my friend, emitting another angry *ffffffff* that elicits further hysteria from Paser's horse and me both.

"Snake!" I cry. Paser scrambles back just as the spotted viper strikes the ground between his legs. His mount rears again, legs flailing as it bucks, kicks, and leaps to the side. Reb's horse, spooked by the commotion and the snake, bolts with Reb still astride, clutching his braided papyrus reins for all the gold in Nubia.

Paser's horse trembles, frothing at the mouth. Nefer, may the gods bless her, hasn't run, but a shudder of fear gallops through her body, matching my own. I strive to make out the viper under all the dust kicked up by the horse. Paser, who seems mostly unharmed, spots it first and points at the mangled body, crushed beneath the horse's trampling feet.

The overwrought animal back-walks, neck stretched, shaking its head from side to side, huffing and snorting. I jump off Nefer and run to Paser to help him up. Giving the snake's body a wide berth, we slowly approach the spooked animal.

"Easy," Paser says soothingly, and I reach for the rope as we try to calm the distraught creature. The horse's eyes roll back in its head and it goes down to its knees.

"Did the viper get it?" I want to check for puncture wounds but am wary of being bitten or kicked.

"I think so." Paser is grim. Minutes later there is no need to look for bite marks, as it becomes apparent from the swelling on the horse's nose that she was indeed bitten. She wheezes, inhaling and exhaling, her breathing growing more and more laboured.

"What should we do?" I ask, knowing the treatment for a human, but not certain about a horse. She is becoming lethargic, which is not a good sign, but at least it allows Paser to remove the rope from around her neck and tie it around her snout while we examine her. This has the dual benefit of preventing her from biting us and hopefully keeping the venom from spreading.

"I think it will be all right." He strokes the animal, murmuring a brief incantation for snakebite into her flickering ears. "She is a large creature. The bigger concern is keeping her airways open. Her breathing tells me the tissues in her nasal passages are swelling. Quick," he urges, "find something hollow we can insert into her nose to keep the air path open."

Frantic, I look around, worrying for Reb and wishing he were here; he is so good with horses. Spotting a clump of reeds, I run over and break off several long and sturdy tube-like rushes at their base.

"Here," I say to Paser, breathless.

"I'll hold her head steady. You must insert them. Push them as high up her nose as you can." He wraps both arms around the animal's head, holding her tight, and continues to mutter incantations over our patient.

With no time to think or consider, I shove the first rush high up into the horse's left nostril. She jerks her head back, but thankfully the reed, which is about the width of my finger, stays in. I grab the second one and jab it deep into the other nostril. The horse shakes her head and snorts, trying to dislodge the hollow rushes, but Paser holds on tight, arms straining, as he tries to calm the animal. There is a faint whistling noise each time a breath enters the horse's airways.

"We need to keep her warm and still, to limit the spread of the venom," Paser says, draping his body across the supine horse, without adding too much weight.

I rummage through the satchel of medicines on Nefer's back for ingredients to make a poultice. In people, skin will usually begin to slough off after a snakebite as the venom devours the healthy tissue. The wound must be kept clean, so it does not become inflamed. Grabbing my pestle and mortar, I grind up some garlic and a few cubeb peppers, add a pinch of fenugreek and several drops of cedar oil. I use my fingertips to apply the paste all around the bite area. The horse looks at me, eyes and face swollen, the sturdy stems sticking out of her nose covered in mucus and snot.

"You are still a pretty creature," I assure her, then glance in the direction of our other friend, who is nowhere to be seen. "What about Reb?"

"He will be all right," Paser says. A strong wind picks up, blowing the horse's mane.

"Do you think he'll be able to find his way back?"

"I hope so." Paser rests his head close to the horse. "He has the map."

I finish applying the paste, smear some honey on the wound, then put the ingredients back in the satchel and go to flank the horse's other side.

"This is my fault." I pat the poor horse, who seems very tired. She rests her head on the ground. I feel like doing the same.

"What makes you say that?" Paser looks across the animal at me.

"I was just thinking how uneventful this journey has been," I confess. "I should've known better than to give Shai a challenge."

"A journey unfolds as it is meant to." Paser's gold-flecked eyes are serious and warm. "We can choose how to react. We can panic and despair, or we can have faith all will be well."

"I will try." I rest my chin on my hands on top of the horse and Paser does the same, our faces very close. "Though I'd feel better if Reb were here with the map."

"The horse's name has revealed itself to me," Paser announces, attempting to distract me. I let him.

"Let's hear it, then."

"Nosy." He grins.

"That is a terrible name." But I allow a small smile. "And not all that creative."

"Who said I was creative?"

"You are a scribe!"

He shrugs. "My strength lies in the drawing of the symbols, not in the composition of the words themselves."

"Princess Merat is quite good with the arrangement of words," I sigh.

"That's right." Paser studies me. "You were teaching her to read and write."

"She is a talented poet."

"You care for her very much, don't you?"

"She is my queen," I say simply, unable to adequately explain my feelings. Paser looks down at the animal between us, fingers threading through the horse's mane. I cover his hand with mine. "But that does not mean I do not care about others just as much." He lifts his eyes to meet mine and we sit there in the sun, looking at one another. My body tingles, as if absorbing the toxins from the horse's skin; I know I am unable to avoid what is coming.

"Before you left for Thebes to get the scroll, you asked me to wait for you," Paser says quietly. "Why?"

"I did not want you falling for the princess," I admit. It is my turn to look down at the horse. Its brown hair is tinged with auburn and roan, the fiery colours matching the burning in my cheeks. I fiddle with Merat's bracelet, which sears my skin, the metal reflecting the sun's rays. "I thought the chieftain would cast you out of the oasis, or even kill you, should he perceive you as a threat for her heart. I wanted to protect you both."

He brings his finger under my chin and lifts it so that I am looking at him straight on. It is impossible to tear my eyes from the green circling his pupils, which are slightly dilated, as if he's ingested the medicine of the poppy. "Is that the only reason?"

I bite my lower lip. "I —"

A loud snore and subsequent fart break the spell.

"It was the horse." Paser holds both hands up. "Swear to the gods."

I laugh so hard it is difficult to breathe. "We lulled her to sleep." He laughs, too, his eyes sparkling, reminding me of priestess stones. "We need to find shade," I announce before the intimacy of the previous moment can restore itself.

"What should we do about Nosy?"

"We will have to leave her for now." I give the creature a regretful pat. "If Reb comes back, he will know we have not gone far. Do you remember passing by any trees?"

He thinks. "Not since the village, and that was some ways back. I think we should go in the direction of Reb's horse."

"Very well." I stand and brush the horsehair from my linen dress. Still flustered from our recent conversation, I busy myself, taking supplies from his animal and repacking the necessary items into one satchel. "I hope Nosy will be all right."

Paser grins. "She is a strong creature, and healthy as a … well, a horse."

"You are the worst at jokes." Reb's voice carries over on the strong breeze, and we whirl to see him walking toward us, leading his steed, firmly under his control.

"Reb!" I run over and embrace him. Paser is right behind me.

"How is your own horse?" I pull back to examine his animal, whose eyes are still a bit wild.

"A sight better than Paser's." Reb takes in the pitiful creature on the ground, hardy rushes protruding from her nostrils. "What in the underworld did you do to her nose?"

"The viper's venom caused her difficulty breathing. We needed to keep the airways open," Paser explains, pushing his hair back. I know whatever is between us two is not over.

"We need to find shade," I repeat. The sun climbs higher, and I feel sweat roll down my back. "Did you see anything we could use as shelter during your, ah, ride?"

Reb shakes his head. "Nothing."

"Let's consult the map," Paser says, shouldering his satchel.

Reb lowers his eyes to the ground.

"What is it?" I ask, alarmed by his expression.

"I . . . I dropped it," Reb blurts out. A mocking wind swirls the dust up at our feet. "It is gone."

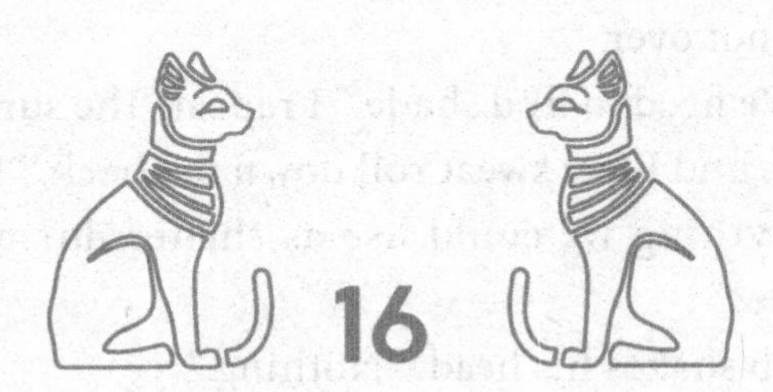


"IT HAS TO BE HERE," I say, looking down from Nefer as we walk back and forth, desperately scanning the terrain for Pepi's map.

"The wind has taken it." Reb looks as miserable as Paser's horse.

Paser strides across the landscape, head bent low. Searching for what feels like hours, we are hot, dehydrated, and decidedly crispy around the edges.

"It's no use." Reb is close to tears.

"It is not your fault," I reassure him. "Your horse bolted. I'm amazed you were able to hang on, never mind holding on to the map."

"Besides, we have it reasonably memorized," Paser adds, walking over to us. "We should keep moving." He doesn't mention we are in danger of falling behind schedule. The eclipse is almost upon us. We must find the oracle before then; if she makes a third prophecy and we miss it, we may not hear it until it is too late. According to Pepi, oracles don't go around revealing prophecies to everyone; Pepi's mother had been a priestess herself and thus been privy to them, sharing what she knew with whom she wanted, as she saw fit. But Kalali is gone now, so it is up to us to learn what we need to know in time to save the kingdom.

"What about Nosy?" I wipe my forehead. "We should go back and check on her."

"Do you think she is all right?" Reb asks. Both boys' faces are flushed from the heat. I imagine mine is, as well.

"I hope so." In defeated silence we walk back to the place where we left the horse and the rest of our supplies. The lump in my stomach grows bigger as we approach the area. The animal is not there. "Is this the right place?" I say, trying to keep the panic at bay.

"Yes." Paser gestures. "There is the body of the snake."

"Do you think the horse staggered off?" Reb looks around, mystified.

"It did not seem like she was in any shape to walk." Paser, too, turns in different directions, scanning the area. There is no blood or body parts that would indicate an animal attack.

"Look!" I point. Hoofprints trail off in the direction we were originally headed. Paser and Reb rush over to examine them.

"I am no skilled tracker, but the gait seems off." Paser crouches low to the ground, touching the dirt. "She may have been forced by something, or someone, to hobble along." He walks a bit farther up to where the ground is softer. "Here. Another set of prints, of the human variety."

"Do you think the Nubian has caught up with us?" Reb asks, and my mouth, already parched, dries up like a sandpit.

Paser shakes his head. "Not unless something happened to his own horse, as there'd be two sets of hoofprints."

"It is a possibility, though," I say, and the boys look uneasy. We have learned that during a trek, anything is possible.

"What supplies were on your mount, Paser?" Reb asks.

"The beer." Paser closes his eyes and curses under his breath. "My weapons. Most of the food. Sesha has the medicines." Reb's horse carries materials for our shelter and another canteen.

"I have a little food." I rifle through the satchel on Nefer's back. "But we will have to be careful with our rations." We look at each other.

"Well," Reb remarks, "it's nothing we haven't done before."

We walk for another hour or so, reviewing everything we can remember about the map, while keeping an eye out for the horse and whoever took it. We see no one else on the trail; it is mid-afternoon, and most people, if there are any around, will be resting, out of the direct, suffocating heat.

"How much farther should we go?" It feels like I'm being roasted alive.

Paser looks up at the sky, estimating Ra's position. "There was another small village on the map. We can stop there. Maybe someone will have seen our horse."

"With luck, they will welcome physicians, as well." Reb gets down off his animal and lets Paser have a turn, so as not to overwork his horse. We alternate between walking and riding at a fair pace, ignoring our thirst and grumbling stomachs as we push on, trying to earn back lost time. "We can trade our expertise for supplies like we did at the last stop. Maybe the inhabitants will have heard of the priestesses and can confirm that we are headed in the right direction."

"What makes you think they will know anything?" I ask. "Pepi said the location of the sect is a highly guarded secret."

"Being this close, someone will have had a daughter or an aunt or a friend who has joined their ranks," Reb says, with the astute experience of one who was nephew to the High Priest of Thebes. I wonder whatever became of his uncle, Nebifu. The last we saw of him he was in a dark hole, put there by Pharaoh for betraying the kingdom. Back then Pepi had been our hostage, an enemy spy. Now he is my mentor and friend. Even more astonishing, we are conspiring to set him up on the throne. How quickly things can change. And yet, I muse, they also remain the same, because here we are on another journey to find something missing — again, in part for our own reasons — and to bring it back to where it needs to be ...

"There." Paser motions at a few small huts ahead and some chickens and goats in the distance. "I do not think this is the village I saw on the map, it is too small, but there must be people who tend these animals."

A few clouds roll overhead, providing some respite from the heat. "Thank the gods," I breathe. The hoofprints trailed off some time ago, and it feels like I'm floating half a cubit off Nefer's back. I blink. A small child with brown curls, about four years, steps onto the path. I think I'm imagining her, but Paser puts his palms up in a show of peace.

"Hello," Paser greets the little girl kindly. "Can you tell us the name of this place?"

The child does not speak, but giggles and runs off, presumably in the direction of her parents. Maybe it is only the heat and lack of water, but the strange dizzying feeling intensifies as we draw closer to the huts.

"I hope the people here are friendly." I can barely make out Reb's voice over the high-pitched ringing in my ears. The buildings are spinning around and around, like a tower of sand spiralling up to the sky.

"Sesha!" I think it is Paser who shouts as I slump forward on Nefer, eyes closing as I descend into darkness.

My eyelids flutter open, and I look up into the concerned faces of Reb and Paser.

"Are you all right?" Paser asks, waving a short palm frond over my face.

"Fine," I croak. "Thirsty." An earthen jug is placed at my lips and a cool drink slides down my scratchy throat. It tastes of honey and passionflower. It's almost dark and I wonder how long I've been out for. Sitting up, I look around. We are in one of the thatch huts. The elderly woman who gave me the drink smiles. The little girl we saw in the road peeks out shyly from behind her. Both are clad in threadbare linens. "Thank you for your kindness," I say.

The woman nods and stands, placing the jug beside me, and tugs gently at the small child to leave the hut. They exit without a word.

I look at Paser and Reb in confusion. "Is she unhappy about us being here?" The woman smiled when giving me a drink of the reviving elixir, but why would she not speak to me?

"She cannot talk," Paser says, watching me carefully.

"She is mute?" I am curious.

"She is, but it appears she was not born with the condition." Paser holds back his next words as if worried they might send me into a faint again. He and Reb exchange a look.

"What is it?" They are not telling me something. The disconcerting sensation I am experiencing increases. Little beads of sweat dot my brow, and all at once I feel nauseous.

"She is missing her tongue."

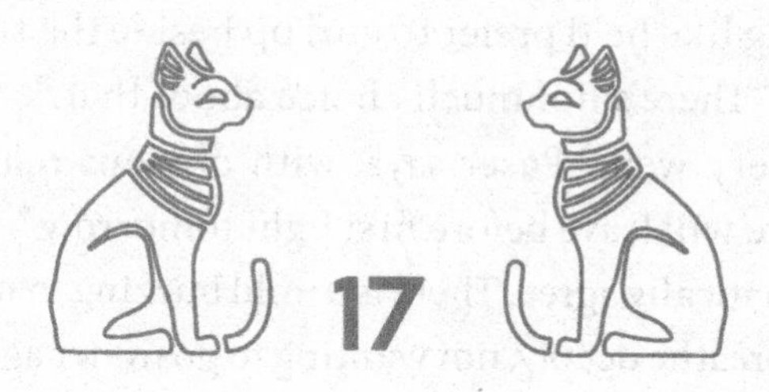

# 17

"WHAT?" I WONDER if I've heard Paser correctly. "Her tongue?" Did the woman suffer from some kind of hereditary anomaly? But Paser said she wasn't born with the condition, meaning …

Reb swallows and lowers his voice. "It was cut out."

I stare at him in horror. "By whom?"

"We do not know." Reb shrugs helplessly. "And she obviously cannot tell us." It is unlikely the woman can write to communicate, either, as the skill is only possessed by trained scribes.

"What do you think happened?" My hand goes to my mouth.

Paser shakes his head. "There is no way of knowing. But I do not think we should stay long in this place."

"We'll have to spend the night," Reb says, despite looking like he'd prefer to curl up beside the trampled viper. "There's not much choice about that."

"Very well," Paser says, with obvious reluctance. "But we will leave before first light tomorrow." Reb and I emphatically agree. There is a mild buzzing in my head, and I breathe deeply, not wanting to go under again. The heat is still oppressive, even inside the hut. "Did you have a chance to ask about Paser's horse? Or the priestesses?"

"That is when she showed us her tongue." Reb pales at the memory.

"She was demonstrating why she was unable to answer your questions?"

"Either that, or ..." Paser pauses.

"Or what?"

He hesitates. "Perhaps it was a warning."

"A warning?" I swallow, my own tongue thick in my mouth. "You cannot think the priestesses had anything to do with ... removing it, do you?" I cannot imagine why Pepi would send us into a cult of priestesses with a proclivity for cutting out tongues.

The child peeks her head in the doorway.

"Hello," Paser says, beckoning her in. "What is your name?" She giggles again but does not come in. "Can you help us?"

The child nods and points at the drink. "Yes, many thanks." Paser holds up his cup in acknowledgement.

"Is there someone here other than your … grandmother? Who we can talk to?"

The little girl shakes her head. Are she and the old woman the only people in this place? There does not seem to be another soul around, but someone must have taught the child language because she understands Paser's questions.

"We are doctors," Paser tries again. "Are there people in this place who need help?" She lifts a finger and points directly at me, causing the hair on my arms to stand up. "Yes, this is Sesha. But she is all right now, only a bit dehydrated."

"What about your grandmother?" I say, licking my dry lips. "Does she need help?"

The child shakes her head and sticks her fingers in her mouth the way children do when they're shy, or uncertain about something. She turns to leave.

"Wait," Paser calls. "Would you like to play a game?" The child comes back over, looking interested. "It's called Bird, River, Arrow." Paser contorts his hands into three different shapes. "Bird beats river because he drinks from it, river beats arrow because it swallows it, and arrow beats bird because it pierces it." He gestures at Reb to help him demonstrate the popular game young scribes often play in temple on their breaks. It provides entertainment between the tediousness of transcribing, but also helps stretch our hands and fingers after gripping reeds and tracing hieroglyphs all day.

"Bird, river, arrow, go," the boys chant, creating shapes with their hands. Reb wins, pointing his finger straight as an arrow, while Paser's thumb and fingers open and close in imitation of a bird's beak. The little girl watches, transfixed, as they play another round. This time Paser wins with his bird dipping its beak into Reb's river: flat palm facing up, fingers spread wide to resemble the Nile and its branches.

"Now, you try," Paser encourages her. "Ready?"

She nods solemnly.

"Bird, river, arrow, go," he says, and the curly-mopped child does it perfectly, forming an arrow to shoot at Paser's bird. She lets out a delighted squeal and we laugh back. She indicates she wants to play again and Paser obliges. He offers her a dried plum each time she wins. "It's more fun when you have something to wager," he confides. An idea occurs to me and I fiddle with Merat's bracelet around my wrist. The glint of it catches the child's eye; I see her staring at the pretty bangle in fascination.

"Why don't we play?" I say to the child with an engaging smile. "If you win, you can have my bracelet." I hold my arm out to her. "If I win, maybe you can answer a few questions for me and my friends?"

"Sesha." Paser is taken aback at my suggestion.

Reb perks up. "It's not a bad idea," he murmurs. The girl tilts her head and nods slowly. I should probably feel more guilty about inducing a child to gamble, but the need to find the oracle and get back to Avaris before the king dies and leaves the kingdom to Yanassi has me desperate.

I put out my hand. "Bird, river, arrow." We contort our hands into their chosen shape. I win with her arrow sinking into my river. We go again. This time the little girl beats me with arrow into bird. Last chance. "Bird, river, arrow." I hold my breath, fingers forming an open beak position. Her hand is face up for river and my bird takes a drink. Face falling, she glances wistfully at the bracelet.

"You did very well," I say, nodding at Paser to give her another plum, which brings back her smile. "Will you answer my questions now?"

She nods, munching away on the dried fruit.

"Thank you," I say. "Have you by chance seen our horse? He was bit on the nose." I playfully grab for hers and pretend to catch it between my fingers. She giggles and shakes her head no. One down. Paser gives her another piece, which she gobbles up, while I draw a map in the dirt floor with my finger. "My second question is this: We are here." I make a small dot to mark the spot and then trace my finger up and over to the triangle I drew. "Is this the way to the priestess sect?" I look into her wide brown eyes. "It is very important we find them."

The child cocks her head and wrinkles her nose, bending down to squat near my rudimentary map. Taking one of her sticky fingers, she draws a triangle to the left of mine. "Thank you," I say, smiling at her. "That is most helpful."

She holds out her hand to play again and Paser obliges with a few more rounds until we hear light footsteps outside. I rub the map away with my foot just as the old woman comes in carrying a large bowl, eyes searching for the little girl. This is obviously their hut, based on the few homey items that furnish it. It is a warm night and so we offer to sleep outside after ravenously consuming the porridge she puts in front of us, sweetened with goat's milk.

We take the linens off Nefer and Reb's horse, whom he names Breakaway — much more clever than Nosy, he informs Paser — and laying them on the ground, we settle back to look up at the stars. I feel better under the open sky, though exhausted from the day's events. By unspoken agreement we face away from Khonsu, who's grown fat and nearly full, not wanting the constant reminder of the upcoming eclipse, hanging so plainly over our heads.

Paser winces, one hand rubbing his inner thigh area.

"Did the snake get you?" Alarmed, I sit up, ready to examine him.

"No." His face flushes. "I am just sore from riding." I almost offer to massage it for him, then think better of it and lie down again.

"Sham said it takes a few days for your body to become accustomed to the horse." Reb yawns. "You can walk all day tomorrow if that helps."

"Many thanks, friend," Paser says dryly. "Your thoughtfulness is touching."

Reb grins. "Think nothing of it." We watch the stars shoot overhead for a few minutes in silence. "Do you think the girl really knows where the sect is located, or is she just playing games?" Reb says.

"She knows," I say. Somehow I can just tell.

"She is only a young child," Reb says.

"I knew most of my hieroglyphs by then," I say. "Perhaps she has travelled to or from there with her grandmother."

"Maybe they supply them with eggs or goat milk." Paser clasps his hands behind his head to cradle it as he looks up at the endless indigo heavens.

"That is a thought." Reb squeezes Paser's bulging bicep affectionately. "You're not as simple as you look, my friend." Paser unclasps his hands and punches Reb in the arm.

"For the love of Isis." Reb rubs his arm. "What was that for?"

"Your compliment." Paser grins. I smile at their good-natured teasing, my eyelids growing heavy. We must find the oracle soon or we will miss out on the prophecy. That cannot happen. I send a heartfelt prayer that she is with the sect. My thoughts return to the old woman's missing appendage and I shiver. Paser moves closer, thinking it is from the evening breeze, and his warmth is comforting. I send up another prayer that the map does not fall into the wrong hands; I do not think the priestesses will be impressed if their secret location ends up becoming public knowledge. I have a strong sensation that we do not want to anger them.

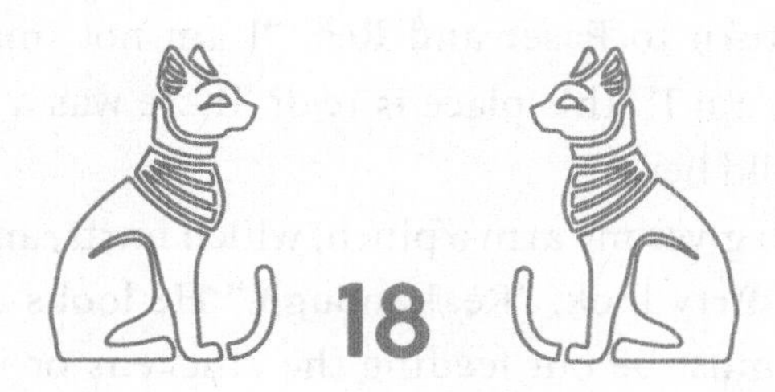

WE WAKE BEFORE the rooster crows and pack our things in the lightening dark.

"Should we say goodbye?" I whisper, listening for movement from the hut. "They were kind." The boys agree, and we walk to the door to offer our thanks. Paser raps on the ramshackle structure and we wait, but it is quiet inside.

"Hello," he calls. "We are on our way and wish to thank you for your hospitality." There is no answer, which is strange; most farmers would be up by now. I push aside the skins covering the door and stick my head in. There is no one inside.

"Do you think they are out tending the animals?" Reb asks.

"Perhaps," I say, looking around. The bowl that held our porridge is gone and, despite the cozy feeling from the night before, I realize the space is quite barren. I turn to Paser and Reb. "I am not imagining things, am I? This place is real? There was a woman and child here?"

Reb gives my arm a pinch, which hurts, and I give him a dirty look. "Real enough." He looks around. "They must be out feeding the chickens or milking the goats."

"I'm surprised I didn't hear them leave," Paser says. "I did not sleep much." I notice the dark circles under his eyes; he must have stayed awake to keep watch.

"Wherever they are, it's time for us to leave this place," Reb says.

"Wait." Paser holds up a hand. "I would like to leave something as payment." He takes off one of his anklets, blue faience beads and shells jingling, and leaves it on their doorstep.

"That is generous of us," Reb remarks, walking quickly over to Breakaway.

Paser sees me hesitating over Merat's bracelet, recalling the way the girl admired it, and shakes his head. "Keep it, Sesha. It is a powerful charm, and we may have need of it yet."

I sigh and climb onto Nefer, knowing he is right. We leave the deserted huts behind.

We go the entire day without seeing another soul. Paser thinks he recognizes a rock formation from the map that signals the entrance to the sect, but after we walk several more miles, he starts to doubt himself.

"We must have somehow bypassed the larger village," he says, walking beside me. Our food and drink are getting low. Early evening is approaching, and the now full moon is visible in the sky. I know what he is thinking, what we are all thinking. We should be there by now.

"We don't even know if the oracle will be with the priestesses," Reb says, atop Breakaway. He gazes at another enormous rock face, as more are appearing, one by one. "Maybe it is that one?" he murmurs to himself.

I keep talking to distract myself from the devastating fact that we are probably lost. "Pepi believes she might be," I say from Nefer's back. "At the very least they might know where she is or what became of her."

"What if we do not find her in time to bring her back and answer our questions?" Reb asks, finally voicing what we are all thinking. "Will Khyan leave the throne to Yanassi?"

"There is something I must tell you both," I say, knowing the time has come at last. I informed Pepi of my decision when we were in his scriptorium. He said I'd earned the right to do what I think best. I square my shoulders and take a deep breath. "Pepi does not think the king is his uncle." The boys look at me in surprise and I continue, bracing myself for their reaction. "He says Khyan is his father." I pray they will understand why I have kept the spy's secret for so long.

"Pepi … is the son of the king?" Reb's jaw drops. "Does Khyan know this?"

"He does not believe it," I say. "That is why it's so important we find the oracle. To prove to Khyan and his followers that Pepi has a lawful right to rule. Perhaps if others believe him to be a viable successor to the throne, Pepi will start to believe it himself."

"That explains much." Paser recovers quickly, his face impassive. "When did you discover this?"

"At the oasis." I prepare myself for their resentment. "He made me promise not to tell anyone. I am sorry for keeping it from you, but Pepi swore me to silence. He said his life depended on it." Holding my breath, I wait for their response.

"He is likely right about that," Paser says, and my shoulders slump in relief. They do not seem angry. A giant wave of gratitude at their understanding rolls through me. "As a cousin, Pepi does not pose the same threat to Yanassi as he does as a brother."

"But by announcing the prophecy, Pepi made Sesha the threat instead." Reb gets off the horse, allowing Paser a turn.

"That's why he volunteered us to search for the oracle," I say, as the boys trade places. "He wanted us away from Avaris as quickly as possible, before Yanassi got any ideas about doing away with the competition."

"Sending a mercenary after us is indication those 'ideas' have already occurred to the chieftain." Reb kicks a small stone out of his path.

"Yanassi does not need to kill you, necessarily." Paser looks at me from Breakaway's back. "He could take a page from Pepi's papyrus and force you to marry him. If the prophecy *is* true, then it would be extra insurance that he or his offspring would end up in power, one way or another."

My blood goes cold. I did not think of that. "What about Merat? The chieftain seems charmed by her."

"Easy solution." Reb shrugs. "He keeps her as a concubine."

"Queen Anat and Pharaoh won't be thrilled with that scenario," Paser says. "Least of all the princess."

"I am still unable to reconcile the idea that *I* could be the one meant to rule the Hyksos kingdom!" I say in exasperated frustration.

"But if you are the one from the prophecy *and* serious about setting Pepi on the throne," Paser says, remaining calm, "then your marriage to him would legitimize his *own* right to rulership, same as the chieftain."

"Our engagement hoax is meant to protect us all." I gesture at my "brothers." "It is not real. Pepi does not need me to rule."

"It appears he does," Reb reasons. "No matter how you spin it, Sesha, you are woven through all of this." He gestures to demonstrate the complex tapestry of political intrigue and prophecies.

I am silent. So much depends on the oracle and what she has to say. Reb is accurate in that it is a lot of pressure for one soul to bear. Perhaps she *has* made herself scarce. I briefly consider doing the same thing. Maybe by the time we get back to the capital Merat will have found Paser's uncle, and we can board a ship for a distant land like we once planned …

"And if we find the oracle and she confirms Pepi's claim that you are the one to rule the kingdoms?" Paser asks. "What will you do?"

My voice comes out barely audible. "I do not know."

"Sesha, Paser." Reb points at the rocky horizon. "Look."

In the distance is a grandiose structure, and my breath catches. I feel the oddest sensation that I've been here before, as the late-day rays of the sun pierce the clouds, illuminating a magnificent temple in brilliant hues of pink and gold. Suddenly, my father's voice comes back to me, and a long-forgotten bedtime story … *There once was a secret sisterhood …*

As we approach, we see a tall woman standing in front, clad in the skin of a panther, signalling her status as High Priestess. Her head is shaven, as is the custom. As she watches our approach, a feeling of trepidation rises up in me. I eye the spear in her right hand, wondering if it is for ceremonial purposes or for something else altogether. At last we come within speaking distance.

"Welcome to the Priestesses of Seshat," she says as we draw near. Her voice is low and gravelly, like the rocks she gives the impression of being carved from. The spear stays by her side. For now. "We have been expecting you."

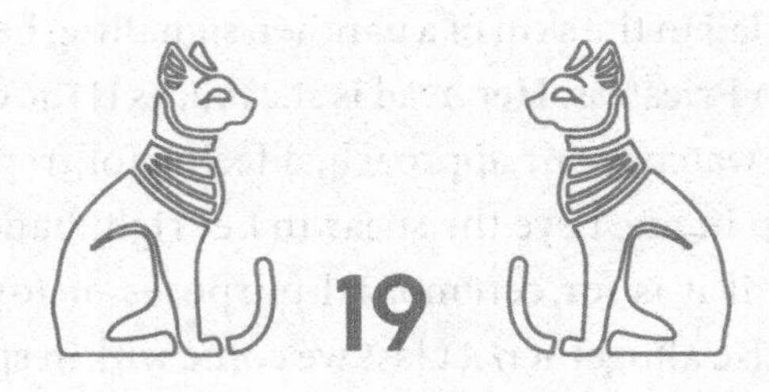

THE TEMPLE IS NOT AS large as the one at Thebes, but it is still breathtaking and gives off a feeling of immense power. Sophisticated, spiralling patterns are carved into the outer walls, and the thick columns lining the entrance are vividly painted, the architecture fusing Theban and Levantine styles. We are instructed to wash in the courtyard to cleanse ourselves and take in the lush gardens and groves surrounding the temple. Several young priestesses are going about the daily tasks of cleaning and caring for the outer space, as we once did, a lifetime ago, seemingly unconcerned with three strangers in their midst.

"The expertise that went into these carvings is incredible." I touch the wall in reverence. The tawny pigments are bright and intense, like the eyes of the High Priestess, who escorts us through the grounds.

"Did you divine we were coming?" Reb asks her with deep respect.

"No." She nods at a four-legged creature a way up and off to our right. "Your horse did."

"Nosy!" Paser exclaims, and we run to inspect the animal, who does not quite look the picture of health, but at least is standing on her own four hooves. "How did you get here?" He examines the horse's face, which is peeling profusely.

"A new initiate beginning her studies found it abandoned on her way to the sect. She is most persuasive with animals and was able to coax the creature to go with her." The priestess looks at the animal with a critical eye. "We have been tending it with medicines and think it will survive."

"You have our deepest thanks." Reb leads Nefer and Breakaway over, tying them to the same post as Nosy. Nefer brays an enthusiastic greeting to her former travelling companion, and Breakaway nuzzles Nosy before guzzling from the trough provided.

Leaving the animals, we follow the High Priestess past a large number of doves nesting in domed coops. Their gentle cooing provides a charming backdrop as we enter the temple's inner sanctum. Most of the girls and women are finishing their duties for the day. The temple is shining and spotless, and there are flowers everywhere, presumably in preparation for the upcoming eclipse ceremony. Their sweet scent mingles with the mouth-watering smell of the evening meal being prepared somewhere close by.

At last, we reach the deepest recess of the temple; the space is hallowed and quiet. The High Priestess turns to face us, the sun's final rays shining down through the opening above. They illuminate a huge lioness-headed statue in the centre of the room and remind us we do not have much time.

"Why are you here?" the High Priestess asks, fierce voice echoing in the chamber. She examines me. "Have you come to join us?" I stand straighter, surprised at the stab of desire that hits me. To return to the peaceful life of a scribe, shielded by cool temple walls, devoting my time to writing and studying, must be what life in the Field of Reeds is like. Yet. There are other obligations and duties that lie before me. Ones that involve the fate of kingdoms. And I would be lying if I said I do not enjoy the occasional adventure.

"We are here to find the oracle," I begin, hoping she will be open to our inquiries. "She was due in Avaris, and the Hyksos king there is most concerned by her absence. We were told you might know of her whereabouts."

The High Priestess places one hand on the large lion goddess, stroking marble as hard and cool as her expression. "Even if I knew where she was, why should I tell you?"

"We need the oracle's help," I begin. "Without her —"

"— the lands will run red with blood," Reb interjects, always to the point.

"There is a set of prophecies surrounding our friend." Paser nods at me. "As you can appreciate, we have a keen interest in clarifying these foretellings ..."

"We also believe a third might occur at the eclipse," Reb adds.

"Please," I urge, "we must speak to —"

"Enough," the High Priestess says in a sharp voice. "Who are you to barge into our temple, demanding counsel with the sacred oracle?"

"Does that mean she's here?" I hazard, with a desperate eye on the sun's rays, which are rapidly receding from the temple walls.

"Our oracle is no longer at Avaris's service." The High Priestess's voice is harsh, a marked contrast with the cooing doves outside.

"What about at the service of a fellow priestess and her son?" I fumble for the gems Pepi gave me, pulling the stones from the bindings around my chest. "We are to show you these." I open my hand and the exquisite stones glint in the softening light. The High Priestess's eyes flicker in recognition of the jewels.

"Whose donkey is that in the courtyard?" a female voice inquires from someplace behind us. There is a giant intake of breath. "Where did you get those stones?" the voice demands, and we turn to see a dark-haired girl standing there, studying us in suspicion. She is familiar, somehow.

"Pepi, Son of Kalali, gave them to me," I say. The girl startles at my words, taking a step toward us.

"Pepi?" she echoes in disbelief. "He is alive?" One hand goes to her heart, the other reaches out, as if to touch the stones.

"You know the King's nephew?" Paser examines the brown-haired girl, who looks about Merat's age.

"Yes." The girl's large eyes well with unshed tears. "He is my brother."

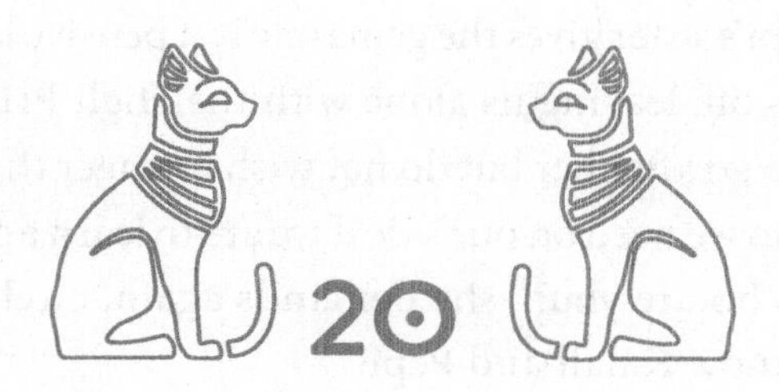

# 20

"YOU ARE PEPI'S SISTER? Tany?" I ask, in shock. "He thinks you are dead."

She offers us a tremulous smile. "I thought the same of him."

"He is alive and well," I assure her, joy filling me on Pepi's behalf. "He sent us here to find the oracle."

"So that *is* Nefer back there?"

"Yes," Reb says.

Tany looks wildly about, like she is about to burst with all the questions she has to ask, but before she can begin, the High Priestess interrupts her.

"Leave us, Tany," she commands, tone gentle, words firm. "You must rest before the ceremony."

The girl nods reluctantly. "Will you be there?" she says.

"I want to," I say. "I —"

"Now, Tany."

Pepi's sister gives the gems one last pensive look and hurries off, leaving us alone with the High Priestess. I want to go after her but do not wish to anger the priestess, who we need on our side if we are to learn anything.

"Who are you?" she demands again, circling me. "You know Kalali and Pepi?"

"Yes." I wonder what to tell her. "I am Sesha, Pepi's betrothed and Daughter to Ay —"

"Ay's daughter?" Still prowling, she takes me in. It is like being stalked by a leopard.

"Is there anyone who does *not* know your father?" Reb murmurs under his breath.

I ignore him. "These are my friends, Paser and Reb, and as we said, we need to find the oracle to help us prevent the kingdoms from erupting in war."

"What makes you think wars can be prevented?" The High Priestess stops her pacing and stands there, studying us all.

"Kalali told her son of a prophecy." Paser faces her. They are the same height. "'One from the line of the physician' is meant to maintain light and learning among the lands and rule in peace for forty years. As Sesha is Ay's daughter, Pepi thinks this might be her."

"And what do you think, Sesha?" The priestess addresses me as if Paser just told her the weather might be warm tomorrow.

I take a deep breath. "I believe that Pepi, Kalali's son, should be the one to rule."

"You would shirk your duty?" the priestess asks.

"It is true, then?" Reb interjects. "Sesha is meant to rule?"

The priestess does not answer him. "Why do you think Pepi should rule and not the other?"

"Yanassi wants Thebes, not only to possess it, but to punish it." I swallow, recalling the chieftain's contempt for my former city and its rulers. "The land is already weakened by famine and plague. Warfare would be catastrophic; innocents would die," I say. "Pepi wants peace. As did his mother, one of your own."

The priestess lifts an eyebrow, as if sensing there is more. "And what do *you* need the oracle for?"

"To prove to the king and his courtiers that Pepi is a legitimate heir," I say, transparent. "That way he stands an equal chance of inheriting the throne."

"What of the other prophecy?" she asks. "Has it been set in motion?"

"The other?" There's been so much focus on the prophecy Kalali relayed, I'd almost forgotten about the one featuring the scroll, and that she would know of it.

"Yes." She recites a part of it:

THE ONE WHO HOLDS THE HEALER'S
PAPYRUS

Is the One Who Wields This Power
Of Life Over Death
When the Gods Come to Devour

"Where is the papyrus?" she asks, eyeing me. "Who holds it?"

"I did," I stammer. "It is in Avaris now." I left it in Pepi's scriptorium. Yanassi would be outraged if we took it, and Pepi wanted to keep things as calm as possible.

She looks at me in sharp appraisal. "You used it to fend off the hungry spirits who came for the sick?"

Swallowing, I think of Ky, Paser, and Akin and nod.

"There are others who desire it," she notes.

"Yes," I admit. Yanassi. Pepi and the king. Queen Anat and Pharaoh. The blood drains from my head. *They have their own copy.* Unless the queen has destroyed it by now?

"The oracle is here," the High Priestess finally announces, stunning us. It is only as she utters the words that I become aware of how rigidly I've been holding myself. Paser and Reb also sag visibly with relief. I am desperate to ask why she did not arrive in Avaris as expected, but I keep silent. There is still a chance to witness the prophecy and ask our questions.

The High Priestess seems to consider her next words carefully. "Daughter of Ay, as you have the gemstones in your possession, I will permit you to attend the ceremony." I feel light-headed again, like I did at the hut. "Kalali was a dear friend and, as you say, one of our own." She gives Reb and Paser a pointed look. "You will come alone."

"You have my gratitude for all lifetimes." I bow my head.

"However" — her eyes narrow at us — "the oracle is *not* going back to the Hyksos capital," she warns, her stark features foreboding. "She is safe inside these walls. Outside, in the world, we can do nothing to protect her. Especially if things are as precarious as you say."

My body goes rigid again. "My friends and I will guard her with our lives," I plead, willing her to understand the necessity of returning with the oracle.

"That is what I am afraid of." She turns, toned back to us. "The eclipse will begin in a few hours. Go and rest now."

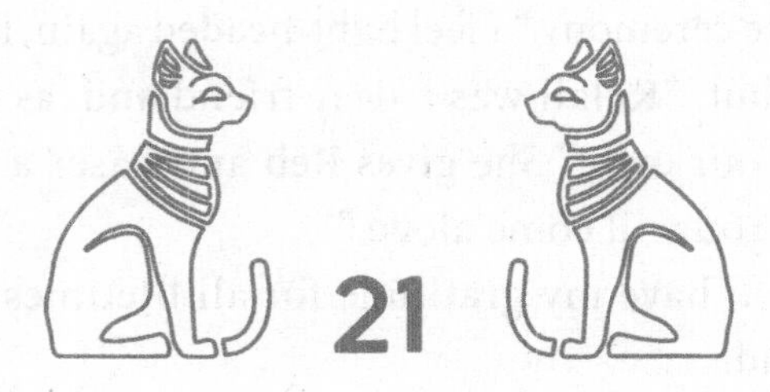

# 21

I STAND IN A CIRCLE of priestesses, their linen dresses pristine and as white as the full moon shining overhead. It bathes the whole of the inner sanctum in a soft glow, shimmering off the natural spring in the cavern's centre. We're deep underground, having descended stone-carved stairs that wind around a large inner shaft, which allows for direct viewing of the sky above. There's been much chanting as the black shadow slowly creeps across Khonsu's face, devouring the god a piece at a time. It is an unnerving sight.

The priestesses rattle their *sistrums*; I'm given one, as well, an indication I'm not only an observer but an active participant in the proceedings. The wooden instrument's metal rods are strung with silver pieces that produce a soft tinkling sound. I flick my wrist at the appropriate times, taking my cues from the women around me, who range as much in age as they do in appearance. Their one shared feature is a stunning gold headdress, inlaid with dazzling green stones. I wear no circlet, but Kalali's matching gems are tucked safely in my robes. I am glad to have them, still incredulous that I am here, attending not only the priestesses' solstice ceremony, but a most special one in which the oracle herself is apparently in attendance.

Pepi's sister, Tany, is also here. She stands next to the High Priestess, who is clad in a rare white panther skin, and whom the others refer to as *Chantress*. Fragrant incense burns low and thick, adding to the heady smell in the air, a by-product of the vapours emanating from the cracks and crags of the smooth cavern floor. Billows of wisping steam rise up from the glittering pool, which lies directly under the open column.

At last, the moon is swallowed whole and Khonsu vanishes from the sky. I gasp as the Chantress lets out a ululating cry, the eerie sound echoing through the chamber. The other priestesses join in, rattling their *sistrums*. They begin moving around the pool, spinning in their own circles within the larger one. I follow their lead, picking up the dance quickly, my knowledge of temple rituals serving me well.

Faster and faster, we circle the open column as the *menats*, the heavy beaded necklaces, swing from the necks of the higher-ranking priestesses. Their clicking beads add to the percussive *sistrums* as we continue to dance and spin until the cavern blurs. Finally, Khonsu emerges, a sliver at a time, but with a different face. He is red, like Ra himself, though it does not burn our eyes to gaze upon him. Clamour from the jangling instruments reaches a feverish pitch until, at last, the moon is entirely ablaze. We halt as one, breath coming hard and fast.

The Chantress steps forward and signals to two of the priestesses, who pick up the sycamore trays behind them that each contain small copper chalices of a dark potion. They walk around the circle, offering each priestess a cup. I take one, as the others do, as the heat from our bodies mixes with the grotto's steamy vapours. We wait, still breathless, in anticipation of the Chantress's command.

The High Priestess lifts her cup, signalling us to drink. The others immediately bring their chalices to their mouths. I hesitate, sniffing the mysterious elixir. *Now or never, Sesha.* Cool liquid quenches the thirst roused from the chanting and dancing, as curious flavours mingle inside my mouth. I try to place some of them. Belladonna. Henbane. Blue lotus. A powerful concoction.

The Chantress finishes her drink and sets it down. "We call upon the oracle." She holds both her arms high, voice echoing through the chamber. It floats up out of the column and into the sky. "Illuminate us in darkness. Speak and reveal to us your truths."

Tany steps forward.

The cup falls from my hand as the red-orange glow from the moon sets her outline on fire. The wreath of gold rests ethereally on her brow, green gemstones sparkling. With the lithe grace of a cat, Tany disrobes and walks slowly into the pool. Moonlit waters lap at her body, as if eager to soothe the fiery radiance of her skin. She submerges herself and I hold my breath along with her. What feels like hours pass before she finally surfaces with a gulping gasp of air. Running her hands over her face, she wipes the water from eyes as black as the dark moon.

Tany is transformed and the oracle is here.

She begins to speak in a deep guttural voice, completely at odds with Tany's honeyed tones, and I blink. The words the oracle speaks are unfamiliar, but I recognize the language of the Hyksos. The other priestesses sway in unison as the Chantress steps forward, holding a dove. The bird is calm and does not make a sound, even when the Chantress breaks its neck, almost as if it knew, and was honoured, that it had been chosen for this great destiny. The Chantress slits the bird with a silver blade, pouring its blood into the pool. A coppery scent mixes with the steamy vapours.

"The sacrifice is made. Those who wish to consult the oracle may now step forward."

One at a time, women approach the pool and dreamily relay their questions through the Chantress, who is the only one permitted to speak directly to the oracle. My mind feels hazy and untethered; I wonder if I will be able to ask a question.

The High Priestess allows my presence here, but will she let me address the oracle? For that matter, what is it I should be asking, exactly? The winking of the green gems reminds me of my own stones tucked away beneath my robes, and I pull one out, gripping it tightly in my palm, which brings things back into focus. The line of questioners is slowing.

I find myself stepping forward, almost floating to the edge of the pool. Before I am quite sure how I get there, I stand before the oracle. Tany's black eyes pass over me, showing no recognition. Then she begins to speak.

"Welcome, young scribe," the Chantress translates in a language I can understand, half startling me from my trancelike state. Some part of Tany must recognize me. "What is it you wish to know?"

*What do I want to know?* I think dazedly. Whether Pepi is truly the son of the king? Clarification of the previous prophecies? And what of the expected third forecast, that Pepi and Khyan thought might happen during the solstice alignment? So far, Tany is only answering questions, as she would at Avaris, though perhaps with more spectacle.

Channeling my courage, as Tany channels the oracle, I open my mouth. "Your brother spoke of two prophecies featuring a healer's papyrus." My voice sounds strange to my ears. "I am here for the third."

Tany does not answer. Instead, she falls back under the water, disappearing from view. Bewildered, I look at the Chantress for guidance, but she stares into the dark pool, waiting for the oracle to emerge. After an eternity she does, thrashing and gasping again for air, like something is being choked out of her. Everyone remains where they are. Apparently, this is not unexpected behaviour.

At last, she gains control of herself, inhaling deeply, and begins to speak in the indecipherable language. The Chantress translates, murmuring the lines I am familiar with, lines that were perhaps first uttered at previous astral events such as this one.

> NEW KINGDOMS, OLD KINGDOMS
> KINGDOMS IN BETWEEN
> FOR THOSE WHO WISH TO RULE THEIR
> PEOPLE
> THE SCROLL IS THE KEY
> THE ONE WHO HOLDS THE HEALER'S

Papyrus
Is the One Who Wields this Power
Of Life over Death
When the Gods Come to Devour

When the Healer's Papyrus
Is Held Firmly in Hand
One from the Line of the Physician
Will Rule the Land
For Forty Years
Light and Learning Will Reign
And Peace and Prosperity
Will Thus Be Maintained

The oracle stops speaking as the hazy moon glowers; the peak of the eclipse is coming to an end. Khonsu will soon turn his face back toward Ra and the alignment will be over. I look up at the column, where the reddish hue begins to vanish.

"Hurry," I urge the oracle, "please." She obliges, her words coming faster, racing against the departing moon.

But Another of the Physician's Line
In Several Years to Come
Will Sneer at Levantine Light and
Learning

And See It All Undone
They Will Wipe the People from
Their Lands
A New Kingdom Will Begin
And the Glories of the Hyksos
Will All but Be Forgotten

The oracle finishes. Her eyes roll up in her head, and she falls back into the water with a soundless splash. Her words turn me to stone; I am unable to move. Some voice in the back of my mind wonders if Tany is going to emerge from the pool, or if someone should go help her?

I am about to wade in when she emerges, spluttering and coughing, and — trance broken — I lean forward to give her my hand, helping her emerge from the pool. Her eyes are their normal shade, and she shivers, arms wrapped around her body, as another priestess brings her a robe.

The Chantress gives me a stern look and I melt back into the circle, while the ceremony concludes. I go through the motions while my mind tries to make sense of the ominous and completely earth-shattering prophecy.

*Another of the physician's line ... will wipe the people from their lands ...*

If what the oracle says is true, then it sounds as if "another" from the line of the physician will be responsible for the destruction and eradication of the Hyksos people. And if, as Pepi claims, I am the one from the other prophecy, then that means the one who would undo "Levantine light and learning" would be ...

Ky.

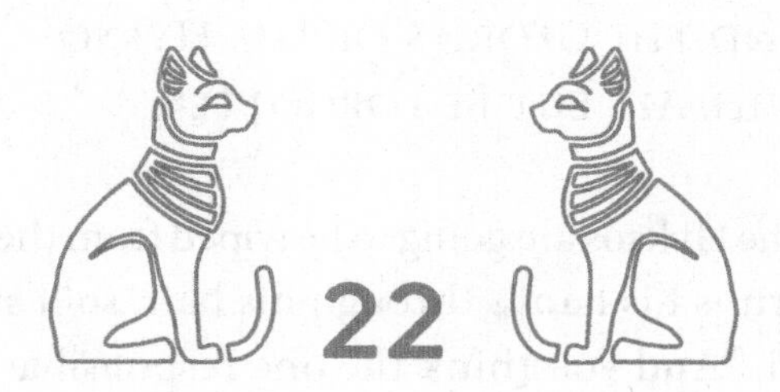

# 22

"SHE SAID WHAT?" Reb and Paser repeat together as we huddle under the stars. The late-night air is sharp and crisp, and after the overwhelming smells of the cavern, it is a relief to breathe it in. I am exhausted, but the evening's revelations leave me unable to sleep. With good reason.

I repeat the prophecy again for my friends.

> BUT ANOTHER OF THE PHYSICIAN'S LINE
> IN SEVERAL YEARS TO COME
> WILL SNEER AT LEVANTINE LIGHT AND LEARNING
> AND SEE IT ALL UNDONE
> THEY WILL WIPE THE PEOPLE FROM THEIR LANDS

A NEW KINGDOM WILL BEGIN
AND THE GLORIES OF THE HYKSOS
WILL ALL BUT BE FORGOTTEN

"The Hyksos are going to be wiped from the lands?" Paser runs his hands through his hair, so it sticks up on end. "And you think the one responsible for this might be *Ky*?"

"I don't know." I shake my head, still dazed and foggy from the evening's ceremony, capped by the oracle's upsetting decree. "If what Pepi believes is true, and I *am* the one from the first prophecies then … perhaps?"

"It might not be him." Paser is pacing. "It could be one of his children or their children. All it says is 'another of the physician's line.'"

"The possibility that it might be Ky's child or grandchild who eradicates the Hyksos does not make me feel any better," I say, head going to my hands.

"Or it might be the reverse, and you could be the one doing the wiping," Reb says to me. I lift my head and glare at him.

"Why did Tany not come to Avaris for solstice?" Paser wonders, trying to work things out. "And how did Pepi not know his sister was the oracle?"

"It is only a recent development," Tany says from behind us. Still wrapped in her robe, her wet hair hangs in tangled ringlets around her wan face. "The previous oracle was unexpectedly indisposed."

"What happened to her?" Reb asks.

"It is nothing I wish to speak of." She eyes us warily. "But the High Priestess felt I needed to be here for the eclipse, as I am somewhat new to prophesizing."

"How new?" Paser asks. "Did *you* make the prophecy Kalali relayed, about one from the line of the physician ruling the lands?"

"That was the previous oracle," Tany says.

"How did your mother learn of it?" I ask.

Tany's eyes go to the coops behind us. Messenger doves. "Our network is vast."

"You really think Sesha is the one to uphold peace throughout the lands?" Reb says.

She looks at us, hesitant. "My brother seems to. He wouldn't've sent her here with my mother's stones otherwise."

"What do you think?" I push, somewhat reluctantly, not sure if I want to hear the answer.

"About what?" Tany hedges. She, too, seems unfocused and pensive, likely even more exhausted than I am.

"About the prophecies," I say. "Are they ever wrong?"

"Some have not come to pass, but it could be their time has simply not yet arrived." She looks at me, tentative. "What *did* I say, exactly?"

We look at her in amazement.

"You don't remember?" Reb asks.

"I am still only an apprentice. It can often take a few days for things to come back to me." She tucks a piece of wet hair behind her ear. "Other times they never do. The High Priestess will tell me the prophecy tomorrow, when I'm better rested, and we will decipher its meaning together."

Paser looks at me. The prophecy seems painfully clear in this case.

"Your brother's heart will be filled with happiness to learn you are alive." I change the subject for now. "His face when we return you to the capital will be something to behold."

A shadow that has nothing to do with the moon eclipses her features. "I cannot go to Avaris," she says, though there is longing in her voice, which I assume has to do with reuniting with her brother. "I need to complete my training. My place is here for now."

"But we must bring you back," I protest. "You have to tell the king, and his court, that Pepi is his son …" I stop as it hits me that she might not know this. Did Tany's mother speak to her of Pepi's parentage? Do they share the same father? Is it offensive to ask such personal questions?

Fortunately, Reb has no such reservations. "Are you also a child of the king?" he asks Tany bluntly. She studies us, as if not quite sure she can trust the three Thebans standing before her.

"Pepi and I share only a mother," she says at last.

"Is Khyan Pepi's father?" Paser says.

"That is what Kalali told him." I wonder if Tany knows what happened to the priestess spy. She looks at me sadly, as if hearing my unspoken thought. "She is dead, I know."

"We are sorry." My heart contracts at the thought of another mother gone too soon.

"How long have you been the oracle?" Reb probes gently.

"I have always been prone to visions." Tany's wide eyes come up again to meet our gaze. "But I was not initiated officially until the other ..." She swallows, her elegant neck like Pepi's. "Could no longer fulfill her duties."

"Does your brother know of your abilities?" Paser asks.

"He knew I was one of several thought to have potential," she admits. "Though my mother swore him to tell no one." And if Pepi thought his sister was dead, there'd be no reason to say anything.

I give my head another shake to clear the lingering buzzing, a hundred cicadas swirling inside my skull. "The oracle before you," I say, "was she the one to relay the prophecies foretelling of Khyan's rule?"

"Yes. The king was most grateful." She turns and looks back at the temple and the grounds. "He helps provide for our home here."

"He wants the oracle to come back to Avaris for her scheduled visit," Paser says softly.

"I will not allow it." The High Priestess, still clad in her ceremonial panther skin, approaches, simmering with supressed temper. "Tany is still a novice. In addition, the last oracle we sent to Avaris got her tongue cut out for her troubles."

Paser, Reb, and I look at each other, aghast. *The woman from the hut!*

"Who would do such a thing?" Reb asks.

"One who did not like what they were told." The High Priestess purses her lips. "Or someone who wished to prevent her from speaking what she knew. Whatever the case, she refuses to discuss the matter." Reb looks confused, and the priestess gives a feline huff. "There are other ways to communicate than by speaking. As scribes, you should know this." My guilt flares for assuming the woman could not read or write. As a priestess and former oracle, she'd be adept at both. In fairness to my friends and me, I suppose that was the impression she wanted to convey to unfamiliar travellers.

"Khyan will be appalled to hear of her fate." I refuse to give up. Tany and the High Priestess look at each other. "Pepi is the king's beloved nephew; he would not let anything endanger his own sister, who is also Khyan's royal niece." I gesture at my friends. "She would have our protection."

"Kalali died with an arrow through her throat, silencing her forever," the High Priestess says with unyielding finality. "I will not allow the same fate to befall her daughter, even if it displeases the powers at Avaris. You may bring back the third prophecy if you wish, which may or may not garner an arrow through your own throats, but she is to stay here. That is final."

# 23

WE EAT BREAKFAST the next morning in the gardens under a statue of Seshat, the goddess of wisdom and knowledge. I am named for her, the creator of scripts. She holds a tablet and a reed in her hands, poised to capture the words of the gods. I cannot help but compare them to my own hands, which are metaphorically empty.

"I cannot believe we are returning to Avaris without the oracle." Glumly, I stir the porridge with my finger, having a hard time connecting it with my mouth. Exhaustion from the late evening and the after-effects of the ceremonial potion leave me feeling disembodied, like my *Ba* is hovering somewhere above my body, waiting to reunite with my *Ka*.

"We learned of the third prophecy," Paser reminds me. "That is no small thing."

"What good will that do?" I give up and put my bowl down. "How can we reveal the oracle's words to the Hyksos rulers? It foretells of their expulsion from the lands!"

"At least they have forty good years ahead of them," Reb says bleakly.

"Only if Sesha holds the healer's papyrus 'firmly in hand,'" Paser reminds him. My friends seem to have fully accepted Pepi's theory that I am the one from the prophecy. And that I may accept the role it foretells.

"I do not want to be the one to inform Yanassi that his people will be struck from the land in forty years." Reb sticks his tongue out and looks down at it, eyes crossing. "I, for one, would like to keep my tongue."

"Pepi and the king will not let Yanassi harm us," I repeat uneasily. *Who would do such a thing — and to a priestess, an* oracle *no less?* I feel my appetite leave me.

"No," Paser says slowly. "But the king and his courtiers might let Yanassi wage his war against Thebes, in a pre-emptive campaign. They already have the Nubians on their side."

Another consideration slowly dawns on me, like the sun in the east, rays of realization piercing my heart like knives. "If one of Ky's line really *is* meant to erase the Hyksos from history, they wouldn't need to wage an entire war to alter the prophecy." I look at my friends. "They would just have to dispose of Ky."

Paser leans forward, lifting a brow in inquiry. "What if we give them another prophecy instead?" Reb and I absorb this, as our uneaten oats absorb water.

"You would tamper with the words of the oracle?" Reb rubs his nose thoughtfully, not sounding terribly shocked. "I suppose priests do it all the time. Those in power often bend words to suit their purpose."

Distress at what the chieftain might do if he learns of Tany's proclamation has me on my feet. "What are we to do?" I pace up and down the gardens. "We need the oracle to prove Pepi is Khyan's son, but if Yanassi finds out about this final prophecy, he may kill us all!"

"At least Ky is safe in Thebes with Pharaoh and Queen Anat," Paser reminds me. "He is one of their sons now, and well protected. Even if Yanassi somehow manages to learn of the prophecy it will be difficult to get at your brother."

"It is a blessing that the High Priestess forbids Tany to come with us," Reb says. "That way, we are free to report back what we wish."

"I am not sure I can lie to Pepi," I say. My skills of deception have come far, but he knows me well, and his spy's instincts are exceptionally honed. And despite his own tendency to withhold information — with good reason, he would say — Pepi is also my mentor, and my friend.

"There will be time on our journey back to debate our options." Paser stands, as well, and brushes himself off. "We need to be on our way soon, though. Only the gods know what is happening in Avaris in our absence."

"What about Nosy?" Reb asks. The two boys gather up the bowls and begin walking toward the temple. "Do you think she is well enough for the return trip?"

"We will check on her again this morning," Paser says. "The extract of juniper berries administered by the priestesses is reducing the swelling some."

I follow them, disoriented, listening to their talk, sensing I am not seeing something right there in front of me. I feel like Paser's horse, nosing at some elusive, shapeless form hidden in the tall grass. I only pray I will be able to work out what is slithering just beyond the grasp of my understanding before it bites me in the face.

"I do not think we should take her." Reb sounds as reluctant as me to admit it. Though the horse's condition is not worsening, large swathes of skin are peeling from her nose. Frequent cleaning and application of herbs will be difficult to perform properly while on a hurried and challenging journey home. And if the demons get into the skin and turn it green or black, things can go badly quite quick, horse *or* human.

"Having only two animals will slow our pace," I fret, though I know he is right. Nosy is in no condition for an arduous trek.

"So will an injured horse." Paser pats the animal. "Reb is right, we must leave her here. We can always return to get her."

"We can ask Tany to care for her. Perhaps she will bring Nosy to Avaris when she is better, to pay an unofficial visit to her brother," Reb says. The thought of Tany visiting seems to cheer him.

"Pepi will be tempted to race out here the moment he discovers his sister is alive and well," I say, knowing I would do the same.

"That could be disastrous with regards to timing," Paser comments. "The kingdom's successorship seems most delicate." I am inclined to agree. "We should not mention Tany right away," he continues. "Reb is right: the High Priestess prohibiting her from going to Avaris benefits our plans. You can tell Khyan whatever you wish about Pepi's parentage, *and* we can tweak the prophecy to suit our aims."

"Making us no better than deceptive temple priests." I sigh, the bitterness of last night's elixir rising up in my throat. We stand there, contemplating the peaceful animal, before Paser speaks again.

"We are trying to do what we believe is right," Paser says. "But if our conscience will not allow us to modify the prophecy, then we need to acknowledge the consequences that sharing the real one will have." He counts on his fingers. "The first being that war is waged on Thebes and our people there. The second being the potential loss of our own tongues, or worse. And the third" — Paser gives me a levelling look — "a dagger in your brother's heart and, again, possibly our own. Are we prepared to accept these consequences?"

"Not for all the fish in the Nile," Reb remarks.

"Sesha?" Paser's golden eyes search mine.

There is no decision to make.

"I will abide by this plan." I glance at Nefer in apology. Is it my imagination or does the donkey give me an accusing look?

"We are scribes." Reb appears relieved at my consent. "Are we not allowed some artistic licence with our words?"

I sigh. "It occurs to me that the oracle perhaps cut out her own tongue, to avoid the headache that comes with being an instrument of betrayal and doom."

"I would not discard that notion," Paser says, in all seriousness.

"You became a spy to make a difference." Reb gives me an encouraging pat on the back. "Is this not all part of the profession?"

I lift my chin high, thinking of Pepi's mother and all the distasteful things she had to do to protect the people she loved. "Yes. It is."

# 24

WE LEAVE AFTER BREAKFAST, saying goodbye to Tany and the other priestesses, who tolerated our presence well, all things considered. It is clear Kalali was their sister and important to them, and so, by extension, are her children and the people they send their way. The High Priestess is conspicuously absent from our departure, but we are told she is busy recording the evening's events.

"Thank you for caring for Nosy." There is sincere appreciation in Reb's voice.

"She is a fine and noble creature," Tany says with a Hyksos's passion for horses. "Please give my love and blessings to my brother." I try not to shift under her assessing stare.

"We will." *Once he is on the throne, and all are safe from Yanassi's wrath and battle plans.* I pray that we find the king alive and Merat still unmarried upon our return.

Holding out my hand, I offer Tany one of the sparkling green gemstones. It was her mother's, after all.

"Keep it." She nods at the gem. "It will bring you luck in your journey."

"You have our thanks." I pocket the stone and climb onto Nefer. We set off, Reb riding Breakaway and Paser walking at my side. Both animals are restocked and ready for the trip home.

"Farewell," Tany calls, face wistful, and we turn to lift our hands in goodbye as we leave the oracle behind. The guilt prickled by Tany's plea to give her brother her love is somewhat soothed by my reasoning that at least Pepi's sister is safe here. Perhaps he would understand our motives after all.

"Do you think the Nubian will find the temple?" Reb asks later that morning. We are searching for some shade where we can stop and eat the lunch prepared by the priestesses. A small cluster of palms lies up to our left and we head for their shelter.

"It depends on if he finds the map," I say. We'd cast the mercenary from our minds for a time, but my stomach churns to think he is still out there somewhere.

"Or whether he's even still tracking us," Paser says. "He might have taken Yanassi's payment and run. It takes more than silver to maintain someone's loyalty when things become difficult."

"Even if he manages to locate the sect, I do not think the High Priestess will tell a man such as that anything." I feel fairly confident in my assessment of their leader, who seems as intelligent as the goddess she worships.

"Not unless he forces her to," Reb mutters.

"There is only one of him, and many of them," I say. The High Priestess and the other women there give the impression they are comfortable with weapons. I am sure Kalali was. Even Tany, with her former training as a spy, would be skilled at basic defensive moves. "They will be fine. Besides, I doubt Yanassi wants his mercenary attacking the priestesses and desecrating the temple; it would only anger the gods who the chieftain wishes to back his rule."

"That is a fair point," Paser says, getting off Breakaway; he and Reb switched some time ago. "But we should not underestimate Yanassi's obsession with Thebes."

"Should we go back to warn the sect?" I look at him, uncertain.

"I think it best if we make our stop here short," he responds, "then continue on to Avaris as quickly as we can."

But we are still tired from the night before and our eyes close in the warmth of the early-afternoon sun. Nefer's loud braying startles us from our dozing and, in the confusion of sudden waking, I think the Nubian has found us. Paser and Reb scramble for their weapons.

But it is not the mercenary who approaches.

"Hello again." Tany stands before us, a bulging satchel strung across her body.

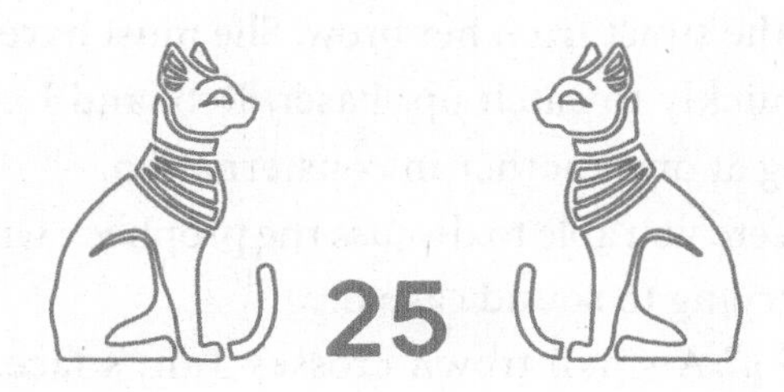

# 25

WE GAPE AT HER. Reb wipes the drool from his mouth and Paser rubs the sleep from his eyes.

"What are you doing here?" Am I dreaming? Or is this a residual hallucination from yesterday's concoction?

"I have decided to come with you to Avaris." Tany's cheeks are flushed, her eyes bright and determined.

"What about the High Priestess?" Paser demands as he lowers his weapon. "Does she know you're here?" The three of us try to hide our panicked dismay. If we are to relay an altered version of the prophecy as planned, having the actual oracle accompany us does not work in our favour.

"She will realize when we meet to go over the ceremony's events and I am not there." Tany plunks herself under one of the palms and takes a large drink. She wipes the sweat from her brow. She must have walked very quickly to catch up. Paser, Reb, and I continue looking at one another in consternation.

"Were you able to discuss the prophecy with her?" I ask, trying to sound casual.

"No." A small frown crosses Tany's face. "But it may come back to me on its own. Often, it is a sound or smell that triggers the memory." She waves a regretful hand. "In the meantime, I could not miss this opportunity to reunite with my brother." Anticipation flickers across her expression like the shadows above. "A little excitement would not go amiss, either. I've been cooped up in that temple for months."

I suppose a taste for adventure does run in her family.

"Paser, Reb, I think I dropped my blade," I say hastily, beckoning them to follow me behind the palms.

"I can help search." Tany starts to stand.

"No! Ah, no, thank you, that is quite all right. You must be exhausted from chasing after us." I gesture for her to remain sitting. "Let your breath catch up."

She eyes us curiously but shrugs in acquiescence, the gesture so like Pepi I blink.

"I think it was over here somewhere," I call, and Reb and Paser follow me. Once behind the trees, I lower my voice to a whisper. "What are we to do?"

"She does not remember what she foretold, so I say we remain as breezy as the palms." Reb points up.

"It could come back to her at any time!" I say in an agitated whisper.

"Or not," Paser reasons. "Don't forget, she is new."

"Are you sure you don't need any help?" Tany calls from the shade.

"Found it!" I say in a high-pitched voice that sounds ridiculous to my own ears and grab the blade strapped to my leg. "Say *nothing* of the prophecy," I murmur as we walk back to Tany, not wanting to further arouse her suspicions. My friends nod and we plaster welcoming looks on our faces for the oracle, who, with much luck, will remain oblivious to our outrageous schemes.

"How did you come to be with the priestesses?" Reb asks Tany, who is riding Breakaway. The boys flank her; the trio have been speaking non-stop about her family background as a spy and current role as oracle. I trail behind them.

"I was with my mother and Pepi on a mission to find an ancient scroll. You are familiar with it, I believe?" Tany lifts a brow. "They were disguised in the Theban marketplace, waiting for an opportunity to sneak into the palace, when things went sideways. Perhaps a soldier became suspicious and inquired after their identity — the details are unclear." She grimaces. "After I learned my mother was dead and my brother captured, I knew I must get to the safety of the sect. Kalali made me swear if anything happened to her or Pepi, I was to get to the temple."

"You didn't try to save him?" Indignation on Pepi's behalf makes my voice sharper than I intend.

"He sacrificed himself for me. Both of them did." She whirls to face me. "Was I to let their lives be wasted? The first days after his capture, I waited for a chance to visit his pit, even just to throw down some food, or let him know that I was all right, but there was a guard stationed beside it from sunrise to sundown, and all the hours between. I could not get close without exposing myself."

*We were able to free him*, I almost say, but remind myself that was during the festival, when watch over the pits was much laxer.

"And then —" she pauses, blinking several times "— I had a vision, where I sensed something terrible befalling the current oracle. Between that, my mother's death, and Pepi's capture, I knew I must return to the sect at once. There, it was declared that I was to be the next oracle, in part due to that very vision. In truth, I did not know if the priestesses chose well or not. That is another reason why I did not come to Avaris this solstice; until I made my first prophecy, my status as oracle was not solidified."

"And so you left Pepi in Thebes?" I struggle to keep my judgment at bay. But my condemnation is not for her — it is for myself, who did the same thing to Ky.

"I did." Her eyes shine with sadness and she looks down. "May the gods forgive me for abandoning my brother, because I never will."

I exhale. "You are not the only one to leave a brother behind." Granted, the pharaoh's palace is somewhat more luxurious than the pits, but I know what it is to have guilt eat at your soul.

"You have a brother?" Tany says, curious.

I freeze at the enormity of my blunder. *For the love of Isis.* Reb's and Paser's shoulders stiffen on either side of her.

"We are her brothers," Paser says quickly, gesturing at himself and Reb.

"Uh, yes, Sesha's always leaving us behind ..." Reb's eyes dart from me to Paser. "Um, in our studies. She is very smart, just swims on by us in lessons, her memory is impressive, as is her hand for hieroglyphs ..." He trails off at Tany's frown.

"That is not quite the same thing," she says, sounding skeptical.

"You are right," Reb continues babbling. "It is not the same thing at all, but —"

"But Pepi will understand." Paser elbows Reb sharply. "You survived, as did he. Your mother's spirit will rest easier for that."

Paser's words have a consoling effect on Tany, and she nods, sitting up on the horse. The three of them continue to speak as they walk; she is hungry for news of the outside world. I follow behind, still cursing myself for my absent-minded slip. Why are we deceiving her? She will discover the truth once we reach Avaris and she confers with Pepi, sooner if her foretelling comes back to her. Yet I think again of my own brother and know why we misled her, even if it buys only a little time. If Tany recalls the prophecy and reveals to the powers at Avaris that Ky, or one of his descendants, is meant to bring about the Hyksos's downfall, I and all of my "brothers" will be in very real danger.

"I want to check." Paser is insistent. Usually the most easygoing of us three, he can be quite stubborn when he wants. Reb and Tany are riding ahead, while Paser and I walk behind. We've been taking turns on the animals, who grow weary as dusk approaches. He and I are discussing whether to bypass the little hut. Knowing it may be the home of a woman who was once Avaris's legendary oracle gives me an odd feeling.

"It's the little girl, isn't it?" I say. The child left an impact on us all, but Paser especially. He'd entertained her and left her his anklet; he feels concern for her welfare. He nods and I sigh. "Your heart is as soft as a sack of ibis feathers, you know that?"

"The better for you to jump into," he teases quietly, and my cheeks grow warm.

"There is a place we can stop just ahead," Tany calls out. "It is not large, but I know the woman there." Paser gives me a look. I suppose that settles things.

"We stayed there on our way to you," Reb says. "She is the former oracle, is she not? There can't be that many women around missing their tongues."

"You'd be surprised." Tany's tone is dry. "But yes, she was the oracle before I."

"And what of the girl?" Paser asks. "Who is she?"

"A future priestess," Tany says.

Reb looks down at Tany. He seems quite taken with her. "Why does the woman prefer to stay here and not at the temple?"

"I do not know," Tany admits, "but if I had to guess, I think out here she is not reminded daily of who she was, and the power and status she once held. Out here she can get lost in the milking of goats, or the feeding of chickens, and forget." Tany shivers. "It wasn't all that long ago, and I imagine her emotional wounds are still raw. The heart heals more slowly than the mouth."

One of the goats in question trots toward us, bleating in frustration. Its issue seems to be a swollen udder that needs milking. I sniff the air, smelling smoke, and Nefer bristles. The others smell it, as well.

"With luck we will have a cooked meal tonight," Tany says, turning back to Paser and me, smiling, but I know first-hand that sometimes smoke means more than dinner. Sometimes it means disaster.

"Hello?" Tany calls out. "Rahibe?" Tany and Reb disembark their animals, and Paser reaches for his bow. It is eerily quiet, like the morning we left this place. We approach cautiously. There is movement inside the hut and the tanned hides are pushed aside. A man steps out, gripping a small child's hand in one of his, the other wrapped around the hilt of a gleaming curved blade.

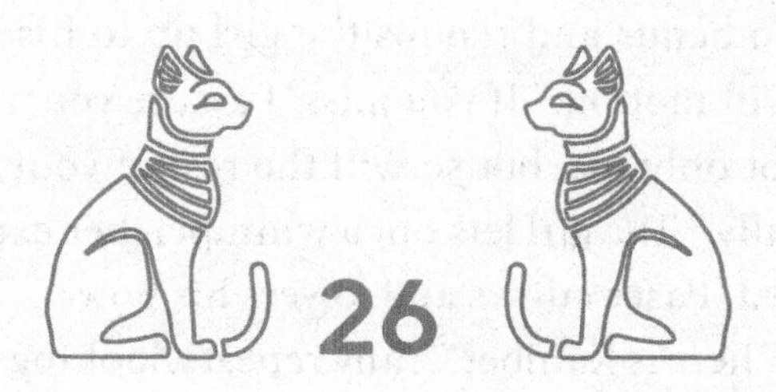

## 26

"GREETINGS," THE NUBIAN SAYS, spitting on the ground beside him.

"Where is Rahibe?" Tany demands, making a move for the child, knowing at once this man is not to be trusted.

"Stay where you are." The Nubian lifts his deadly sword, his hand tightening on the little girl. "Or I will give her a tongue to match the old woman's."

"Let her go," Paser commands, bow already sighted. I know that only the girl's small hand in the mercenary's is keeping him from releasing his arrow.

"I might," the Nubian says. "But first you will drop your weapon."

"And I will do that, once you let her go," Paser repeats evenly, fingers holding the string taut.

"Do you have that much faith in your skill?" The Nubian bends and scoops the girl up to his chest in one swift motion. "If you miss, I assure you, the child will not only die, but so will the rest of your friends. Painfully." The girl lets out a whimper, her expression terrified. Paser curses and lowers his bow.

"Where is Rahibe?" Tany repeats, looking around.

"Who are you?" the Nubian demands.

"I am Tany, Daughter to Kalali and Sister to Apepi, nephew to the king at Avaris. Who are *you*?" she demands. "Other than a flea-bitten whelp of a jackal, that is."

"I am the man your cousin hired." He brandishes his blade in a mocking subservient gesture.

"Hired to do what?" She keeps her eyes on his weapon.

"To bring back the oracle." I notice a map peeking out of the mercenary's robes. *Donkey dung.* "There are a few things he would like clarified," he sneers.

"I am now she, and would be happy to accompany you," Tany says politely. "In exchange for you releasing the child."

The mercenary blinks at this unexpected turn of events. "You seek to deceive me."

"I assure you, I do not," Tany says. "Now, let the little one go, and depart peacefully from this place."

He contemplates us a moment, a wicked grin spreading across his face. "Where's the fun in that?" He lifts his blade high.

The girl bites down on the Nubian's shoulder with the ferocity of a hippo. He curses, half dropping her to the ground. Paser lifts his bow and fires. The arrow whirs past the mercenary's head, burrowing itself with a *thunk* in the hide behind him.

The child uses the arrow's distraction to scramble beyond her captor's reach. He lunges, but she is quick, his fingertips only graze her. Reb grabs his dagger and hurls it with all his strength at the mercenary.

The Nubian looks down at the knife sticking out of his thigh. It is hard to tell who is more shocked — him or Reb. I bolt for the child, knowing I must get between her and the mercenary, who is now yanking the knife from his leg. He launches it back at Reb, who dives into the scrubby underbrush.

"Stop!" Tany shouts, just as I reach the girl and pull her into my arms, pushing her head into my chest. Paser's bow is reloaded, and the Nubian grips his *khopesh* sword with both hands, blood seeping from the gash in his leg. "I said I would accompany you." She grabs Breakaway's lead and walks boldly toward the mercenary. "Leave them be, and we will go to Avaris where you can claim your reward, because only a fool would pay everything up front before the task is completed. And whatever my cousin is, he is no fool." She gives the Nubian's bleeding leg a pointed look. "Are you?"

The Nubian does not respond. Instead he rips a strip of linen from his robes and ties it around his upper thigh. He limps over to his horse, which he had left behind the hut, and Tany follows.

"Tany," Paser shouts. "You do not have to go with him."

"He will not harm me," she says calmly. "I am needed alive."

"What about Rahibe?" Reb calls out, slowly extracting himself from the bush. The child lifts her head from my chest and points toward the hut, sticking the fingers of her other hand in her mouth.

Paser dashes in and back out. "She is safe. Bound, but alive." He dives back into the dwelling, presumably to untie her.

"Do not worry." Tany unties our bag of medicines from Breakaway and leaves it on the ground. "My brother and uncle will protect me once we reach Avaris."

"There is much you don't know —" I protest, but she cuts me off earnestly.

"I am aware, Sesha, Daughter of Ay." She gives me an arch look. "But the prophecy will come back to me, I am sure of it."

*That is the worry.*

Paser comes out with Rahibe. I expect to see her visibly distraught, but instead of tears in her eyes, there are flaming arrows. Tany rushes to the former oracle and hugs her fiercely while the Nubian, who mounts his horse, begins to ride in the direction of Avaris. Tany whispers something in Rahibe's ear, who nods, then she runs back over to Breakaway.

"I must take your animal." She climbs on top of Reb's horse with the skill of a seasoned horsewoman. "If my uncle is as ill as you say, I don't have much time. I would like to see him before he departs this world."

"Help your brother," I burst out.

She gives me a funny look from astride the creature, who's packed with the rest of our supplies. "Of course." She manoeuvres Breakaway in the direction of the Nubian. "I will see you three back in the city of Avaris, I know it. Travel safe." She kicks the horse, and they take off, leaving us with our donkey.

We cobble together a meal for the woman and child. Reb collects some eggs while I milk the goats, much to their bleating relief, and Paser rekindles the fire. We eat a simple dinner of soft-boiled eggs and milk, still warm from the animals. Sharing our bread and beer rations, we pour an extra-large cup for the former oracle. I watch the priestess more closely this time, knowing who she is. If she was prophesizing when Khyan came to rule, she must be in her fiftieth or sixtieth year, making her one of the oldest people I have met. There are many things I want to ask, but I do not want to pester her — she's been through much already.

Fairly quickly, though, it becomes apparent that Rahibe has other ideas. After we finish clearing our meal, she makes a sound, and we look up. She points at us then spreads her hands wide to make a "Who are you?" gesture, having discerned from recent events and former company that we are not your typical passers-by.

Paser and Reb both introduce themselves, then it is my turn. "I am Sesha, Daughter to Ay, the former royal physician to the exalted pharaoh of Thebes, his Great Royal Wife, their family, and the court there."

Her eyes light in recognition and she beckons us to follow her outside. We leave the little girl curled up in a ball, belly full and fast asleep on a mat. Outside the night air is fresh. Rahibe points to the sky, where the three stars line up to form Osiris's crown, and then back at me, insistent.

My friends and I look at one another, unsure of what she is trying to tell us. She lets out a garbled noise, the first we've heard her speak. It sounds like "ah-ah-ee."

Being who she is, I attempt a guess. "Prophecy?"

She nods and points again, this time at the two brighter stars first, then at the third one that lies slightly farther away.

"Yes, we know about the first two prophecies concerning the healer's scroll. Tany just made a third." I hope she does not want me to go into details. Thankfully, in the excitement of her escape from the sect, Pepi's sister had not thought to ask if I recalled it.

Rahibe shakes her head impatiently and points at me and then at Reb and Paser. "They are my friends, my brothers," I say, baffled. She nods emphatically at my words.

A sudden cry from the hut sends her rushing back to check on the girl, woken by a bad dream. Little wonder, with the day the child had.

"What do you think she is trying to tell us?" Reb says.

"I don't know." Feeling helpless, I consider the night sky above. "Perhaps that we are stronger together?"

"Of course we are," Paser says. "Like the stars above and three points of a pyramid, we are a formidable unit."

"That is very poetic for someone who says they are not creative, Paser." I give him a tired smile, suddenly utterly drained. "We can clarify tomorrow. I need to rest. Now that we only have Nefer, we will be at least a day or two behind Tany and the mercenary. And if the third prophecy comes back to her before we get there, we will be up the Nile without a paddle." Particularly if Yanassi gets wind of it.

The old woman does not come back out of the hut. She, too, is probably exhausted and has likely fallen asleep comforting the child. We make our bed as we did the last time we stopped, albeit with fewer linens, and finally lie down to rest. Reb is out instantly, but despite the fatigue that settles in my bones, I am unable to fall asleep. I breathe deeply and release the air slowly, trying to relax my body cubit by cubit, an old trick that usually works. This time it does not.

Paser senses my agitation and takes my hand in his, breath warm on my cheek. "Remember, there is no sense worrying about what we cannot control." His touch comforts me and, at last, I fall into a restless sleep, dreaming of Yanassi's face and the mercenary's crocodile grin, swimming languid laps around us, as if they know it is only a matter of time.

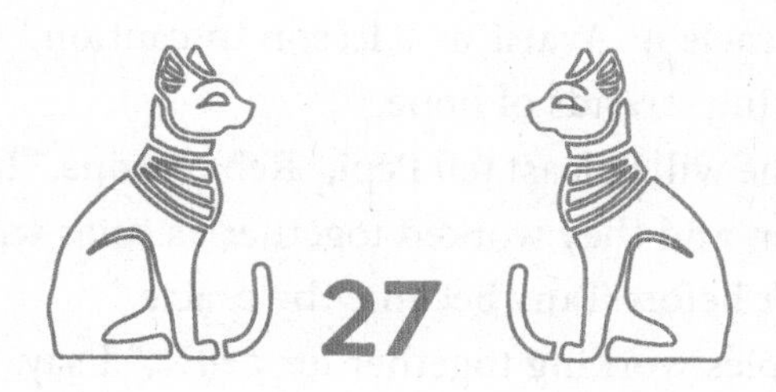

# 27

WHEN WE WAKE, the woman and child are gone again, as last time, and I feel a fist in my gut at my questions going unanswered. Paser thinks they've headed for the safety of the priestesses' temple. I hope so. We take no rest the next day, nor the one after that, stopping only to sleep a few hours each night.

*Avaris. Avaris. Avaris.* The city's name runs more urgently through my mind the closer we get. There is no knowing what to expect after our absence. Is the king still alive? Is Yanassi ruler, are he and Merat wed? Will Tany remember the final prophecy and relay it to the powers there?

"You know." I bite my lip. "On the odds Tany *does* remember the third prophecy, she may keep it to herself."

"Why would she do that?" Paser asks.

"Maybe she will take what happened to the former Oracle of Avaris as a lesson in caution." I clutch at fleeting strands of hope.

"She will at least tell Pepi," Reb reasons. "He is her brother, and they worked together as spies with their mother before Tany became the oracle."

"Spies working together for *peace*," I say. "That is what Kalali was doing, maybe what all the priestesses do, what Pepi swears he is also trying to achieve."

Reb looks up. "That was before Tany made the final prophecy, predicting the erasure of his people," he points out.

"Yes." I take another breath, feeling the strands slip through my fingers. "There's that." I stop to take a drink from the canteen. Paser and Reb halt, as well. I pass the drink to them as we use a little of our precious time to catch our breath.

"With luck, she will not remember the third prophecy at all," Paser says. "And even if she does, they may not immediately believe her. She is a young oracle, not finished her training, and though the king trusted the last one's word implicitly, Tany may have to prove herself, and her skills, to the court."

"I can also foresee Yanassi casting doubt on her abilities if she claims Pepi is the king's son," Reb adds. "He will accuse her of trying to set her own brother up on the throne."

"That is a fair point," I admit. Tany's initiation as oracle *is* fairly recent.

"Do you think she even wants her brother on the throne?" Paser asks.

"I imagine she would support him, if that is what he wants," I say.

"But is it?" Reb inquires. "He seems intent on setting you upon there."

"We spoke of it once, on our way to get the scroll." The Hyksos's words, their sincerity and suppressed longing, remain scorched in my mind from that desert crossing. "He said if he were king, he would let anyone who wants to learn glyphs do so, regardless of their station." This sentiment, as much as his character, convinces me Pepi will be a worthy ruler. "A king who values learning and shares this gift with the masses, instead of hoarding it for the few, strikes me as incredibly generous, revolutionary, even." I look at my fellow scribes. "I may not be an oracle, but I feel in my heart that Pepi is the one meant to rule, and that it is our destiny to help him."

"He is a far better option than Yanassi," Reb agrees.

"What is our plan when we reach the city?" Paser asks.

"That will depend on several factors, the major one being whether the king is still alive. We need to demonstrate, with Tany's help, that Pepi is the best choice as a legitimate heir, whereas the chieftain would lead the kingdom to ruin."

"If the prophecy is true, it appears things are headed that way regardless," Reb says.

"Shall we give up, then, and let Yanassi wage his war with the suffering of hundreds of thousands on our conscience? Forty years is a long time, Reb," I retort. "A lot can change. New prophecies are made all the time."

Reb holds up his hands. "Easy, Sesha. We are with you. Or at least I am?" He looks over at Paser.

"Always," Paser says simply and holds up his hand, palm facing forward. I touch my fingertips to his and Reb puts up his hand, as well, fingertips meeting at the vertex of our triangle.

Then Paser is putting the lid back on the canteen, and we continue with our relentless walking. "All will be well when we get to Avaris," I say, partly to reassure myself, as well as them.

As it turns out, I would be very wrong about this.

We arrive in the capital, not by way of its impressive port this time, but through the Egyptian quarter; three ragged Thebans and one exhausted donkey. We see several people as we get closer to the city and learn the king still lives, thank Ra, though it does not sound like for long. It appears the royal wedding will take place in a *decan*, ten days' time. More messengers have been sent out to the surrounding areas, inviting neighbouring chieftains and nobles to attend, while Avaris readies itself for a wedding and looming funeral.

"Do you not think it odd that for one so bent on dominating the land, Yanassi seems very invested in this wedding?" Reb says. "I know Princess Merat is not without her charms, but it feels peculiar for one who's professed to see Thebes brought low — and prepared to shed significant blood for that to happen — to be concerning himself with flower arrangements?"

"Merat is likely doing most of the work," I say. "She is trying her best to distract the chieftain from his battle plans."

"I wonder if Pharaoh and Queen Anat will attend," Paser muses as we stop to let Nefer drink thirstily from a dusty trough.

My palms go slick at the mere thought of Queen Anat here in Avaris. "I pray not," I say fervently. "That would be yet one more thing to worry about."

"Do you think she still bears us a grudge?" Reb asks.

"I do not think, I know." I give Nefer an encouraging pat. "If you think *my* pride is something to behold, Queen Anat's is on an entirely different tier." Reb snorts. "But that's not my main concern. If Yanassi learns of the prophecy and Ky accompanies the royal family to Avaris ..." I stop speaking, heart pounding, not wanting to give malicious gods any ideas.

"We should find Tany and Pepi as soon as possible," Paser says. "What do you think is the quickest way to the palace?"

"I can take you there," a friendly voice says. We look over to see a man leaning against a stone wall, arms folded across his broad chest, still handsome despite having left his youth behind some years ago. It strikes me that this is what Paser will look like when he's in his middling years. My friend stands still, expression carefully composed so as to not give away the strong emotion he is feeling, but knowing him well, I detect it in his shoulders and face. The man's eyes crinkle kindly at their corners as he considers the young man before him. "It warms my heart to know your face at last, beloved Paser."

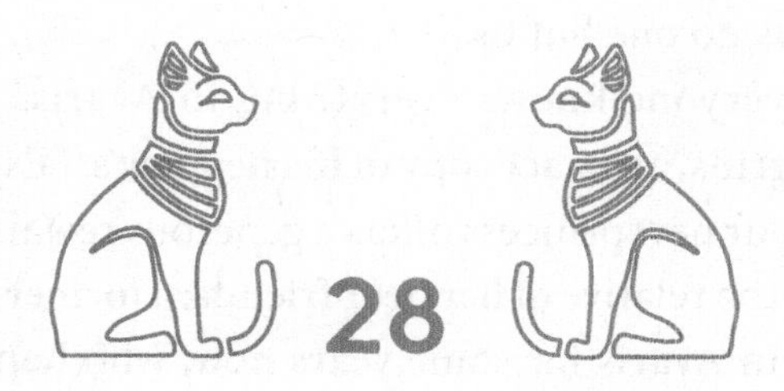

# 28

"UNCLE?" PASER'S MOUTH hangs open.

The man breaks into a huge grin. Uncrossing his arms, he steps forward and pulls his nephew close to his chest in a tight embrace. Happy tears stream down the man's face and he casts his eyes skyward, uttering a woman's name — likely Paser's mother's — while he embraces her son. Paser's uncle pulls back from his stunned nephew. "I have been waiting for you."

"What … how …?" Paser is unable to form a coherent sentence.

"We only just returned to the city," Reb butts in, "how did you know it was him?" Yet to see them side by side it is obvious they share the same blood. Reb watches the reunion, slightly wistful, and I put my arm around his waist. At least my own brother still lives. Reb has no one but us.

"Everyone knows everything in Avaris." Paser's uncle grins, an exact copy of his nephew's. "Especially when our new princess offers a generous reward for locating the relative of her dear friends; a former Theban living in Avaris for some years now, who happens to roughly match my description." He puts a hand on Paser's shoulder. "I've been keeping watch for you, Nephew." Then he looks at us. "I was unaware that I also have another nephew and a niece." He lifts an inquisitive eyebrow, the same burnished shade as Paser's.

We look at each other, at a loss. Merat kept up our ruse so as not to alert Yanassi that we've been deceiving him all this time. And though this man is Paser's family, we've known him less than a blink of Ra's eye.

"This is Sesha and Reb." Paser gestures. "They are my family."

"Then they are my family, as well." He comes toward us and embraces us as tightly as he did Paser. He smells of the sea and fish, leading me to guess what his profession is. "Your aunt and cousins will be most elated to meet you all. Come, I will take you to our home."

"We need to be getting to the palace," I whisper to Reb some hours later. We are in Paser's uncle's small house. Or perhaps it is not that the house is small, but that so many people fill it, it only feels that way. The food is mouth-watering, and we stuff ourselves, half-starved after our rationed trek.

Reb burps in response. "I am trying to remember why."

I narrow my eyes at him. "Oh, merely to prevent the outbreak of war."

"The chieftain is getting married." Reb waves a shank. "He is not thinking of war."

Ari, one of Paser's older cousins, overhears. "Tell that to our commander," he groans, stretching. Paser's cousin resembles him, as well, though shorter and stockier. "Our training regimen has only intensified these past weeks. This is my first night home with family in days."

Paser and I exchange a look.

"We are blessed to have you home, my love." Paser's aunt bends down with another tray loaded with delicious foods and places it in the centre of the circle. Leaning over, she kisses Ari on his forehead. She is Hyksos and beautiful still; it is obvious that she and Paser's uncle, Ramose, are very much in love.

We do not recognize the solider from the oasis and say as much. "It was mostly the horsemen out there."

Ari picks up a chunk of lamb and tosses it in his mouth, chewing. "My own skills lie with an ax, which is as easy to train with here, in Avaris."

"By chance, do you know how Yanassi's man Akin fares?" I ask tentatively.

Ari shakes his head, regret crossing his features. "We are told he will not walk again." I feel a pang at his words, although I am not altogether surprised by this news.

"I left Thebes so I wouldn't have to be a soldier, and now my own son is one." Ramose throws his hands up in mock dismay. "How is that for a twist of the gods?"

"But unlike your own father, you let me choose for myself," his son reminds him.

"If we ever disagree as strongly on politics as he and I did, I hope you will be more compassionate than I was with him." Paser's uncle looks down, somber. "I left to find my own way, but there is no excuse for not going back. Despite our opposing views, I loved your grandfather." He looks at Paser. "And your mother and grandmother."

"Why didn't you go back?" Paser says. I see the hurt behind his eyes, but he is careful to keep any accusation from his voice.

"I did once," his uncle admits. "When your mother married your father. She was overjoyed but worried your grandfather would be angered by my presence.

Not wanting to tarnish her happy occasion, I watched from afar as she married her handsome scribe. By then I was married, with children of my own, and life was busy. I planned to return, to bring the family, but something always came up. Then the plague struck, and it was too late. I couldn't take my children to a place where people were dying so easily. Nor could I risk going and bringing it back to them. Or catching it myself and leaving my young wife with hungry mouths to feed." He blinks at Paser's cousin's thick stature. "You see how much this one eats?"

The mood lightens momentarily, but Paser's uncle cannot quite shake off the melancholy that has taken him. "It is my deepest regret I never got to tell my family how much I cared for them," he addresses the room's occupants. "And that is why I say do not let a day pass where you don't speak your feelings to those you love. You never know when it will be the last time you see them."

"Praise Hadad." Paser's aunt lifts a cup, tears in her eyes. More food and drinks are brought out as the family celebrates its new additions.

Paser's uncle picks up a lyre-like instrument and begins to sing. His voice is low and melodious, as soothing as honey on a hot burn. The sun has been down for hours and the last few days leave me weary. I lean my head on Paser's shoulder, eyes fluttering. I try to keep them open but can't, and so I give up and let the music take me to a place where I feel nothing but lightness and the love and warmth of a family welcoming home their own.

I wake the next morning to find someone has covered me with a thin blanket. Paser is curled around me like a shrimp, his left arm slung across my body, weighted but not uncomfortable. I feel safe. Last night was a reprieve, one I could not deny my friend, nor myself or Reb, if I am honest. To be cared for and doted on by his uncle, aunt, and cousins, after everything that has befallen us, eases something jagged inside me. Something I've become so accustomed to that I do not even notice how sharp it is anymore, like the blade strapped to my leg.

"Paser," I whisper. "Wake up." I feel consciousness come back to his body. "We must get to the palace." I sit up, surveying the slumbering bodies lying every which way, tucked cozy and warm against children, partners, and siblings. I recall the joy shining from Paser last night as he laughed non-stop during a humorous story told by his uncle, as skilled a teller of tales as any at Pharaoh's court. Can I really make my friend leave his newfound family so soon?

"It is early, Sesha," he murmurs. On impulse I lean over and kiss him on the cheek.

"You are right, my friend. Rest, I will be back." I get up quietly. It will be a few hours before the sun rises. Carefully, I tiptoe around the slumbering family members. Reb lies snoring by the door and he opens one eye blearily as I walk by. He closes it when I motion I'm only going to relieve myself.

I leave the fug of the peaceful dwelling, letting my friends sleep, and walk the mostly deserted streets alone. There is no sense dragging them along when only one of us is required to do what needs to be done. I have taken Paser and Reb far from their home, across deserts and up rivers, and they have come, two points to the tip of my arrow, as I drive us toward some destiny, a fate we will only recognize after slamming headlong into it. The least I can do is allow them a lie-in.

I reach the palace without incident and nod at the guards who let me pass. The sky is lightening, though Ra has yet to make his appearance, and I walk past servants going about their morning preparations. I consider going to Merat's room, but the impulse that woke me and an unexpected frisson in the air make me turn to the king's ward.

*Something is happening.*

I find myself outside the entrance to Khyan's chambers. Abisha is there speaking with Kazir, the physician, and someone else I am both surprised and delighted to see.

"Min!" I rush toward the small doctor, who turns at my voice, opening his arms in time to catch me.

"Sesha!" He gives me a warm hug. "You have returned."

"What are you doing here?" I ask.

"The people of the oasis have made a full recovery. And when a messenger came to invite those of us remaining to the wedding, we agreed a celebration of life and love would be most welcome after our recent battle with illness." The grey-haired healer smiles, but it does not quite reach his eyes.

"How is the king?" I ask, though I read from their expressions what my own instincts are telling me.

"It is difficult to say how long he has," Kazir admits. "He is suffering and in great pain, yet his heart is strong. It could be days, or he could languish for weeks."

"He commands us to put an end to his torment," Min says. "Kazir and I were discussing how best to allow him a peaceful departure into the underworld."

"When?" I ask.

"In the next day or so. Every hour for him is an agony."

"Before Yanassi and Merat's marriage, then?"

"The king believes the occasion will give the people something to look forward to and take their minds off his parting."

"He is a good king," I say quietly, "to be so concerned for his subjects." Many others would demand elaborate and extended mourning periods.

"He is the best," Abisha finally speaks. The guard has tears in his eyes.

"If it is done this evening people will have several days to mourn before the ceremony," Kazir says to Min.

"This evening?" It seems too fast, but things can roll downhill quickly once the demons find their momentum. "Does Pepi know?"

"He does," Kazir says. "His sister is with him. She has returned, in a most happy and unexpected turn of events."

"Where are they?"

"I am not sure." Kazir seems distracted, and I realize he has more pressing concerns, such as helping the king depart for the afterlife as effortlessly as possible.

"No matter, I will find them." I look at the doctors. "Is there anything I can do to help?"

"I think we are all right, Sesha," Min says. "Be there for Pepi. Kazir and I will take care of the rest."

I nod, then go in search of my friend and his sister. I have some idea of where they might be.

# 29

ON MY WAY TO Pepi's sanctum of scrolls, I'm left wondering who knows what exactly. Tany will have told Pepi everything, or at least everything she knows, but how much is that? I doubt she's remembered her prophecy, or if she has, she has not made it widely known, as evidenced by the fact that my "brothers" and I are still alive. The urgency to find the pair has me quickening my pace, and I arrive at the sanctuary out of breath, hoping I am right that they are there.

Entering the scriptorium, I see two dark heads close together, poring over the healer's scroll in front of them. My scroll. Both of them look up as I enter the quiet room.

"Sesha," Pepi cries, relief appearing on his face.

"You made it," Tany remarks, crossing her arms. "Where are your friends?" she asks pointedly. Friends, not brothers. So, she is aware of our deception, at least.

I look at Pepi, who nods. "It is safe." He rolls up the papyrus. "I cannot thank you, Paser, and Reb enough for returning my sister to me." He puts an arm around Tany to squeeze her tightly to him. "To discover she is alive — and the new oracle, no less! — brings me unmatched joy."

"Have you remembered the third prophecy?" I ask Tany, careful not to let my apprehension show.

"No," Tany says shortly, and I exhale. "We were discussing the first two and looking to see if the scroll held any illumination as to the third. But now you are here, you can tell us."

"Me?" I falter.

"You were there, at the ceremony." Tany inspects me, rubbing at her eyes. The last few days must be taking their toll on her, as well. "I can't believe I did not think to ask before."

"It is understandable," I babble, stalling for time. "Things were somewhat chaotic, what with Yanassi's hired mercenary threatening children and elderly women."

"Tany told me." Pepi shakes his head. "I will speak to my cousin about this detestable act. But first, tell us the prophecy, Sesha. The king does not have much time; I think having the final prophecy in hand will ease his mind." He swallows. "And his journey into the next realm."

I hesitate. Hearing that his people might be wiped from the land in forty years may not ease Khyan's mind — or his journey — all that much. "The Nubian captured your map to the sect," I say, again avoiding answering.

"No." Tany watches me closely. "On our journey back, I put it in the fire while he slept."

"Oh, Reb will be most relieved to hear that," I say.

"The prophecy, Sesha," Pepi urges.

"I cannot recall it word for word. The ceremony is … hazy," I begin, and words tumble from my mouth before I can think too much on them. "But what was clear is that it claimed *you* are the one destined to rule, not me." Because I believe in my heart this to be true, the statement does not feel like a lie. Pepi and Tany sense my sincerity.

"What?" Pepi is in shock. "You are certain?"

Tany looks at me, then her brother. "We must tell the king."

"I don't understand," says Pepi. "The third prophecy contradicts the second one? What about the 'one from the line of the physician'?"

I scramble to answer. "I wish I could remember it exactly, but the third one seemed … definitive."

Pepi looks incredulous but, as the son of a priestess, I know he puts great stock in the prophecies, and I can see his mind turning as he adjusts to this new information.

"What will happen when Khyan learns of this?" I say, pushing aside my guilt at my manipulation. "Will he make you king after he is gone?"

"I do not know, but at least he will have the prophecy to aid his final decision, which we expect shortly," Pepi says. "According to my inquiries, there seems a significant amount of support for the principles I believe in." He looks abashed as he says this, as if he still cannot quite comprehend that others might believe in or back him, that they might prefer peace, and not war.

"Yanassi will have difficulty accepting it." Tany crosses her arms again. "One doesn't need to be an oracle to see that."

"He will have to, once you inform the king and the court of this," I say.

She gives me another piercing look, as if evaluating my truthfulness. "You are sure?" Her question speaks to several levels.

"It is what is best for the kingdom," I say firmly, and turn to Pepi. "You once said you are nothing but a prince of sand and secrets, but you must believe in yourself. Think of the good you can do. You will be a great ruler; Tany knows it, all of Avaris knows it, even the king knows it. Khyan's son or not, you are worthy, Pepi." The sentiment rings out in the sanctum's hollowed space.

Pepi gazes at the priceless documents he, his mother, and his uncle have spent years collecting, knowledge he wishes to share with his people and preserve for future generations. He nods slowly, as the weight of this moment settles around his shoulders, like the finest of linens. "I have long been a boy seeking adventures and escapades, eluding responsibility. Perhaps it is time to become a man."

"Our mother said a good man acknowledges the responsibility laid at his feet," Tany says, putting a hand on his shoulder. Pepi nods at the familiar words. "A great one accepts it with honour."

"The king is a great man," Pepi says softly. "May the gods help me to be like him."

"You already are," I say. "Now go claim your throne."

The king lies dying, one agonizing breath at a time. Only close family are permitted to enter his chambers. Strong incense burns, and the room has the feel of a tomb, dark and hushed. Pepi and Tany are there, as well as Abisha, the physician Min, and the healer-priest Kazir. Yanassi is not there, nor Merat. I wonder if Paser and Reb are on their way to the palace or are staying with Paser's family a while longer.

"Where is the chieftain?" I whisper to Pepi, who presses his lips together tightly in disapproval at his cousin's absence.

"He says he finds his father's illness difficult to bear." He keeps his voice low. "Though if the king can endure it with such grace and bravery, I do not see why his son is unable to." Pepi seems angry that the chieftain prolongs Khyan's suffering by delaying his appearance.

The door to the chamber bangs open and Yanassi appears, cheeks flushed. Merat is not with him.

"What is happening?" he demands, looking around the room at our faces, the king lying there, the healers at his bedside.

"I am leaving this realm for the next, my son." The king's voice is frail. He looks much worse than the last time I saw him. According to Kazir, the disease has spread to his bones, causing them to fracture and break from the slightest movement, leaving him in intolerable pain. He is propped up by numerous pillows to ease his discomfort but has now come to the point where only one thing will ease his agony. And it is a permanent solution. "I wish I could attend your marriage to your beautiful bride, but I hope to seek a dignified death while I still have the ability to do so."

Yanassi blanches, his accusing gaze falling on Tany. "I hear my pretty cousin has assumed the role of the oracle." His voice holds sarcasm. "Can you confirm the prophecies?"

"That is partly why we are gathered," Pepi says, terse. "To officially witness them, and to hear Khyan's final words."

Yanassi folds his arms across his body. "Get on with it, then."

Tany meet his eyes. "You are familiar with the first two?" She still holds the scroll.

"Yes, that document in your hands is the key to an empire which, as my delusional cousin believes" — he motions at me with a derisive hand — "this scrap of a Theban is meant to rule." He turns to his father and snorts. "Preposterous."

"Yanassi is right," I say loudly, heart ringing in my ears. "I am not the one from the prophecy." The words rush out of me, defiant, assured. I sense Yanassi's surprise as he whips around to face me. Offering up my soul to the gods, I prepare for the consequences as I continue. "It is not me, but Pepi. He is the one who is destined to rule in peace for forty years."

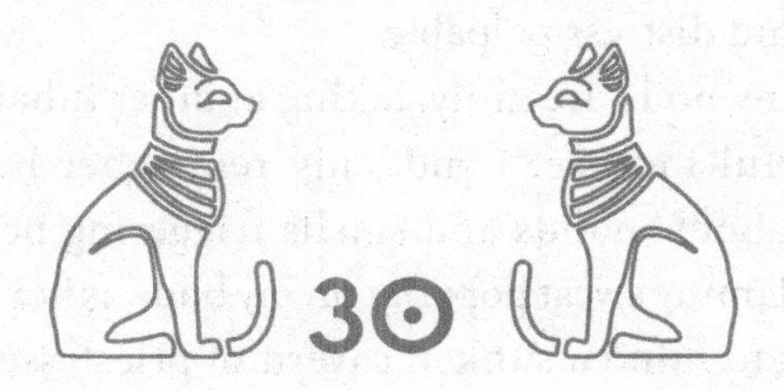

# 30

YANASSI'S SURPRISE AT MY denial of my own destiny morphs into outrage upon my declaration of Pepi's. I glance at Tany for support. She stands beside the smoking incense, swaying, vague and unfocused. No help there. I turn back to the king, hoping my expression conveys the importance of declaring Pepi his heir.

"How convenient," Yanassi snarls, giving his cousin a fierce glare. "How did you come to be the oracle anyway?"

"The previous oracle was unable to fulfill her duties after her tongue was removed." Tany's brow furrows as she tries to focus. She must be more tired than I thought. "Likely by someone who was unhappy with her divinations."

There is a sharp inhale from the king who begins to wheeze and cough. Kazir quickly reaches for a draught and helps Khyan drink. “Is this true?” The king winces, pain and distress palpable.

Tany nods dreamily, taking another inhale of the powerful incense. I suddenly remember her comment about sounds and smells triggering her memory. Clammy sweat pops out on my body as her manner brings to mind a sunken cavern of priestesses under a bloody moon.

Pepi is staring at Tany, as well. Their mother was shot by an arrow right before passing on the second prophecy to him. He’s always assumed it was loosed by one of Pharaoh’s guards, but now, hearing about the previous oracle, I can see other ideas are occurring to him.

“Tell me the final prophecy,” the king rasps. “From the beginning.”

I look at Tany, alarm still prickling, and she takes a deep breath. For the love of Isis, is it coming back to her?

“Wait,” Pepi says, and everyone in the room looks at him. My heart pounds so loud I think they all must hear it. “Of two who relayed prophecies connected to the scroll, both are no longer able to speak.” He keeps his eyes on the king. “My sister has just returned to me; I will not have the same fate befall her.” He refrains from looking at Yanassi, who grasps the subtle implication nonetheless.

"Are you alleging I had something to do with either occurrence?" the chieftain growls, massive fists clenching.

Abisha's deep voice echoes through the chamber. "Perhaps it is best if Tany converses with the king alone." The giant soldier looks at Khyan, to see if this is acceptable. Both Pepi and Yanassi start to say something, but stern looks from the doctors silence them. For now.

The king nods his assent, and we move toward the doorway. I cast a helpless glance over my shoulder, but Tany does not meet my eyes. Her face is unfocused as she approaches the king's bedside. Is she about to reveal everything? I am not sure who is most reluctant to leave the room, but we shuffle out into the corridor, allowing the king and the new Oracle of Avaris their privacy. Min and Kazir quietly confer on the readiness of the medicines necessary for this evening, leaving Abisha, Yanassi, Pepi, and me standing there.

"What have you put your sister up to?" Yanassi says through gritted teeth, eyeing Pepi with deep suspicion.

"You know she's always had a gift," Pepi retorts. "Whatever she says in there will be the oracle's words alone, not anything I told her to say."

I swallow. But it might be something *I* said. I'd give anything to be inside that room at this moment. Min frowns at me.

"Sesha, are you all right? Your colour is poor."

"I do feel dizzy." I fan myself, my voice sounding far away from my own ears. "The incense is potent."

"You should stay out here when we go inside," Kazir says gently.

Not for all the gold in Nubia.

"I will be all right," I say, forcing a smile. They do not appear convinced.

Tany opens the door at last. "The king has something he wishes to say."

We file back in, Abisha inserting himself between Pepi and Yanassi. Min and Kazir follow, then me. Whatever Tany said to the king seems to have had an animating effect.

"My son," he addresses Yanassi. He pauses frequently, gasping for air. "Did your … hired mercenary … threaten … an innocent child?"

Yanassi flushes. "He is a man who makes his own choices."

"He is … under your employ," the king says. "I wish to leave my kingdom … in the hands of one who defends innocents … not threatens them. Your cousin shows compassion" — he looks at Pepi, then back at Yanassi — "while you embody aggression." The king licks his dry lips, the talking taking its toll, but presses on. "There are times when both are needed … Though I hoped your betrothal to Princess Merat … would strengthen our truce with Thebes … instead, I am informed … envoys were sent to neighbouring kingdoms and villages … rallying them to Avaris."

"Yes," Yanassi says calmly, "messengers have been inviting guests to my wedding."

The king is silent. "Our people have worked hard … to maintain a certain cordiality … if not quite friendship … with the pharaoh … and those before him … Will you see that work undone?" Yanassi keeps his face blank. He can tell what is coming, as can the rest of us.

"You and Pepi … have always made a good team …" the king says at last. "My last command is that … you rule together, as co-regents." His words strike the room's occupants like Set's bolts of light.

Co-regents?

Pepi, appearing only mildly singed, holds out his hand. "Cousin, can you let go of your anger and work with me for the good of Avaris and its people?"

Yanassi ignores Pepi's outstretched hand and rounds on Tany, his hair almost on end, the electric pulse around him visible. "What did you say to him?" His voice is low and hissing. Abisha steps forward, spear at his side.

"Nothing I did not already know." The king is aware of the shock waves his announcement is making through the room. "Kalali's daughter is indeed the next oracle."

Yanassi turns back to confront Pepi and his father.

"You would take my birthright from me?" the burly chieftain says to Khyan, making an effort to speak evenly.

"We are not Theban," the king reminds him, gently. "We do not always inherit our titles … we earn them … As our fathers' grandfathers gained their place here at Avaris with hard work and skill … so do its rulers."

"I have heard enough." Yanassi's voice is hoarse, perhaps from the screaming he is doing on the inside. Spinning on his heel, he storms from the room.

"Farewell, my son," Khyan whispers, barely able to lift a hand from the bed. He looks at Abisha. "See that this proclamation is made at once … to the court and the people." Abisha nods and leaves the room after Yanassi. The king looks at Pepi, summoning his last scrap of strength. "I am sorry, Nephew … I do not leave you with an easy task," he says, "but I know you will do all you can for this city and its occupants."

"I will" — Pepi's voice breaks on his next word — "Father."

The king clears his throat, voice barely audible. "As much as that would be my honour … it is not the case."

Pepi stiffens. "Of course." He stands back from Khyan's bedside. "Forgive me, Uncle, I will go check on my cousin."

He rushes from the room, and the king sighs, his breath rattling through the hollow bones that are almost visible through his skin. He looks at Kazir and Min. "Shall we begin?"

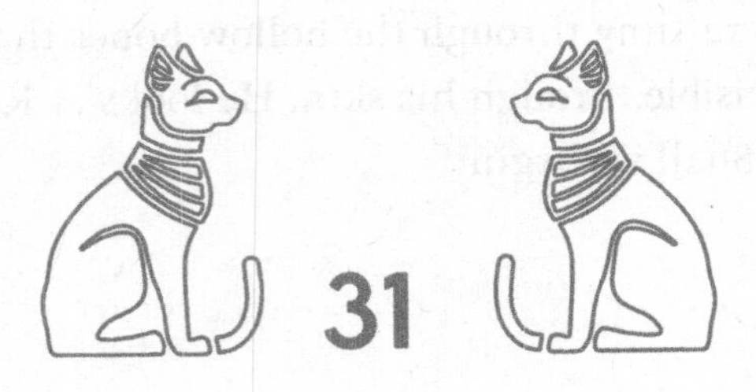

# 31

HALF AN HOUR PASSES while Kazir and Min make the king as comfortable as possible, giving him a potion to relax. They begin reciting the incantations that will see him safely to the other realm. Though obviously hurt by the king's denial of siring him, Pepi has rallied to be at his uncle's side. I am there, with the scroll, as are Tany and Abisha. Yanassi is noticeably absent, and I still have not seen the princess. I wish for Paser and Reb's presence, and anxiously wonder what's keeping them.

*Paser's uncle is a fisherman,* a small voice says. *He has a boat ... you told them they could leave ...*

*Stop,* I command the voice, taking a deep breath of herb-scented air. If there's one thing I've come to trust these past months — make that two things — it is my "brothers." They will come.

I look at Tany, desperate to know what she and the king spoke of. If she's remembered the prophecy, she excels at keeping her emotions in check, a trick learned from her mother, no doubt. Pepi has this same trick, only he hides nothing as he stands there, gazing at the man he has worshipped his whole life, father or not.

"Are you comfortable?" he asks, putting a solicitous hand on the king's brow. Khyan blinks and nods. The potion is having an effect, and he stares off into the distance, pupils wide and dark, fixed on something only he can see.

"It is time for the final rights and incantations," Kazir says quietly. He lifts his hands to speak the sacred words that will see the king's soul safely to the afterlife. Candles flicker, casting their long shadows on the walls. A trio of musicians play instruments and sing melodiously in one corner, while dancers perform the sacred steps to escort the soul; they are the only other people allowed in the chambers.

The king gave his consent earlier, but Min asks him again, "Is it your wish, Khyan, to leave this realm of existence for a new one, at this time?"

"Yes," the king breathes, "to leave behind the pains … of this broken body … and join my wife … on a more peaceful plane …" I wonder briefly about Yanassi's mother. I don't know much about her, only that she died of an illness many years back. "Has Yanassi … come?" His voice holds hope.

Pepi's features tighten. "I'm sure he will be here any moment." I can see he is furious with his cousin for not coming back to bid farewell to the man lying before us. I, too, feel angry at the chieftain for allowing his feelings to stand in the way of sending his father off.

"Would you like to say the final prayer for your uncle?" Min asks Pepi.

"Yes. There's an incantation from the healer's papyrus I wish to use." He takes the scroll. Tany puts a hand on his shoulder, tears already welling at her eyes. My own eyes are burning with tears, too, along with the incense and herbs. Pepi unrolls the papyrus, locates the spell, and begins to recite. Both Kazir and Min step forward, each holding a vial.

"May the gods enfold you into their arms and bring you to the land of peace. There, you will be restored to your full glory and might." Min offers the vial to the king to drink.

The king nods his assent, and Min puts the dark liquid to his lips. It undoubtably contains blue lotus and opium, to enhance the king's tranquil state. Kazir steps forward to administer the next vial. This is the concoction that will ease the king's breathing until it stops altogether. Some priests do not approve of this, but my father, too, believed the choice to end a dying man's life, one who is in great pain, should be his and his alone. To make those we love most suffer the longest, for our sakes and not theirs, is callous, even if our intentions are good.

Khyan considers each of us. "Thank you … for allowing me … a dignified departure." He nods at his loyal healers, then looks out on Abisha, Pepi, and Tany. "Until we meet again … beloveds." Khyan takes the vial from Kazir; his hands do not tremble as he drains the potion to the last drop. "Additional wine … would've made it slightly more palatable," he says, his old humour shining through. Kazir smiles as he takes the vial from the king, tears in his eyes.

Khyan lies back as Abisha and Tany murmur their choked goodbyes. Pepi holds his uncle's hand, continuing with the incantation. Khyan closes his eyes. Finally Pepi's voice breaks as he is overcome, unable to go on. I step forward and put a hand on his back, picking up where he left off, having memorized the spell.

I do not know if it is the sound of my voice that rouses him, but the king's eyes fly open and he gazes directly into mine. "Sesha … make sure the Hyksos are not forgotten." He nods weakly at the papyrus in Pepi's hands. "Tell … our stories."

"I swear it," I vow, tears now trailing down my own cheeks.

The king nods, satisfied. An expression of peaceful contentment settles on his face, as he appears to be tucking in for a nap. The musicians play on, increasing their volume to a fevered pitch.

The singers weep between their songs, as Kazir and Min lift their hands over Khyan's body. Their joined final incantation echoes through the chamber as they repeat the words until, after an eternity, Kazir bends his ear to Khyan's mouth, one hand on his sunken chest feeling for a heartbeat that does not come. The spirit of the great Hyksos king is finally free from its suffering, leaving behind those who will mourn and remember him, which it is our utmost privilege to do.

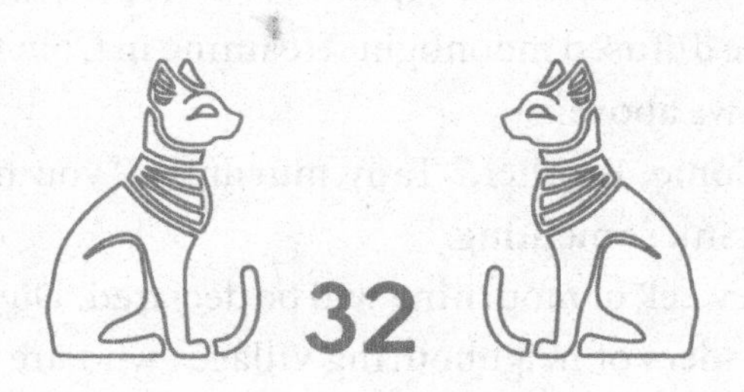

# 32

"HOW ARE YOU?" I say to Pepi after he emerges from his uncle's chambers with Tany. Abisha has gone with Kazir to inform the people of the king's passing and to begin preparations for the upcoming ceremony that will honour the ruler's life. Min stays and tends to the body, readying it for the next world.

"I feel his *Ba* close by." Pepi looks around, as if expecting to see it perched somewhere. "I know he is not gone, just … in another place."

"He is with the others who went before him," I say, putting a hand on his arm. "Perhaps he will find your mother there."

"It was quite peaceful, don't you think?" Emotion makes his voice crack.

"A most dignified departure." I keep my voice soft, like the diffused moonlight streaming in from the high windows above.

"Come, Brother," Tany murmurs, "you must eat and drink something."

"A week of mourning will be declared. Dignitaries and leaders of neighbouring villages who are coming for Yanassi's wedding will want to pay their respects," Pepi says, but his face darkens at the mention of his absent cousin's name.

"How is Princess Merat?" I am hungry myself, but for news of my friend rather than food. I have not seen her since my return.

"The princess is … well," Pepi says with an odd look, one that sounds a small gong in my head.

"Have you been spending much time with her?" I am careful to mind my face.

Pepi is just as careful with his own, his expression giving nothing away. "We've been working together on an operation she requested my assistance with."

"And what operation is that?" I inquire.

"A diplomatic mission." The gong sounds again, louder. "She sent an emissary to Thebes, to invite her family to attend her wedding ceremony."

Blood drains from my head, pooling somewhere around my feet, which feel like bags of sand, the only thing keeping me upright. "The royal family is coming here?" I say faintly. I knew it was a possibility, but to hear of their official invitation is a shock.

"That will hinge upon their acceptance of our invitation," Pepi says. "Merat feels if we can get her parents and the chieftain on improved terms, it might ease Yanassi's resentment for the Theban dynasty." The *and dissuade him from declaring war on her home* goes unspoken.

"Pharaoh and Queen Anat gave the chieftain their daughter," I say shortly. "What more can Yanassi want of them?" But the depth of his bitterness toward Thebes makes oceans seem shallow.

"Their respect," he says simply. "As you are aware, Queen Anat is most contemptuous when it comes to those whom she … disapproves of."

"Yanassi has agreed to this?" I do not bother to hide my incredulity.

"He has," Pepi affirms. "If I am to co-rule with my cousin, then I need to appease his ire for the Thebans. If Queen Anat and Pharaoh come to see for themselves the things our people have done and who we *really* are, perhaps we may earn their respect, in addition to their tribute." Pepi turns to Tany, who has remained silent through our revelatory exchange. "You must tell me the final prophecy you relayed to our uncle in its entirety."

Tany looks down, avoiding Pepi's eyes.

Panicked dismay shoots the pooled blood back up my body. I feel last night's meal rise along with it. "The prophecy *has* come to you?" They will both know I lied.

"We should go some place private," Tany whispers, glancing over her shoulder.

"Follow me," Pepi says. We walk down the hallway leading from the king's room. How will Pepi react when he hears the prediction of the Hyksos's fate? I give Tany a sidelong glance; it must be difficult, shattering hearts with your words. I think of the previous oracle. *Maybe she did cut out her own tongue.*

There is a loud commotion from the bottom of the grand stairway, out of place with the solemnity that has fallen upon the palace at Khyan's passing. We race to the top of the landing.

Yanassi stands below, a knife to Paser's throat. My friend's hands are bound. Reb is there, too, his hands also bound, restrained by the Nubian, who has his sword at Reb's back. It appears the reason for my friends' delay was a fight. One they lost, apparently.

"We were just looking for you, Cousin." Yanassi's courteous tone is at odds with the scene. "And your sister."

Pepi evaluates the situation, hands coming up in a pacifying gesture. "Grief can make us act in strange ways, Cousin." He keeps his voice as level as the landing. "Whatever you plan on doing to our young friends will not ease our loss."

"*Our* loss?" Yanassi gives a bitter laugh. "He was *my* father. Yet, despite my being his only son, the man cared for you more than he ever cared for me."

"That is not true." Pepi walks down the stairs, one cautious step at a time. Tany and I are right behind him. "I know there was discord between you, but please, for the sake of the kingdom, let us put it aside and rule together, as Khyan wanted."

"I do not give a donkey's behind for what he wanted," Yanassi barks, dropping the fake geniality. "I, alone, will rule this kingdom." He looks at Tany. "Tell me the prophecy."

"Release them first." She nods at the boys.

"I do not think so." Yanassi's eyes cut to the mercenary holding Reb. The scribe has a graze on his temple, yet retains his defiant look, as does Paser. "If you wish to test my sincerity, he will kill that one to start." He gives Paser a shake, snapping my friend's head back. "I myself will take great pleasure in ending this son of a jackal here." The chieftain does not appear to be bluffing.

"Tell him, then," I whisper to Tany, mouth dry.

"I do not know it," she whispers, shocking me further. "*You* must reveal it."

"Do not say a word, Sesha," Paser says calmly, gold-flecked eyes holding mine. Though one is shot through with blood, it is still beautiful.

"If I tell you, how can I be sure you won't harm them?" I'm thinking furiously.

"You have my word." Yanassi gives a mock bow. "But I am running out of patience." The knife slides gently across Paser's throat and a thin line of blood wells in its wake. *For the love of Isis!*

I take a deep breath, smelling my own sweat, feral and rank. Pepi says what Yanassi wants most is respect. Fine, then. I will give it to him.

"Very well." My throat feels raw. Am I making a huge mistake? "On your word and honour as a Hyksos and prince of the great king, now recently departed for the afterlife, I will tell you, and you will *not* harm my friends." I hold Yanassi's ferocious gaze and jeopardize one brother's safety for the sake of the two before me. "The prophecy was this."

BUT ANOTHER OF THE PHYSICIAN'S LINE
IN SEVERAL YEARS TO COME
WILL SNEER AT LEVANTINE LIGHT AND
LEARNING
AND SEE IT ALL UNDONE
THEY WILL WIPE THE PEOPLE FROM
THEIR LANDS

A NEW KINGDOM WILL BEGIN
AND THE GLORIES OF THE HYKSOS
WILL ALL BUT BE FORGOTTEN

Yanassi's eyes grow wider, if possible, and he stares at me in disbelief as he takes in the oracle's words.

"Now release Paser and Reb," I command.

"Our people, forgotten?" His voice is dull, horror-stricken. "You are lying." I shake my head, praying he doesn't make the connection that, as far as he is aware, he and the Nubian have my "brothers," or "another of the physician's line," in their clutches.

Unfortunately, Yanassi is not without some sense.

"Another of the physician's line?" he repeats, with a look at Pepi, who appears as stunned and stricken as the chieftain. "Did you hear that, Cousin? One of these two will be responsible for the demise of our people. We cannot let them live."

"If you believe the third prophecy, then you must believe the second, that one from the physician's line will rule in prosperity and peace for forty years," Tany interjects. "You do not know which one it is, realistically. They are all scribes, healers, it could be any of them."

Tany makes a fair point, but as Yanassi wishes to rule himself, I do not think this argument will have any effect.

"I say we kill them all, just to be certain," says the Nubian, his vile reptilian smirk having returned. "Who needs peace? War is much more profitable."

"True," Yanassi agrees, recovering some. "Forget the line of the physician, *I* will rule for forty years, and if in blood and war, so be it."

"Enough," Merat's voice rings out. "Prophecies aside, those two are *not* Sesha's brothers."

*Holy mother of Osiris.*

The princess, and future queen of Avaris, walks toward us, as impossibly beautiful as always. "They are her companions, temple scribes." Yanassi stares at her, mouth agape. "It is the truth, dearest one." Her voice is soothing, melodious, like a sweet rainfall in the desert. "They only told you that when they first arrived at the oasis so you would not kill them."

"Pity they only delayed the inevitable." The mercenary raises his hooked blade, poised to slash down across Reb's chest. "Because they are going to die now."

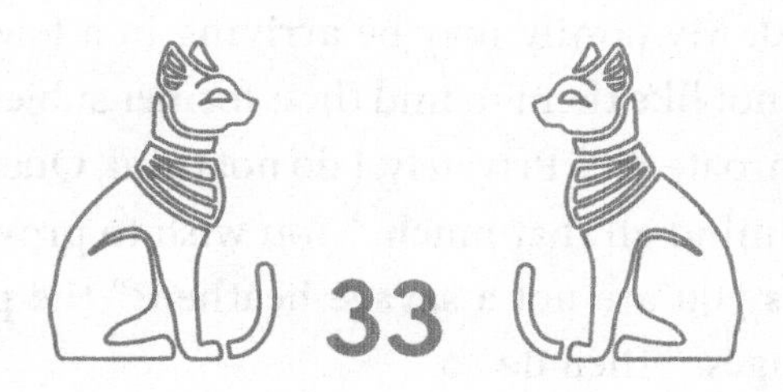

# 33

"WAIT!" PEPI SHOUTS at the mercenary. "I, too, am now ruler of this kingdom, and if you kill these men, you will meet a slow and tortuous death." He entreats his cousin. "You gave your word, Yanassi. I know that means something."

"You lied to me," Yanassi retorts. "You said they were the brothers of your betrothed."

"They saved my life, and I was honour-bound to do the same for them." Pepi appeals to the chieftain, the cousin he has known since birth. "They were under my protection. You understand honour, Yanassi, I know this."

"You promised to let them go," I remind the chieftain, striving for calm, keeping my manner respectful, deferential. "As they are not of a physician's line, they are no threat to you."

Merat floats over to the chieftain's side. "Please, my beloved. My family may be arriving in a few days. I would not like them to find their former subjects with their throats slit." Privately, I do not think Queen Anat would mind all that much. "You wish to prove to my parents you are not a savage heathen?" the princess challenges. "Then do so."

Abisha and Kazir enter from a corridor, taking in the brutal tableau in front of them. Abisha lifts his long spear, going to stand by Pepi. "What is happening?"

Yanassi knows he is outnumbered. He lowers his knife and pushes Paser forward. The tall scribe stumbles but does not fall and rounds on the chieftain.

"What of the man who was with us?" Paser demands, hands still bound. Did Yanassi do something to Paser's uncle? Or was it Ramose himself who turned them in to the chieftain and the mercenary?

Yanassi ignores him and gestures at the Nubian to release Reb. With a disgruntled snort, he pushes Reb forward. Reb scrambles to stand beside Paser, face pale. I run to my friends, reach for my blade, and saw at their ropes, heart thudding.

"My apologies," Yanassi says, with another mock bow. "You are right, Cousin, I am not thinking clearly. The grief of my father's passing affects my reason." He turns to Merat and lifts a hand to her face. To her credit, she does not flinch. "Forgive me, my beloved.

I will not let violence taint the hour of my father's departure or our upcoming wedding." He turns to the Nubian. "Your services here are no longer required."

The Nubian scowls but lowers his sword and leaves without a word.

"Come, My Prince," Kazir murmurs, stepping toward the chieftain. "I will fix you a calming tonic to help you relax. It's been a most eventful day."

Yanassi nods and follows the doctor out toward the healers' wing, leaving the rest of us standing there in various states of stupefaction. Abisha shakes his head and goes into the king's room, where Min is still, oblivious to the drama outside the royal chambers. I can hear the musicians faintly, playing for the king's recently departed spirit. Paser, Reb, Merat, Pepi, Tany, and I stand there looking at one another as the tune changes.

"Can this be true, Sesha?" Pepi seems shaken by my revelation and the events of the past few moments. "Another of the physician's line will erase our people from the lands?"

"Those were the oracle's words," I admit. "What did you say to the king in private?" I ask Tany, wondering at his final request to me.

"That is between he and I." Her curt tone takes me aback.

"Why did you reveal the prophecy to the chieftain?" Paser rubs his wrists, which are red and chafed from the rope. He looks very much like he wants to punch something.

"I had little choice." I am sick at the thought of endangering Ky. But the guilt on my friends' faces makes me add, "It is no one's fault but Yanassi's."

"So, you *are* the one to reign in peace?" Merat asks, uncertain.

"I do not know." I look helplessly to Tany again, hoping she can offer some insight.

"One from the physician's line is destined to rule," she says. "Rahibe confirmed it."

Something occurs to me. "Does Kazir have children?" I demand. I know Min doesn't. Pepi shakes his head.

"It will be all right." Reb's hands massage his wrists, as well. "Ky is far from Avaris."

"But there's a chance the royal family could be coming here," I say, pacing. "If the chieftain discovers who my real brother is, he will be at risk." And it will be my fault.

Tany startles. "You have a brother in Thebes?

I nod, close to tears. Pepi will tell her anyway. I am surprised he did not mention it already.

"Do not worry, Sesha," Merat says soothingly. "Ky is son of the pharaoh and Great Royal Wife now. Yanassi will not be able to touch him, even if he accompanies my parents to Avaris."

"Our cousin said he was distraught and not thinking clearly." Tany steps forward. "Perhaps, if the royal family comes here and we celebrate together, he will abandon his resentments at last."

Despite Merat's considerable charms, I am not sold on Yanassi's sudden change of temperament. One look at Pepi tells me he isn't, either.

"Yanassi cannot find out about Ky," I beg my mentor, unsure of what he will make of the third prophecy. Pepi is our friend, but he is also Hyksos, and this is his kingdom now. His and Yanassi's.

"Sesha, in addition to this evening's events, this foretelling devastates me." He runs a hand through his short hair. Tany glances at me, then goes to her brother, who looks staggered, maybe in part by the extent of my manipulations; he can't fault me, though, I learned from the best. Tany knows now why we lied to her about my "brothers." They both do. My eyes plead with them for understanding. Pepi shakes his head. "I need time to think."

"Kazir is right." Tany takes her brother's arm. "It's been a long day. And you and the city need to mourn the king."

"We should all rest," Merat concurs. "The hour is late. Tany, take Pepi to his chambers. I will take Sesha." She looks at Paser and Reb. "Though it pains me, my friends, now that it is known you are not, in fact, Sesha's brothers, perhaps you should leave the palace. It will be safest."

"We can stay with my family," Paser says. It sounds like he, at least, fully trusts his mother's brother. "Let's go, Reb." Paser doesn't look at me as he leaves. I know him well enough to see he is angry at himself for being captured. Reb turns at the door, lifting one shoulder in a helpless shrug, and then they are gone, taking all the air in the room with them.

Tany and Pepi walk away, as well, their dark heads bowed together, leaving Merat and me alone.

"Are you well, Sesha?" Merat asks. I do not answer her question. Instead, I grab her hands. Her eyes fall on the bracelet she gave me. "It brought you back safely."

"Is your family really coming here?"

"Shall we retire to my chambers?" She motions to indicate that although the hallways appear deserted, there is never any certainty about who is listening. I manage a short nod, and we walk toward her rooms at the far end of the wing.

"Why did you invite Pharaoh and Queen Anat to Avaris?" The short walk did not lessen my agitated state.

Merat's eyes narrow. "Is it wrong to want my family at my wedding celebration?"

"Your family gave you away like a 'prized cow,'" I repeat her words from when we arrived at the oasis to rescue her from a marriage she did not want. Now she is planning an elaborate menu and sending emissaries inviting others to revel in it, including her mother, who — not so long ago — tried to have my friends and me killed. My temper is rising, and one look at Merat's face tells me hers is, as well. "Paser, Reb, and I risked everything to save you, and now you throw it back in our faces?" I am being harsh, but cannot seem to stop myself.

"What am I supposed to do, Sesha?" Merat fires back. "Would you rather I fling myself from the top of a pyramid? Because that is the only way I am getting out of this marriage."

"You could leave with me," I say, knowing how shameful and weak I sound. And also knowing that despite my plea, I could never leave my friends, would not even want to, but I am pushing her to see her response.

She is silent for a moment. "A queen does not run away," she says at last, her voice gentler. "I am trying to make the best of things, to soothe the tensions between our cities and peoples."

"And you think throwing a big party is going to make Yanassi forget his burning need to make Thebes bow to him?" I retort. "How did he even agree to such a thing?"

"Perhaps he loves me." Her eyes flash dangerously. "Is that so hard to believe?"

"No," I say, anger dissipating at once. "No, it is quite easy." A tear slides down my cheek, a trail of salty grief in its wake.

"Sesha." My name is both the start and end to her sentence. The pain in my chest makes it difficult to breathe.

"I need to know, Merat." I take a gulp of air, forcing it past my lungs. "What are the chances that Ky will accompany the royal family to Avaris, if they indeed decide to come?"

Merat hesitates.

"Tell me," I demand.

"If my family honours my request and attends my wedding, there is a good chance Ky will be among them," she says, reluctant to confirm my fears. "He is a future prince of Thebes."

I turn.

"Where are you going?"

"I need to find Paser and Reb."

"You must sleep first. Here, with me."

I want to, oh how I want to, but I shake my head.

"It is not safe alone on the streets at this hour." Merat puts a soft hand on my bare shoulder. She smells of lavender and cinnamon, and I am tempted to curl up beside her and breathe in her sweetness all night.

"There is no time to waste," I say instead. "The kingship of the realm is precarious, the third prophecy has been revealed, and my brother may well be on his way to Avaris with the pharaoh. And your mother." Who, presumably, would still enjoy seeing me at the bottom of the Nile with a rock tied around my ankle. I do not know how the next few days will play out, but I don't need an oracle to tell me that the person I swore to always protect is in great danger.

"Goodbye, Merat." I remove her bracelet and leave it on the ornate wooden dresser by the door. "I do not want to cause any more friction by being here when your mother arrives."

"Sesha." Her tone is insistent. "Please stay."

But I don't. Instead, I walk out of her room and out of the palace. The king is dead. Yanassi knows about the prophecy proclaiming the obliteration of the Hyksos. My brother, supposedly responsible for that erasure, could arrive in Avaris at any time, along with the vengeful Queen Anat, whom the chieftain despises. There is little doubt that the combination of these volatile ingredients equals a highly explosive situation. I need my friends at my side now, more than ever.

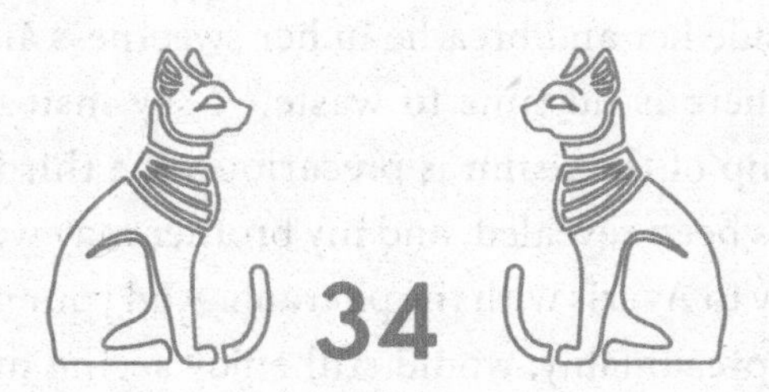

# 34

THE STREETS ARE DESERTED. It is the darkest hour of night. The sky, usually brilliant with stars, is pitch-black, as if the gods conjured clouds to block the light, marking the Hyksos king's passing.

Like Pepi, I feel Khyan's spirit lingering. I wonder if it senses the turmoil brewing in the kingdom and is reluctant to move on. I think of Pepi and pray it's only his grief and exhaustion that made him withdraw from me. Might he really give up my brother, and me, on the words of a newly indoctrinated, not fully trained oracle? Even if she is his sister, not all oracles are created equal. She could be wrong.

I feel a prick of shame at this dismissal of Tany and recognize it for what it is, what others have done to me: the underestimation of the skills and strengths of a female because she is young. But as I proved wrong those who doubted me, I suspect that Tany, too, though fresh into officially prophesizing, is legitimate.

A skittering noise on my left makes me jump. A scavenging rat scampers by, bringing back my time on the streets after my parents' deaths, when I was forced to catch them to feed myself and my sick brother. Then I fought with every resource available to protect Ky, who I still miss with the ferocity of a thousand lionesses. I will do no less now. Prophecy or not, no one is going to harm my brother.

No one.

Another quarter of an hour goes by before I admit I am lost. There is also a brewing sensation that someone is following me. Keeping an even pace, I resist looking over my shoulder, cursing myself for not paying attention the night before and for leaving the palace in the depth of night. Avaris, for the most part, is safe, but there are always those with ill in their hearts, who use the cloak of darkness to cover their transgressions. Irrationally, I think of the fruit vendor and his wife from the Theban marketplace, think I smell his wicked breath, see the blood-coloured stains on his clothes, his meaty, hairy arm reaching for me. I can bear it no longer and whirl to confront who or whatever is stalking me.

It is a kitten.

I almost fall over with relief. “What are you doing here?” I ask, crouching low and holding out cajoling fingers. “Should you not be in a temple somewhere?” Worshipped in Thebes, the protective creatures embody Ra; as the Hyksos revere their horses, we adore our cats.

It lets out a mewling sound and, on a whim, I pick it up. The small warm body begins to purr, a comforting weight against my chest. It consoles me somehow, as if Ra himself has sent a sign everything will be well.

Sighing, I put the cat down. “You cannot come with me. There is much that needs to be done.” It looks up at me, cocking its tiny head, and mewls again. I compel myself to turn and keep walking. It follows and, in a blur of spotted fur, launches itself at something at my feet. I stop and look down to see a small scorpion trapped between its paws. The cat bats it around, then promptly eats it.

I consider the animal and sigh again. “So long as you can feed yourself, then.”

Waking to a wet scratchy sensation on my cheek, I crack a crusty eye to see the kitten. I sit up, taking it in my lap. Unable to find Paser's uncle's house, or any sign of my friends, I curled up in an alley, trusting the kitten to keep any hungry rats from nipping at my toes. I pet her soft fur to distract myself from the fact that I haven't eaten much since the feast at Paser's uncle's, the night before last.

"Perhaps you might catch me a scorpion for breakfast?" I murmur to the purring cat.

"Sesha?" I look up to see Amara, standing there in disbelief, baby strapped to her chest. She blinks, as if having a difficult time reconciling me with the person she knows. "What are you doing here?" I am not sure if she means here in this alley or back in Avaris.

"It is a long story," I admit, feeling most heartened to see her. "How did you find me?"

Her mouth twitches. "I was looking for my sister's cat." Amara motions at the kitten, then down a side street. "She lives just this way. Come, you must join us for our morning meal."

"Thank you," I say, cheered additionally at the thought of breakfast. And maybe Amara or her sister will know where Paser's uncle resides. "How is Akin?" I ask as we walk down the narrow alley, the scents of food from other homes increasing my appetite. The cat trails behind us.

Amara's face tightens. "I do not know. He will not see me."

"What?!"

"He bid me to leave him" — Amara's voice catches — "to find another who could properly care for myself and our child."

"He is still in despair, then?" A searing flash of disappointment and sorrow tears through me. I thought the scroll might heal Akin's spirit, that the incantation might at least help him come to accept his fate in some way. And I must admit that I even held out a small hope it might have helped him walk again. We thread through the people of Avaris, who are beginning their mornings subdued, out of respect for the king's passing, the news blanketing the households like a heavy dust.

"Part of me wants to beg the chieftain to let me see my husband, and the other part is furious at them both. Akin for his pride, and Yanassi for complying with his wishes."

"Akin likely thinks he is doing what's best for you," I say, wanting to comfort her. The injured soldier is correct in that things would be simpler for Amara if she were to find another partner, one she need not constantly tend to, who could help with the household. But just because something seems simple, does not always mean it is easy.

"Where is my say in the matter?" She is angry, but I hear the heartbreak in her voice. "It would serve him right if I found another."

"Did Yanassi ever let Akin ride?" I wonder.

She shakes her head. "Akin refused. He does not want to make a spectacle of himself or suffer what he sees as the humiliation. I can still picture him on his horse before the accident, so handsome and noble."

"Perhaps he just needs more time." I put a comforting arm around her shoulder, and she nods as we approach a cozy dwelling, the cat at our heels. Suddenly, I recognize where I am. The docks are not far from here. "Amara, do you know a man named Ramose?" I say excitedly as a woman who looks identical to my friend, minus the height and baby strapped to her chest, sticks her head out the doorway.

"Did you find Temit?" the tiny woman calls out.

"Yes," Amara says. I'm not sure which of us she's answering.

"Who's that with you?" The woman eyes me with curiosity. She appears to be no more than a year or two older than Amara.

"This is Sesha, the healer I spoke of," Amara says, going up the walkway to the front of the house. "Sesha, this is my sister, Alit."

"The Theban?" Alit's curiosity switches to open suspicion.

"The one who risked the desert to retrieve the scroll for Akin," Amara corrects her sister, who snorts.

"Little good that did."

I cannot argue with her there.

Amara ignores Alit's remark. "Sesha is having breakfast with us this morning." She begins unwrapping the snug sling, taking the baby off her chest. "You will recall my daughter is named for her, as she helped bring your niece safely into this world."

I look down humbly, forbearing to add that Amara did most of the work.

Alit's expression softens, like butter in the sun. She takes the baby from her sister and clucks her tongue at the child. My namesake, now free of her swaddling, beams up at her auntie, gurgling.

"Come in, then." Alit turns to go back into the house, Amara following her. I am torn. Should I keep looking for Paser and Reb, or do I stay with Amara and eat? Dizzy with hunger and the sporadic and limited sleep of this past *decan*, I reluctantly conclude that without food, I will not have the energy to keep up the search for my friends.

Following Amara into the main room of the tidy house, I repeat my question in case she did not hear me. "Does the fisherman Ramose live nearby?" Temit strolls in along with me, tail swishing in the air.

"Not far, I think," Alit answers for my friend. "We buy our fish off him." She lays the baby on a soft blanket in the corner of the room, charcoal animals drawn on the wall. "Speaking of fish, did you get the salted tilapia?"

"Yes, but from another." Amara opens a basket and starts taking out the food. Fresh bread, vegetables, fruit, and eggs. "Ramose was not there this morning."

Amara's sister glances up from putting a small bowl of water out for Temit. "Perhaps the king's death keeps him at home." Her face fills with sorrow. Though Khyan's passing was not unanticipated, his people loved him, and their grief is genuine. I wonder if they will respect his appointment of Yanassi and Pepi as co-regents? For that matter, will Yanassi?

"Only a few fishermen were there." Amara breaks the bread into smaller chunks and places them in a bowl. "Many of them were already out; likely stocking up for the chieftain's wedding."

"I imagine everyone from here to Nubia has been invited," Amara's sister says. The sisters flit about the kitchen like a pair of butterflies, chatting and darting here and there, alighting for only a blink of Ra's eye before moving on to the next task. Amara offers me some bread and I dip it in the safflower oil Alit puts out. The food is fresh and restores my ability to think clearly.

"Is it possible Ramose went out early, as well?" I ask, after swallowing. Perhaps Paser and Reb went out with him.

Alit nods her head. "Nothing can keep that man away from his boat."

"Even on the day after the king's passing?" I ask. While they keep many Egyptian customs, some Hyksos traditions are different from our own.

"People will be doing what they can today, so they may have the next few days to mourn and remember our king," Amara's sister explains, pouring me a small cup of pomegranate juice.

Despite Alit's reassuring words, I detect an uneasy feeling swimming though my veins, like agitated specimens of Ramose's catch. Is Paser's uncle out on his boat, or is there another, more sinister, reason for his absence? And wherever he is, are my friends with him? Paser's question to Yanassi the night before comes back to me.

*What of the man who was with us?*

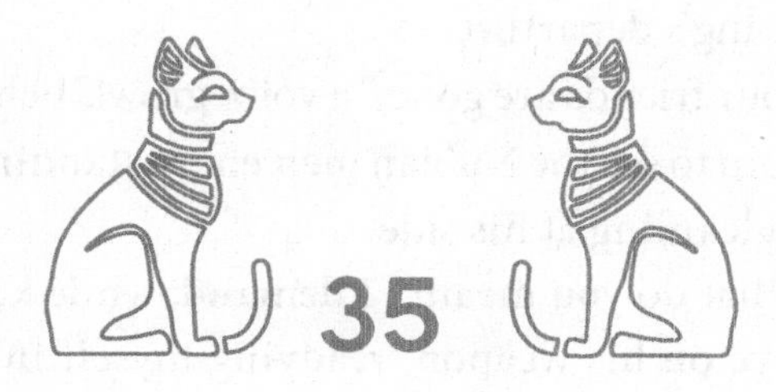

# 35

"CAN YOU POINT ME IN the direction of the fisherman's house?" Alarm sweeps the fatigue from my body.

"I don't know the exact location," Alit says, "but if you go to the port, someone should be able to tell you." Temit pounces on a locust that buzzes its way into the house, earning an approving glance from Amara's sister. I see why she values him.

After stuffing myself full of bread, juice, and sweet grapes and getting directions from Alit, I thank Amara and her sister for their kindness and head toward the water, reaching the docks in quick time. But aside from a few scraps of rotting fish, they are empty, the hunters out for the day's catch. I look around for someone to ask directions of, but the harbour is quiet, devoid of its usual lively atmosphere, likely another symptom of the king's departure.

"Your friends are gone," a voice growls behind me, and I spin to see the Nubian mercenary standing there, sword gleaming at his side.

"What do you mean?" I demand, while keeping a wary eye on his weapon, readying myself in case he takes a single step toward me.

"They left early this morning, on a fisher's boat." He crosses his arms and leans against a weathered beam.

"How do you know this?" And why is he telling me? I find it odd that Paser and Reb would go fishing at such an unsettled time as this.

"I came here seeking passage back to my land, as my services are no longer required in Avaris." His mouth twists.

"As you are still here, I take it you were unsuccessful in finding anyone to transport you?" Little wonder, the mercenary cuts a menacing figure. It will be a relief once he is finally gone from these shores.

"Most of the boats are staying close to home. They do not want to miss their king's life ceremony." The Nubian spits on the ground. The man seems to have an excess of saliva, likely due to a chronic condition. "Though one craft seemed laden with provisions for a lengthy journey, almost as if its occupants were sneaking away. I suppose Thebans do not feel obligated to show respect for a dead Hyksos king."

Thebans. He need not tell me outright it was Ramose's craft. The gleam in his eye and smirk on his face are indication enough. My heart sinks like a boat with a giant hole.

"You are lying," I say, and the mercenary brings his sword close to his face, examining the curved blade.

"Think what you want. It does not alter the fact that your friends have left you on the deserted banks of a place that is not your home, with people who are not your own."

"They would not abandon me," I say firmly, trying not to heed his cruel words. But they are like an invasion of locusts that swarms my heart, devouring what is left of my confidence. I look around for someone else to ask directions of, a friendly face, but there is no one. I leave the Nubian standing there, needing to get away from him, his corrosive smirk, his spittle.

"Your friends are smart," he calls after me. "You should leave, too, scribe. There is nothing for you in Avaris." I ignore him and keep walking, despite the small voice telling me he may be right.

At last, I spot someone, an elderly man sweeping wood shavings from his shop. Based on the abundance of carpentry items surrounding the place, I assume he or his sons are woodworkers. Drawing closer to the shop, I notice dozens upon dozens of large disks stacked high, one on top of the other.

"Do you know where Ramose, the fisher, lives?" I ask him, looking around and wondering what all these massive sun-shaped objects are for. Perhaps a structure to commemorate the king's life? Khyan is referred to as *the one whom Ra has caused to be strong.*

"Ramose?" The man rubs at his white beard. "I believe he resides that way."

Bless Shai.

"My thanks to you," I reply and am gone, running in the direction he pointed, at last reaching a set of houses that look familiar. Paser's aunt walks out of one, carrying some linens, and I race toward her. She looks up in surprise.

"Have you seen Paser and Reb?" Relief at seeing her has my speech rushed, desperate. "Are they with your husband?"

"With him where?" She sets the basket of linens down and puts her hands to her back.

"On his boat? Someone saw them leaving from the docks this morning." Though I have no illusions about the trustworthiness of the source.

She looks doubtful. "I have not seen either boy since they left to find you." My chest tightens — she hasn't seen them since yesterday? "But it is a possibility. Many people will arrive soon, and I know Ramose wanted to stock up before the incoming sea traffic scares the fish away."

Ramose's son Ari comes out of the house, carrying a bow, his ax belted at his waist. His mother crosses her arms. "Where are you going with your weapons, on the day after the king's passing?"

"We received word we are to assemble at the palace." He shoulders the quiver holding his arrows.

"Are they planning a military tribute for Khyan?"

Her son shakes his head. "I was given no additional information other than we are to gather after dawn."

That sounds ominous. I feel torn between searching for my friends and checking back in with Pepi. "If you see Paser and Reb, will you tell them I need them?" I ask and Paser's aunt nods, slightly taken aback by my intensity. "Thank you." I spin and take off toward the palace, leaving Paser's baffled relatives behind me.

"I must see Pepi," I say to Tany.

"He is resting." She crosses her arms.

"Pepi always rises before dawn," I say, stubbornly.

"Leave him be." Her eyes flash in warning, and I recognize a sister protecting her brother. Tany and I are very much alike. "He lost the man he was closest to in the world last night. He must work out how to rule in tandem with his warmongering cousin, and he has half the countryside arriving in the next few days for a wedding, potentially even the Theban royals." She does not mention the latest prophecy and the elimination of their people, but it hangs in the air between us.

"I want to help …" I begin.

"You can help by not giving him another thing to worry about," she says sharply. "According to the first two prophecies — and in his mind — *you* are still meant to rule. Which means you will lie low during these next few days, particularly if the Great Royal Wife is coming. I am told she bears a grudge against you, and we must keep tensions calm."

"But soldiers have been summoned —"

"Please, Sesha." Pepi appears at the door. "We don't know how the events of the next weeks are to play out, but Tany feels there is something still to come. Also, the mere sight of you riles Yanassi — I'd feel much better if you were hidden, protected. Can you do that for me?" He looks directly into my eyes, his grief-ravaged expression pleading, and I am unable to deny the worry on his face. Pepi has come to mean more to me than a mentor, or even a friend. There is an ease and familiarity there, one that is almost paternal, and I find myself wanting to please him, especially after my earlier deception. I take a deep breath. I suppose I could use a moment to plan my next move. "Where will you have me go?"

"She should go to the priestesses." Tany looks at Pepi. "They will keep her safe."

"No." I shake my head, vehement. "I promise to conceal myself, but I will not leave the capital." Reb and Paser's whereabouts are yet to be confirmed, and Ky may be on his way to Avaris this very moment.

Pepi studies me. "Why don't you stay in the scriptorium? You can keep yourself busy organizing scrolls, perhaps making a copy or two of some of the older medical papyri."

"And my brother?" I look at both of them. "Swear you will say nothing of him to Yanassi." The siblings exchange a look. "I returned your sister to you," I say to Pepi, and then look back to Tany, "and your brother to you. Do not endanger the life of mine. He is an innocent who has seen far too much grief for his age."

"Who among us has not seen grief?" Tany demands, hands on her hips.

"Please," I say again, begging for what feels like my brother's life. "Your word, Pepi."

"No harm will come to your brother, Sesha." He holds a hand over his heart. "Now, I must address the people. I will speak with you later." He turns to Tany. "Why don't you both go to the scriptorium until things settle here?"

Tany's mouth drops open. "Will the people of Avaris not be happy to hear the oracle has returned?"

"Not if they hear you have forecasted the erasure of our people from these lands," Pepi points out gently.

"Prophecies can change," Tany protests. "New details reveal themselves all the time."

I look at her sharply. Is she suggesting that preordained fate can be altered?

"I understand." Pepi keeps his voice placating. "But for now, I think it best if you also remain as inconspicuous as possible. I don't want anything happening to you, either." I think of Rahibe and her missing tongue. Perhaps Tany does, as well, because she nods reluctantly. "Just until I get a sense of which way the wind is blowing." Pepi looks out the window at the channels criss-crossing the landscape with an expression as premonitory as an oracle's. "And what the changing tides might be bringing to our doorstep."

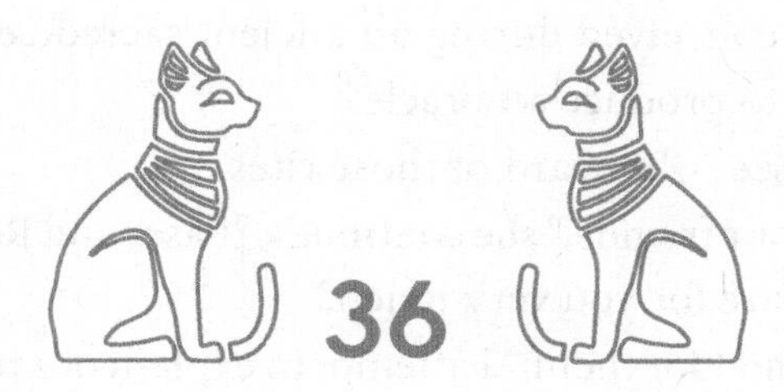

# 36

I CONTEMPLATE TANY, HER HEAD bent over the scrolls. She is different here than she was at the priestesses' temple. I think of her bravely riding off with the mercenary and guess at the reason for her annoyance. "I am sorry we deceived you."

She looks up, wariness crossing her features. "You were protecting your family. I know something of that."

"Your mother must've been extraordinary," I remark.

"She was." Tany looks down at one of the scrolls. "More fearless than any man or woman I've known." She fingers one of the documents, smoothing down the curled-up edges. "I miss her very much."

"What of your father?" I ask. Tany mentioned she and Pepi shared only a mother.

"A temple priest." She waves an unconcerned hand. "I was conceived during an ancient sacred ceremony meant to produce an oracle."

"I see." I'd heard of those rites.

"Your friends," she continues, "Paser and Reb. They must care for you very much."

"And I for them." I attempt to explain our pretense. "We did not mean to lie, exactly. They *are* my brothers in spirit, if not in flesh." Again, I wonder if the Nubian was telling the truth about their leaving.

"Your real brother," Tany says, "Ky is his name? Is he younger or older than you?"

"Younger." His sweet face, his warm brown eyes come to my mind. "He has held my heart since his birth. When my parents died, I cared for him."

"How did they die?" she asks.

"In a fire." I swallow. "I got him off the roof just in time. We lived roughly for a while, in hiding, before being brought to the palace."

"Where your father had been the Great Royal Physician?"

I nod.

"You say you were in hiding? The fire was not an accident, then." She studies me, as if I am something to decipher, like one of the scrolls before her.

"It was set by one of Queen Anat's soldiers." I walk over to the shelf where my transcription of Imhotep's papyrus sits in its protective casing. "She was looking for this."

"Many people have hunted in vain for that document." She eyes it. "It is legendary among the priestesses."

"Because whoever holds it is meant to rule their people?" I take the scroll down to examine it, wishing I had had time to complete the full transcription.

"Power of life over death is a most alluring prospect," Tany says. "Your father thought the scroll had great magic."

"He believed it could heal my brother, and it did." It also healed Paser, though not Akin. Tany's words sink in. "How do *you* know what my father thought?"

"It is a fair assumption, with him being who he was, is it not?" Tany says. Her elusiveness does not escape my attention. She continues, "My mother was your age when she began searching for the scroll, after the first prophecy was made. The Priestesses of Seshat are sworn protectors of the written word, and she was tasked with finding and gathering them." Tany gestures at the plethora of papyri around the room. "Khyan built this sanctum for her. She collected most of these, and when we were old enough, my brother and I helped."

"Pepi mentioned your mother passed on her love of scripts to him."

"And to me." Tany trails her fingertips over one of the baskets. "Many compositions contained within these walls are incredibly rare, and powerful."

"And I thought the guard outside was meant for us." I try again, sensing there is something she is not telling me. "What first brought you to Thebes in search of the scroll?"

Tany hesitates, then says, "Your father sent word to my mother that he thought he'd found it."

"What?" I wonder if I misheard her. "My father knew your mother?"

"They must have met in Avaris while he was training physicians here," Tany says. "Of course, Pepi and I had no idea it was your father who was her source. My mother only said a contact had reached out with information regarding the scroll she was seeking. But now that we know it was he who found it, we can only assume it was him."

"That is why you came to Thebes?" My mind races to trace out the glyphs. "How did my father even know your mother was seeking the healer's papyrus?" Had he sensed the risk from Queen Anat and her priests even then, and sought to keep a copy safe in the Hyksos capital after completing his transcription?

Tany shakes her head. "I do not know. Though if your father was in our capital, as a physician and famed scribe, it is likely he visited this place." She looks around at the sanctum's precious documents, painstakingly compiled. "They obviously shared a passion for hieroglyphs. It's possible she told him about her quest. She may have even sought him out, feeling that the prophecy concerned him, and his future children, though whether she told him the precise details, I cannot say."

I look around the room, imagining my father here. I can see it, can see him reverently picking up the scrolls, maybe even transcribing a copy or two. I inhale the intoxicating smells, musty pulped papyrus, the metallic tang of the ink, the woodsy scent of the reed brushes. I feel him here …

Blaring horns startle me out of my reverie. Tany and I look at each other. "What is that?" I ask uneasily. The sound brings to mind a battle cry.

"Likely it is in remembrance for the king," Tany says. But she looks uneasy, as well.

"I need to know what's happening." I expect her to argue, but she doesn't.

"Shall we go to the roof?"

"What if Pepi sees us? Or Yanassi?"

"Both are involved in the ceremony." She raises an eyebrow. "Besides, I'm sure you know how to move in a stealthy manner."

"I do."

"Good."

"What about the guard? Will he not immediately alert Pepi if we leave?"

Tany picks up the scroll, turns, and walks to the back of the scriptorium. She moves aside one of the large woven baskets, revealing a hole one can walk through with their head ducked. I stare at the passageway in amazement. "There is a hidden exit. Come."

She does not need to ask me twice.

From the roof we can see for miles in every direction. The palace sits upon a hill which, aside from protecting it from flooding, acts as natural fortification and defence from invaders. The harbour basin stretches out before us, the Hyksos nautical fleet occupying a large fraction of the bay. My eyes go to the docked fishing vessels, wondering if Paser and Reb have returned with Paser's uncle. Tany puts the rolled-up papyrus to her eye and peers down the circular tube, training it on the proceedings below. I cringe at this use of the document, but at least it's not the original.

"A formal military send-off," Tany says, relieved. Thousands of people crowd around gathered archers, swordsmen, and the Hyksos's horses.

"What is *that*?" I gawk. A gleaming black stallion pulls a handsomely carved ... thing behind it, bringing to mind the sled-like transportation we used to traverse the desert with the horses. Only instead of flat runners on the bottom, the half-enclosed cart rests on a long axle, framed by two large-spoked wheels. Gaping at this marvel of engineering, I recognize the circular objects from outside the carpenter's shop.

"A chariot." Tany looks through the tube again, as more of the extraordinary carts appear, carrying two Hyksos soldiers apiece; one holding the reins, the other a bow. The speed with which the chariots assemble is astonishing, lining up side by side. The horses must have been trained extensively to perform such an act.

Another vigorous blast of horn, and a magnificent chariot emerges, more elaborately painted than the rest. Yanassi stands in it, proud, holding his duck-billed ax aloft. My eyes go to his skilled driver. He sits on a bench supported by a backrest, a clever modification to the chieftain's grand chariot.

By the gods, it is Akin.

I cannot make out the expression on his face but imagine it to be one of exaltation. The sight of Yanassi's formerly fallen best man electrifies the crowd and their triumphant roars ring out. Despite the battle-laced undertones of the ceremony, my heart cheers along with them. Perhaps the incantation from the scroll could not repair Akin's spine, but it seems to have stopped the demons from consuming his spirit after all. *When the gods come to devour ...* I shiver. The first prophecy is true. Akin lifts a hand from his reins, acknowledging the crowd's cries. He has, quite literally, found a new way forward.

The soldier guides the horses, and advanced mobile technology, to the front. It is both striking and discomfiting to see a portion of the Hyksos army with their exceptional weaponry on display. They raise their bows on Yanassi's shouted command, sighting their arrows.

The chieftain yells something, which I imagine to be "Fire your weapons!" as thousands of arrows are loosed in unison. They arc gracefully up into the air, over the platform holding the king's body, and into the water beyond. Our eyes follow them.

"Look," Tany says, pointing at the water in the distance. "Ships."

I squint to see countless specks on the shimmering horizon. My heart flutters at the thought that one of them might be carrying Ky.

"Diplomats?" I ask and Tany nods.

"Foreign dignitaries, neighbouring nomarchs, and curious courtiers who will be most pleased to discover they get to attend two significant events for the expense of one trip," she says.

"May I look?" She hands me the scroll, my reluctance to use the document as a sight aid forgotten. The incoming crafts range from small to large blobs, as if dotted with different tips of reed brushes. We go between watching them and the ceremony below.

Yanassi holds up his arms. I make out Pepi, on a horse, riding to join his brother. The pair begin to address the crowd, and I strain to hear, but there's no way I can at this distance. I look back to the water, where the specks are floating closer.

One of them, judging by its size against the others, appears to be extremely large. I squint through the scroll again, making out an enormous sail and long powerful oars, manned by a hundred men. Though far away, the lines and curves of the handsomely crafted boat are familiar; it's been in the royal family for generations, the pride and joy of Thebes's fleet.

It seems Pharaoh and Queen Anat have accepted their daughter's invitation.

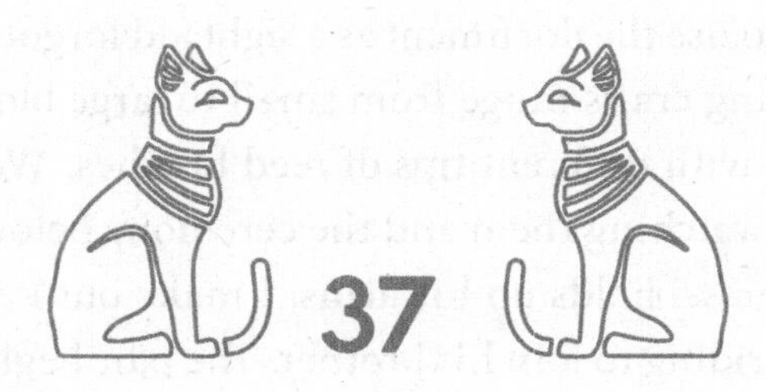


BLACK DOTS BEFORE MY EYES alert me to the fact that I've neglected to breathe these past moments. I gasp for air and exhale in such a gust it's a wonder it doesn't blow the boats back. Is Ky on that ship?

I turn to Tany. "I need to get near that boat." Despite my acceptance of Pepi's request to lie low, Pharoah's arrival in Thebes changes everything.

"Coming up to the rooftop is one thing," Tany says. "Going into the streets again is another. Pepi wants us to stay here."

"The last time you stayed where you were told, what happened?" It is a harsh ploy, reminding her of her mother's death, her brother's capture, but I am desperate.

A shadow crosses her face. "Very well," she says

testily, "but you can be the one to explain to my brother when he finds out."

"So be it."

We slip out of the palace, slinking down side streets. Most are deserted, the people still at the ceremony. With the ships arriving, they will soon fill up. Worry creeps up and down my spine like a sure-footed spider. Where are Paser and Reb? If the boys only went fishing, wouldn't they be back by now? Was the Nubian telling the truth? Maybe Ramose is bringing them to safety somewhere, perhaps to Crete, that large island in the sea. Or somewhere northeast?

"Where are your friends?" Tany senses my thoughts, whether through her ability as an oracle or an intuitive female.

"Fishing," I say shortly.

"For food? Or information?"

"Does it matter?" Her accusation brushes up against my ruffled nerves, teasing them on end, like a lion's mane.

"Forgive me." Her tone is cool. "I'm trying to better understand what business three Theban scribes have with my brother, and this kingdom. Perhaps you are counter spies, working for Pharaoh and the queen." I look at her, mouth hanging open. "Maybe you 'rescued' Pepi from the pits to gain his trust."

I almost trip over a rock. "You think we are capable of something like that?"

"It's a possibility," she says, as we walk briskly. "After all, I — we — only have your word regarding things, particularly the claims of the third prophecy. Which *you* already lied once about." The reproach in her voice causes me to flush.

"As I'm sure you are aware, I was trying to protect my brother." *Tany still doesn't remember the prophecy.* My blood, hot, now turns cold, not knowing which way to run. I force myself to speak calmly. "Why would I then invent something that would put us directly in harm's way?"

Tany gives me a sidelong glance. "There are some who believe an oracle's words are a self-fulfilling phenomenon."

"What do you mean by that?"

"What I mean is, do an oracle's words come true merely because they are spoken, or is it the hearing of and *belief* in them that bring them about?"

"How can one know such a thing?" More and more people are appearing in the streets. The ceremony must be finished.

"I am not sure," she says, "but it's conceivable our own beliefs, whatever they are, cause *us,* not only the gods, to create our realities, to manifest our destinies." Tany's reasoning echoes my own. "Healing, for example."

"Healing is science and medicine, in addition to the gods."

"What about the healer?" she asks. "You are the one to invoke that magic. Pepi told me how you brought Paser back with the scroll and my mother's stones."

"I do not deny their power," I admit, thinking also of Akin. "But it could've been the medicines and Paser's own fighting spirit, or the gods' will ..."

"And *your* will," Tany emphasizes. "Whatever else, it was also you. Our will is magic, as much as an ordained prophecy, maybe more so," she says. "Yet many forget we all possess this power."

"Back to your accusation." I wonder if Tany is testing me. Her brother is very fond of doing so. "You think I'd proclaim the Hyksos's expulsion from the lands in order to bring it about? What would be my reasons for doing so?"

She shrugs, Pepi to the life. "You are Theban, your father an honorary member of the royal family, your brother now a legitimate one."

"Thebes wants peace," I protest. Or at least Pharaoh did. Queen Anat, I'm still not sure of. "Their presence here indicates that."

Tany studies me. "Does it?"

I glare down my nose at her, a look Merat is quite adept at. It's difficult to perform on someone taller; I must ask the princess how she does it. "If I *were* to invent a prophecy, it wouldn't entangle my brother or myself in the demise of the Hyksos people." Only fear for Paser and Reb made me blurt out the real prophecy. "As for your own brother, he means much to me. My friends and I envision setting *him* on the throne."

Tany interrupts. "Why?"

I give an exasperated huff. "Why would one not want a leader who advocates peace over war?" I say. "As healers who regularly see broken and injured bodies up close — we prefer to limit people's suffering rather than multiply it, whether they be Theban, Hyksos, or of any nation!"

"Would that not render your profession unnecessary?"

"There are plenty of accidents and naturally occurring health issues to deal with," I snap. "Never mind adding gratuitous violence to the list. Not only soldiers face injury in war, but so do the people who love them, and the children, especially vulnerable ones ..." I struggle to master my emotions. "It is why we came to Avaris, why we retrieved you from the priestesses. We thought you could prove Pepi is the king's son with a legitimate right to rule. Pepi is for peace and we are for Pepi."

"So, you would put it all on me, as well?" Tany sounds unhappy. "I am merely a vessel."

"Yours is a great destiny," I say uncertainly. Tany seems conflicted about the responsibility that comes with being the oracle. As one currently cast in the role of upholding light through the lands, I have a sense of the emotional muck she's stuck in.

"And what of your own destiny?" Tany again seems to divine my thoughts. "If Pepi believes you are the one to rule, does that then make it true?"

I do not know how to respond. My hand goes to her mother's stones in my pocket, and I pull the small pouch out. "I believe these stones have healing powers. Yet they are still stones. They are not onions, and believing they are vegetables does not make them so. But an onion *also* has healing powers, and believing it does not will not necessarily negate them."

"What you are saying, Sesha?"

"Maybe *Heka*, magic, does not speak only to the mind, but to the heart. It is a feeling, as well as a belief, so it does not always need to be logical. And feelings are real, whether they are based on truth or imagined truths." I put the stones back in my pocket. "Might we pause this perplexing conversation and focus on the task at hand? I must find out if my brother is on that ship."

"Then what?" Tany asks. The streets are filling up as people go back to their homes, to be with their families, to prepare for the incoming ships and the people they carry.

"If Ky did not come and is safe in Thebes, I will search for Paser and Reb."

"I thought they were fishing," she says pointedly.

I give her a look. "Once I find them, we will stay out of everyone's way while supporting Pepi as co-regent."

"And if your brother *is* with Pharaoh?" Tany asks.

"Then I will need to warn him." While remaining unseen by the queen and her guardsmen, particularly Crooked Nose. *Eye of Ra, where are Reb and Paser?*

"Why not just let sleeping lizards lie?" Tany reasons. "Even if your brother is here, Yanassi does not know he is of the physician's line."

"I can't take that risk. If Ky *is* among the royal family, there's a chance Yanassi may learn of the details surrounding his adoption. People love talking about others and their circumstances."

"It was one of the ways my mother acquired her information," she admits.

"And if the chieftain finds out ..." A meaty fist squeezes my heart. "It does not take an oracle to know what he will do to Ky."

"Sesha, I know Ky is your brother, but if the prophecy is true ..." She hesitates, not needing, and perhaps not wanting, to finish her sentence.

"If Yanassi attacks a son of the pharaoh, we will not have to wait forty years for the destruction of your city." I look at the people walking around us. "It will happen before our very eyes."

"You forget, the Hyksos have the superior weapons." Tany is referring to the warriors' incredible chariots and horses, the advanced bows, the axes, and the daggers.

"Regardless of the outcome, it will not be pretty for either side, or for neighbouring villages swept up in a current of violence." We reach the docks as Pharaoh's enormous craft comes into full view. Large crowds are gathering to witness the ship's arrival. "We can worry about the past and we can fret about the future, but then we will miss our chance to do what needs to be done *right now*."

"And if it only delays the inevitable?" Tany says sadly, and I know she speaks of the third prophecy.

"Then at least we buy your people forty more years to figure something else out."

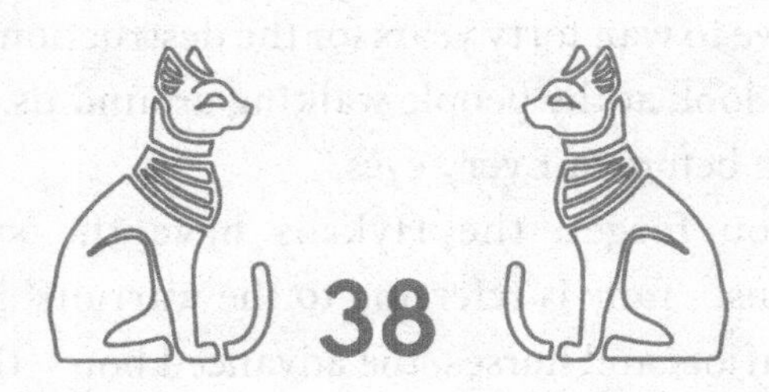

# 38

TANY AND I BLEND IN with the crowd. No one knows us, and we slip around faces reflecting a range of emotions: awe, excitement, and — here and there — fear. Muscled soldiers row Pharaoh's massive boat inland, biceps rippling in unison. I step forward, scanning, trying to make out Ky's shape. Tany yanks me back into the shadows as Yanassi thunders past in his chariot, still driven by Akin, who looks a bit pale.

"Don't overdo it," I murmur to my former patient's back. Another chariot rumbles by, the horses' groomed coats gleaming in the late-afternoon sun. Pepi and the princess. Merat is not dressed in her usual fine linens but rather in a stunning creation the palace seamstresses must've made for this occasion. The form-fitting sheath is composed entirely of brilliant blue faience beads and carnelian crystals, in an intricate criss-cross pattern. The garment's stones catch and reflect the sun's rays, making her sparkle like the stars. A thick band of gold and turquoise encircles her throat, and her eyes are boldly lined, her lips stained an ochre red. Pepi, too, is dressed in his finest linen skirt, his chest and shoulders glistening with precious oils, as Merat's and Yanassi's do. Both he and his cousin carry no weapons, in recognition of this being a welcoming and conciliatory occasion.

Will Pharaoh and Queen Anat recognize Pepi as my accomplice in Thebes? I wonder what their reaction will be when they realize the spy they tossed into the pits — though by his own design — is now co-ruler of the Hyksos kingdom and cousin to the chieftain, the man they sought to appease with their daughter?

The ship anchors just offshore; it is too large to bring into port with all the other docked boats, and more arriving. Trailing behind it is a majestic golden barge. It is untied and brought round to ferry the royals to shore.

I expect to see them, yet it is still a jolt to watch Pharaoh and Queen Anat emerge from the flurry of attendants and guards who are assisting their masters in boarding the smaller, but no less beautifully crafted barge. There is still no sign of Prince Tutan, Ky, or little Tabira, but another familiar figure disembarks the larger ship to join the king and queen on their platform.

Wujat.

I am surprised to see the former High Priest and Grand Vizier, who my friends and I believe is in love with the queen. Whatever the drama between he and the royal couple, it appears settled, as evidenced by his presence here.

"So that is Pharaoh and his Great Royal Wife," Tany murmurs.

"Yes." My eyes scan the ship for the younger members of the Theban dynasty. When they fail to materialize, a wave of relief washes over me. The children must have stayed in Thebes. Tany and I are pushed along by the crowd as people jostle to get a look at the most famous couple of the Black Land and beyond.

"They are shorter than I expected," Tany muses.

"They are still some distance away," I say, unsure why I feel defensive about this dismissive comment, though she is not wrong. Godlike status notwithstanding, the pair *do* seem smaller than I remember. Yet the magnetism emanating from that golden barge is as powerful as always. Their presence is a strong adhesive; everyone's eyes are glued to the famous figures who, fittingly, are illuminated by the setting sun, their arrival well timed.

"I don't think —" The words dry up in my throat as two figures appear. It is Kewat, with her small pregnant bump, and Bebi, my old friend and handmaiden to little Tabira.

*Hathor, help me.*

Where her handmaidens are, a princess is not far behind. My eyeballs feel like they are about to pop out of my head as they strain to see, watering in the sun's light.

Three small shapes emerge from the ship and are assisted onto the large floating platform, which now seems to hold half the original ship's crew. At last, the well-muscled soldiers begin rowing their precious cargo to shore. I find myself moving, as well, heedless of Pepi's warning to remain hidden. I swim my way to the front of the crowd, Tany in my wake.

As the royals draw closer, Merat gracefully exits her chariot, holding her hand out for Yanassi, who disembarks from his own cart to join her. She turns and offers her other hand to Pepi and the trio walk, united, to greet her family. Queen Anat and Pharaoh stand regally, the children behind them, as the craft floats forward.

Joy grapples with panic as I behold Ky, here in Avaris. My gaze does not leave his face.

"Is that your brother?" Tany grabs my arm, jarring me, her voice oddly strangled. Only her tight grip keeps me from launching myself off the dock at the floating vessel.

"Yes," I say, sounding choked myself. The platform reaches the docks, and the royals disembark elegantly, aided by their handlers. We are close enough now to make out some of what is said.

Merat lets go of Yanassi's and Pepi's hands and steps forward to greet her parents; she remains dignified and does not run to embrace them. "Father. Mother. Welcome to the Kingdom of Avaris."

I see nothing more as the two royal families greet one another, my eyes are all for Ky. He looks confident and calm beside the shorter Prince Tutan and tiny Tabira, both of whom blink at their elder sister in awe. One of the soldiers who helped the family off the ship turns, and another jolt runs through me.

It's Queen Anat's favourite parasite and my parents' killer: Crooked Nose.

"Come," I whisper to Tany, melting back into the crowd, not wanting the vengeful soldier to notice me. Despite longing to go to my brother, I don't need to add another piece of dung to the mounting pile.

"Make up your mind," Tany hisses in my ear.

I ignore her, at a loss for what to do, as my two worlds collide. Ky is here with the royal family. My friends are nowhere to be found. I stand in the throng, pulled in so many directions that I am paralyzed.

Tany makes an impatient sound and grabs my hand, yanking me away from the commotion. "Your brother is here," she whispers, stating the obvious. "Now what?"

"I do not know." I look at her. "I need to devise a way to speak with him alone, to warn him." So far Yanassi appears to be playing nice, but if he finds out who Ky's real father is, things could change in the flip of a temple dancer. Perhaps there is a way to communicate with Bebi and Kewat? Or even Wujat? The royal family is escorted to where the chariots wait. Pepi shows them the horses. The children's eyes are wide, and he gestures for them to step inside.

I can tell the royal couple is trying not to look impressed, but Pharaoh seems fascinated as he examines the intriguing mechanisms affixed to the equally magnificent animals. Queen Anat's features are arrayed in impassive sophistication, while the children squeal in delight as their chariot moves forward, pulled by the horses. Other chariots arrive to transport Pharaoh and Queen Anat. Another takes Wujat and a second man who was ferried over on a smaller raft with additional soldiers and handmaidens. The bald head is recognizable and my heart, put through quite the obstacle course already, jumps. It is the physician Ahmes. Pharaoh and Queen Anat have brought their entire entourage.

"Where will they take them?" I ask as the chariots begin to move. Some of the crowd follows behind. Others, hungry after a tumultuous day of both sorrow and excitement, depart for their homes and evening meal. I need to speak to Ky, but should check back first with Paser's relatives for any word of my friends.

"The new palace is almost finished, they will reside there for now," Tany says as we walk with the crowd. I'd heard of the large construction project, meant to house Khyan's successor. The current palace will be filled and closed as tribute to the king, who will be buried close by. Merat said the Hyksos prefer to keep their dead interred within their settlements, in contrast to Thebans, who bury theirs in tombs on the west bank of the Nile.

"We should be getting back," Tany insists. "Pepi will be worried if he checks and we're not there."

"I need to find Paser and Reb," I say stubbornly.

"It has only been a day, Sesha!" she exclaims, exasperated. "They are fine, they ..." A funny expression crosses her face. "They are ... on a boat."

Her words make me feel seasick. "A boat?" The Nubian was telling the truth?

Tany looks as surprised as me, but hers is likely a result of this random expression of her oracle powers.

"Yes" — she closes her eyes — "I can see them ..."

"Is it a fishing boat?" I demand.

Tany's eyes fly open. "I can't tell."

I must speak to Paser's relatives, their home is not far. "I'm going to make an inquiry. Will you come with me?"

She shakes her head. "I need to return to the script sanctum. My brother will wish to consult with me this evening and I need to be there for him."

"I understand," I say.

"Will *you* not come with *me*?" she tries one last time.

"I, too, cannot."

"Then we must each do what we are compelled to," she says, expression serious. We leave each other's company, with a warning from the other to stay safe.

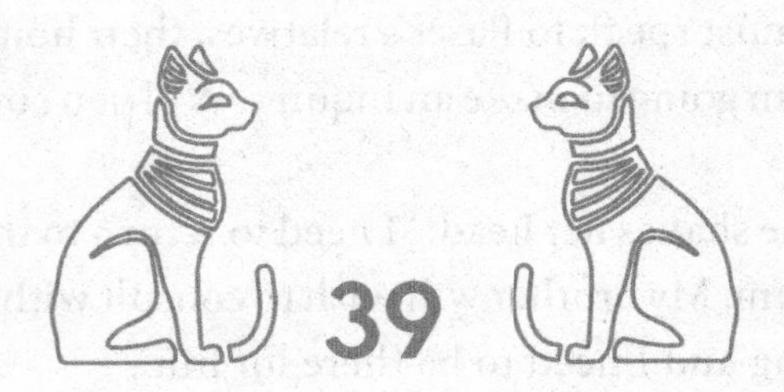

# 39

THE CITY IS BECOMING more familiar and eventually I find myself at Ramose's house. It is quiet and fairly dark. A single candle burns, in honour of the king.

"Hello?" I call. Low murmurs come from the back room, and I walk toward the voices. If I'm not mistaken, it is Paser's cousin, the husky soldier Ari, speaking to his mother, Paser's aunt. I'm about to call out again when suddenly I make out several words that stop me in mid-stride.

"… lull the Thebans into a sense of security …"

The aunt's voice breaks in, confused. "Yanassi is really planning to …"

"Sesha." A voice behind me makes me jump.

I turn to see Paser's uncle. "Where are Reb and Paser?" I demand.

Paser's uncle rubs his chin, the candle's shadows playing over his introspective face. "They are … gone."

"Gone?" I repeat. "Gone where?" He sighs, and I notice a bruise on his forehead. "Please!" Panic makes my voice rise. It brings Paser's aunt and Ari out from the back room.

"My nephew bid me to give you a message," Ramose says. "He said you were to 'trust all would be well.'"

"There were no other details?" I ask.

"He did not want to endanger me or my family with unnecessary knowledge," Ramose says. My eyes go to Ari, one of Yanassi's loyal soldiers. Paser would want to protect his family, but their allegiances to this kingdom, and its rulers, would also make him and Reb cautious about revealing too much.

"Tell me this," I say, "are he and Reb safe?"

"I hope so," Ramose says, but he hesitates a fraction too long.

I leave then, rushing out the front door.

"Sesha, wait!" Ramose calls after me but I don't turn back. Despite Paser's assurances delivered via his uncle, I cannot shake the feeling that I am one of the last pieces left standing on a senet board and rapidly running out of moves.

I make my way back to the palace in the dark, wishing for the presence of Amara's sister's cat, Temit. I attempt to distract myself, wondering if Amara and Akin will reconcile after the soldier's triumph today. Keeping my eyes open and my head down, I move silently though the narrow streets. I spot a familiar form that sends me darting behind one of the stalls, and I slice my foot on a broken piece of pottery. Ignoring the sting, I keep my eyes on my parents' killer. Crooked Nose's menacing face is intent, the look of a man on a mission.

"Where are you going?" I mutter under my breath. Why is he not at the queen's side?

Instinct urges me to follow, and I wait for him to pass, keeping to the shadows, slipping behind structures at a safe distance. We end up at the docks, where he stands a moment, peering out at Pharaoh's ship. Then he turns abruptly, as if making a decision. Untying the smaller raft that ferried Ahmes across earlier, he boards and begins rowing himself out to the enormous vessel. I watch for a minute, confused. Did the royals leave something back on the ship? Or someone? Tany's vision flashes through my mind: *They are on a boat.*

*Paser and Reb.*

I must get to Pharaoh's ship! I glance around for a craft to follow in. Something light and small, and not well secured to the docks. A small fire burns off to the right, tended by a guardsman who leans watchfully on his spear. Eye of Ra. If he sees me, he'll know at once I'm not an owner.

"You there," the guard calls and I freeze, thinking he's caught me. "Bit late for fishing, is it not?" But it's not me he's spoken to. Another man is approaching.

"Some big ones come out at night," the man says heartily. With a start, I realize it is Ramose. "As we have extra mouths here to feed, I figure why not catch a few of them?" He hops on a boat as weather-beaten as his face and busies himself unmooring his vessel from the dock. I slip silently into the dark water, quietly stroking my way to his craft.

Ramose pushes off, and I grab for a net dangling from the back of his boat as he begins to row himself out. Clinging tightly, I wait until we're a distance from the docks before clambering up the net, my muscles trembling from fatigue and the cool water.

Ramose only looks mildly surprised to see me heave myself up, panting, over the side of his boat. He does not miss a stroke. "Hello again, Sesha, how are the fish biting this evening?"

"Take me … to Paser … and Reb," I gasp, sounding like the king on his deathbed.

"Coincidentally, I am on my way to see them now," he says, his face betraying nothing.

I sit up, wiping the water from my eyes, preparing myself to fight Paser's uncle if I have to. "What have you and Crooked Nose done with them?" I demand.

"Crooked Nose?" A seemingly genuine look of puzzlement crosses his face, but I ignore it. I will not be played like a lyre.

"Queen Anat's bodyguard, my parents' murderer. Are you in league with him? I saw him steer another craft toward the ship just moments before you got here."

Concern creases Ramose's features. "This soldier is headed toward the ship? Sesha, on my honour, I swear I am not working against you and my nephew. On the contrary! We must hurry." He begins to row faster. "I told him this was a dangerous idea," he mutters.

"Who?" I ask, unsure of whether or not to believe him. If he's on our side, why did he lie about knowing where Paser and Reb were?

"Paser," he says.

"He is as stubborn as the sign he was born under," I say, shivering. "What idea?"

"I took them out early this morning to meet Pharaoh's ship as it approached," he says ruefully.

I resolve to stay on my guard, but my mistrust of him is weakening. "You did? But how did you know the royals were close?"

"We didn't," Ramose admits. "We prepared for a longer journey, just in case. Paser and Reb were certain the Thebans would accept their daughter's invitation, so we assumed they'd be along in due time."

"What was the plan?" Breath caught, I grab an oar to assist with rowing.

"The boys felt they needed to be warned."

"About what?" My heart thumps loudly in my ears. Does Ramose know?

"Apparently, they felt your brother might be in some danger. They did not tell me why, nor did I ask," Ramose says. He seems genuine. It strikes me that although he's originally from Thebes, Paser's uncle has long made his home among the Hyksos people, having married into the culture. His remorse over abandoning his family and his love for Paser's mother must be strong for him to risk angering Yanassi and his councillors. If indeed that is what he did. "I expected them to exit the ship with the royal family, but they were not among them." He looks very worried, a feeling that is contagious. "Both Paser and Reb assured me they would be all right."

*Likely because they knew you would not take them otherwise.* If Ramose is telling the truth, then my friends took a huge gamble in going to warn Pharaoh and Queen Anat, presumably, to protect Ky. They took that risk for my brother. For me.

"He cares deeply for you, you know," Paser's uncle says bluntly, as if reading my thoughts.

"And I, him." Why am I telling this to a man I barely know? But there is something about Ramose, I realize, now that I'm looking at him, my suspicions evaporating along with the water from my skin as I row. Perhaps it is his resemblance to Paser, not only in looks, but in how he is making me feel. Warm. Calm. Safe. I fear the monumental weight of my admission might sink the ship, but it is buoyed by Ramose's acknowledging grin, a twin of Paser's.

We near the ship. Crooked Nose's smaller raft is tied to one end of the colossal vessel, so we approach silently from the other. Whatever the queen's murderous soldier is up to, I do not think he means my friends well. As if to punctuate this opinion, there is a loud *crack*, followed by a sudden shout and a yelp of pain.

# 40

RAMOSE AND I look at each other.

"Go," he urges, "I'll secure the boat."

Unsheathing my blade, I stick it between my teeth, then launch myself onto Pharaoh's ship, ready for anything that might jump out at me. My knee slams hard into the gold-trimmed deck. Ignoring the painful throbbing, as well as the sting from the slice in my foot, I take the blade in hand and pad slowly down the length of the vessel, soundless as a cheetah sighting its prey.

"Tell me!" There is another loud cracking sound.

The hairs on the back of my neck lift. Crooked Nose.

"Why do you wish to keep Prince Ky's parentage a secret?" the soldier growls. "The queen thinks it has to do with that sandblasted scroll your friend stole." I stick my head slightly above the windowsill, like a crocodile with its eyes just above the surface. Crooked Nose stands there, an evil-looking whip in his hand. Paser and Reb are bound together, standing back to back, red lashes marking their tied arms and legs.

"Sesha and her father transcribed that copy." Paser is defiant. "It was their work and thus not stolen."

"We came to warn the royal family." Reb sounds incensed. "I do not think Pharaoh would approve of our treatment."

"The queen told me to get some answers. Since you refuse to co-operate, it is clear some stronger persuasion is in order." He cracks the short whip again. My friends and I flinch.

"We've experienced worse." Reb eyes the weapon like it is a many-headed cobra.

"Is that a challenge, scribe?" Crooked Nose puts down the whip and pulls his own sharp dagger from his belt. "What I've given you is nothing but a sting compared to what I *can* do."

"The pharaoh said you were not to harm us," Paser instructs him, forceful. "You need us alive."

"Perhaps," Crooked Nose says, "but I do not need you whole." He cocks his head, contemplating them. "I've waited so long to crush you roaches, I hardly know where to start." Thoughtfully, he brings his knife up to his cheek, as if evaluating, and takes a step forward.

"Hello there, fellow seafarer!" Paser's uncle's jovial voice rings out. "I seem to be having some trouble with my nets. Might I get your assistance? There is some fine tilapia in it for you!"

A scowl crosses Crooked Nose's face and he sheaths his blade. "Do not call out, or I'll take off more than a finger," he warns Reb and Paser.

He leaves the cabin, and I immediately hop over the sill and am at my friends' side, sawing through their ropes in the time it takes them to blink.

"Sesha!" Paser whispers. "What are you doing here?"

"Fishing," I reply shortly, severing the bindings around their wrists for the second time in the same number of days.

I'm almost through the one encircling their ankles when Reb yells, "Watch out!"

A blade whizzes past my head as I duck, barely in time. Crooked Nose stands there, enraged, yet oddly triumphant. "So glad you could join us, Daughter of Ay. I thought you might come for your friends." He picks up the whip from the small table where he left it and stalks toward us.

"You cannot harm the prince's sister," Paser shouts, about to lunge, regardless of Reb still attached.

"She is his sister no longer." Crooked Nose smacks the whip against his palm and comes toward me, one eager step at a time.

Ramose bursts into the room and with the practised ease of years of experience, casts his net in a graceful arc, ensnaring the soldier. The fisherman then pushes Crooked Nose, who stumbles sideways, off balance. Paser, who's gotten a leg free from the rope, sticks it out and the soldier trips, arms flailing, as he crashes to the ground. Snatching up one of the severed bindings, I thread the rope though the bottom of the net, trying to avoid the soldier's furious thrashing. His foot connects with my ear and leopard's spots flicker before my eyes, but I manage to tie off the knot. The four of us look at one another, panting, as our catch flops and writhes on the floor.

"Now, that's an ugly-looking fish," Ramose says, folding his arms. "Should we throw it back?"

"Or we could chop *him* up and use him for bait." Reb scowls down at Crooked Nose.

"One toe at a time," Paser agrees.

"I have a few questions first." I toss Paser my knife so he can cut through the final strands entangling his and Reb's legs, and face Crooked Nose. "Why is the royal family really here?" I demand. If there's one thing I know about the queen, it's that the woman has an ulterior motive for every move she makes.

"For a wedding, of course." Queen Anat's soldier sneers, and only my lack of sandals prevents me from kicking him.

"It is a reconnaissance mission, Sesha," Paser says, freeing himself and Reb at last and kicking the rope aside.

"We overheard Wujat and Pharaoh discussing the matter." Reb rubs his skinned ankle, wincing. "They came to inspect the Hyksos's technology."

"What?" I look at my friends.

"Apparently the last time you were in Thebes you mentioned some impressive weapons?" Paser raises an eyebrow.

"I did not think they believed me," I murmur.

"They did," Paser says, "and they came here in hopes of leveling the battlefield. They want the technology. And, in the odds that Yanassi gets any ideas, there are more troops heading this way, as we speak."

"You think you're the only one with intrigue skills?" Crooked Nose snarls from his net.

More soldiers. Coming to Avaris. "The royals are planning for battle?"

"As if I'd tell you," he jeers.

I motion for my friends to step away from the trussed soldier so he cannot hear. "We need to get back to the palace." My relief that Paser and Reb managed to warn Pharaoh and not reveal the prophecy is displaced by the feeling that both Yanassi and the royals have arrows sighted on one another, ready to let them fly at any moment.

"Wait," Ramose says, beckoning in the direction of his craft. "You three can take my boat. Why don't you leave the city and disappear for a while, until things calm down?"

My friends stand before me, beaten and bruised, as Ramose temptingly offers us what we once imagined: freedom. Their welts sting my own flesh. "Paser, Reb," I begin, "you need not walk with me back into the fray. Again."

"How many times must we go over this?" Reb rolls his eyes. "We're in this together."

"You've been through enough ..." I protest.

"So have you," Paser says firmly. "We know you will not abandon Ky and we will not abandon you."

"In that case, shall we be going?" Ramose inquires as I am overwhelmed with gratitude.

"What should we do with him?" Reb nods at our tangled trout.

"A good thunk will render him senseless for a while." Ramose smacks a fist into his hand. "He could be useful."

"As much as I like the idea, if the queen discovers we've assaulted and abducted her soldier, the Thebans may view it as an act of aggression." Paser studies the sullen form on the floor. "It could start a war."

"We'll have to leave him." I walk over to my parents' killer and bend low. "You do not deserve the mercy you are being shown today. When the gods come to weigh your heart, it will sink like a stone and you will never know the Land of Reeds." The soldier stares balefully up at me through the net and I stand.

"Let's go."

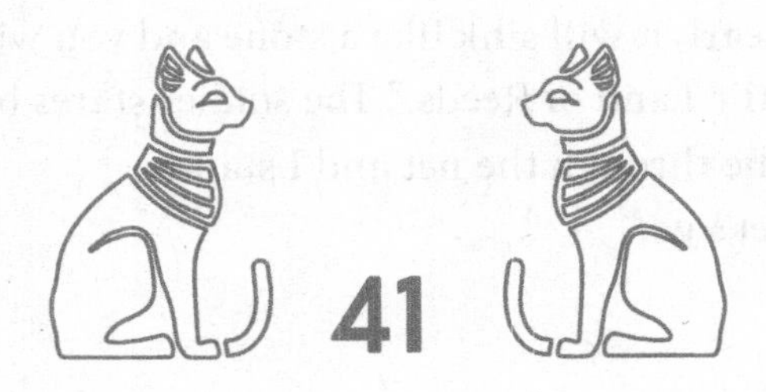

# 41

"YOU ALL MUST REST FIRST," Ramose insists as we disembark from his boat. "The hour is late."

"I won't be able to." I step down carefully onto the dock, knee and foot throbbing. "When did you last sleep?" I ask my friends.

"We had a brief rest before we left to greet Pharaoh." Paser helps his uncle tie up the craft, water lapping at its papyrus hull. "I can manage a bit longer. Reb?"

"I will be all right." Reb stretches. "Let's go see what's happened in our absence."

"We will have to remain hidden," I warn. "We do not want Yanassi *or* Queen Anat catching sight of us."

"With luck, everyone is relaxing after a nice meal, anticipating the upcoming celebration, where two great dynasties will join together as one," Ramose says. Bless his optimistic spirit.

"The wedding will certainly be on Merat's mind." I am slightly more doubtful than Paser's uncle. "As for Yanassi ... I am wary of this sudden shift to benevolent host he portrays. And the Thebans are probably devising a way to steal the Hyksos's technology as we speak."

"Are we to stop them?" Paser brushes his hair back from his eyes. There is a graze above his brow, and I am struck by the urge to kiss it.

"I do not see how that is possible." I look up at the stars instead, sending a wish to the gods. "If only they could eat their honeycake, then leave in peace, without Yanassi finding out who Ky is, all might be well."

"Have we thought about lacing their beer with blue lotus?" Reb names the powerful flower that stirs love and fondness for others. "Instead of fighting one another, it will have people embracing."

"Where would we get such a large quantity of the plant?" Paser looks bemused at this bizarre suggestion. I suppose Reb *is* a healer; it is natural he thinks of an herbal solution.

"I know," Ramose muses, and we look at him in surprise. "Not where to find vast quantities of blue lotus," he admits, "but the Hyksos have another medicinal plant they revere. They call it mandrake, or the love root. It produces a most wondrous feeling of well-being. But you must be careful," he warns. "It is toxic if not properly prepared. There's an entire section devoted to it in the palace orchards."

I can tell my friends are fascinated by his description of this potent medicine. "It is not without risk," I say.

"If our goal is to keep conflicts at bay, and everyone happy, it may be worth asking Min about," Paser says. "Perhaps an infusion could be prepared for the wedding feast?"

"Nothing brings out people's emotions like funerals and weddings," Ramose remarks, crossing his arms over his chest.

"How fortunate we have both occurring at the same time," I sigh. "At the moment, I cannot think of a better plan."

"You want to what?" Min looks at me, incredulous.

"Attempt to ease tensions with a concoction of mandrake," I say promptly. "Apparently it has calming and harmonious properties?"

"Well, yes." Min looks dubious. "But it is a dicey thing you suggest. And difficult to monitor. Those who like to indulge could end up taking too much."

"What if it's not prepared for everyone, but just the royal families?" Paser asks. "Presumably they will want to remain alert and avoid consuming too much drink."

Min sighs. "I cannot aid you in this endeavour."

"The tensions between the families are high," I urge the healer.

"We are only asking for the proper way to brew the herb," Reb adds.

Pentu comes to the door, blinking blearily. "What does Pepi say about all of this?" The beekeeper, who accompanied Min to the capital, was snoring away when we first knocked, sounding like one of his droning winged wards. We apologize for waking him, but he waves a hand telling us not to worry.

"We haven't told him," I appeal to Min's partner. Thick butter-yellow propolis cream coats Pentu's entire face, making it hard for me not to smile, despite the circumstances. "He wants us to stay out of sight as he's been occupied with the king's passing and Pharaoh's arrival."

"Yanassi had me prepare hundreds of jars of honey for this occasion," Pentu says, yawning. "He wanted to gift them to his bride's family."

"Or have them on hand for battle," I hear Reb murmur to Paser behind me. A powerful healing substance, honey keeps wounds clean and prevents infections.

"I'm sure the queen will be most impressed by your beauty balms," I assure Pentu.

"Yes, pity she'll never have a face as lovely as mine." He grins his gapped smile and pats his creamy cheek. "Though beauty can be a terrible curse."

"Oh, listen to you," Min yawns. "You've been stung in the head one too many times." He turns to us. "He slathers on his balm every night," he confides.

Pentu bats his thick lashes at Min. "I do not hear you complaining."

Min gives him a fond look, then turns back to us, firm. "Seek counsel with Pepi first, before any of this business with the mandrake root."

I realize we're not getting any further with the doctor. "Very well," I sigh. "We apologize for disturbing your slumber." Min leads Pentu by the hand back into their room — I recall that the keeper's eyesight is poor — and I catch a glimpse of the tenderness between them, something I would like to have when I'm older.

"What now?" Reb asks as we leave their quarters. "The honey is obviously for treating any injuries from military action." It feels like events are spiralling out of our control, wider and wider, sucking us into a vortex of unknown peril.

"Let's speak with Pepi as Min suggests," I say, not seeing any other solution. "His chambers are this way."

We sneak through the corridor, furtive as mice. It is the darkest part of night and the palace slumbers deeply around us. Reb and Paser follow me up a set of stairs leading to another wing. Just as we reach Pepi's room, his door cracks open. Frantically, I motion my friends back into the shadows. A slight figure slips out of his chambers and shuts the door quietly. As she turns to leave, moonlight from the high window bathes her lovely face.

Merat.

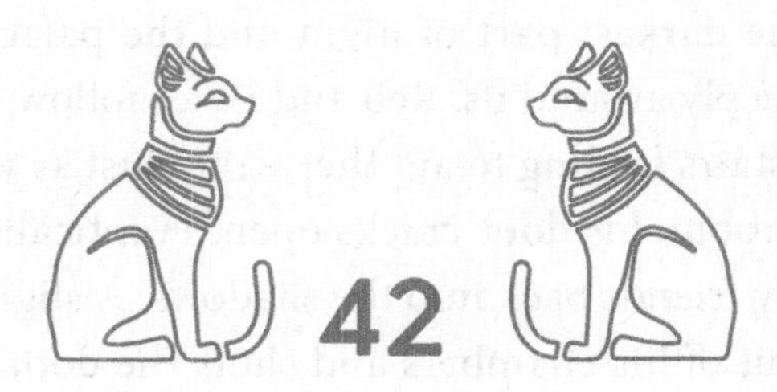

# 42

WE STEP OUT OF THE SHADOWS, and she blinks at us, her chin lifting. "What are you doing here?"

I'm about to ask her the same thing when Pepi pokes his head out the door. "Princess, did you forget some—" He stops, seeing us standing there. The five of us remain motionless for several heartbeats. "Get inside, before someone sees you," Pepi hisses, motioning us into his chambers.

We bumble obediently into his room, bringing the awkwardness from the hallway along with us. Merat's eyes flash as if daring us to say something.

It is Reb who breaks the silence. "How is your family, Princess?"

A cautious look crosses Merat's features. "They are well. Fatigued from their journey and resting at the new palace."

"And my brother?" I ask.

"*Our* brother," she corrects, "is also well. He is fully recovered from his previous illness and thrives at the court in Thebes."

"Does Yanassi know … of Ky's lineage?" Paser says.

"No." Merat says, relieved. "We will keep it that way." She looks at Pepi. "Will we not?"

"For now," Pepi says.

It goes quiet. I clear my throat. "Where is Tany?"

"In the scriptorium" — Pepi narrows his gaze at me — "where I said to stay."

"I had to know if Ky was here …" I begin.

"You could've learned that by staying put," he says shortly. "Nothing can happen to you." He lifts his hands in frustration. "You are the one to rule our kingdom, remember?"

Paser comes to my defence. "If not for Sesha, Reb and I would be missing a few fingers right now." He looks at Merat. "A certain soldier of your mother's was about to get creative with his interrogation."

"I wonder if he has a Nubian cousin," Reb mutters.

"Why are you here?" Pepi asks, impatient.

"We have an idea to ensure the royal visit goes off without any … hiccups," I say, though that is not entirely true; there may be a few of them after consumption of the mandrake.

Pepi is skeptical. "What is it?"

"It involves the love root —" I begin.

"The *what*?"

"The mandrake plant." I appeal to the former spy's sense of intrigue. "It produces friendly feelings; we wish to dose the royals and Yanassi."

"You want to sedate them?" Merat is agog.

"Only a little bit," Reb offers.

"The chieftain is fine." A fleeting look — guilt? — crosses Pepi's features. "My cousin assures both Merat and me that he is putting the past behind him."

"And you believe him?" Paser says.

"Regardless, we are keeping a close eye," Pepi says stiffly. "This is what the princess and I were discussing, before you three took it upon yourselves to burst up to my chambers."

"You invited us in," Reb reminds him.

"It looks suspicious for you to be congregating outside my room in the middle of night!" Pepi snaps. "Everything is under control. Now go get some rest. Tomorrow is a big day, as is the one after that." Pepi tries to appeal to me again to hide. "Sesha, you must keep out of sight. It is for everyone's sake, including your brother's. If Yanassi or one of his men catches you attempting to speak with Ky, it will only arouse his suspicions."

"The royals are here to copy your technology," I burst out. "They want it for themselves."

"Then we will share it with them," Pepi says simply. "They will acknowledge the Hyksos's superiority and Yanassi will be gratified. Now, go. To. Sleep."

Still protesting, we are ushered from Pepi's room. He calls for Abisha, who is stationed not far off, and the hulking guard escorts us back to the script sanctuary, while Merat departs for her own chambers.

Tany is curled on the floor, sleeping, a large pile of fresh linens on her right. We tiptoe past, into the back corner of the room, each grabbing a sheet on our way. Despite everything, Pepi is right. We must rest.

"Do you believe Yanassi has had a change of heart?" Paser whispers to us.

"Let us hope so," Reb whispers back. "What do you think, Sesha?"

"I am not sure. The honey is suspicious." I try and fail to stifle a yawn, which both Paser and Reb immediately mirror. "It wouldn't hurt to have a batch of mandrake potion on hand, in any case."

"Yes," I hear Reb murmur as we drift off. "Yanassi will likely need a drink when he discovers Princess Merat and Pepi are in love."

I wake the next morning to the sound of rustling. I hope it's not rats. Opening one bleary eye, I see Paser and Reb scanning through piles of documents. Tany is not there, perhaps she's off getting some food. Pepi has strict rules about eating and drinking in his sanctum.

"What are you doing?" I wince, and bend to examine my bruised knee and the cut on my foot.

Paser looks up. "That wound needs a stitch or two, Sesha."

"It can bide," I say. "Reb?" My friend is reaching up high to another shelf.

"The mandrake potion," he responds. "There's a chance we might find a recipe for it among the other medical texts."

"Good thinking," I say approvingly, now alert and getting up to help search. The smell of fresh bread reaches my nostrils, and there is a noise outside the room. "Would you like your midday meal?" Tany's voice calls from outside.

I look at my friends. "Midday?!"

"We needed the rest, Sesha," Paser reminds me. I suppose it was only an hour or two until sunrise when we fell asleep. We exit the sanctum to find servants laying out a delicious spread.

"Thank you," Tany bids them, and they depart as we sit in a circle to eat. Paser and Reb fall ravenously upon the food, and we tell Tany about the previous night's events, omitting our discovery of Merat outside Pepi's room.

Tany is appalled when she hears of Crooked Nose's actions. "What are the odds this soldier has a Nubian cousin?"

Reb's mouth falls open. "That is what I said!"

Tany smiles at him and he smiles back. Paser and I look at each other.

"You seem to know this space well," I say to Pepi's sister, gesturing at the sanctum behind us. "Can you tell us where we might find a recipe for mandrake?" She takes her eyes off Reb to look at me.

"Why do you wish to know it?" She is curious, but not judgmental.

"We want to have it on hand." Reb is honest. "In case there are any … tensions that need soothing."

Tany shakes her head. "That script is rarely written down. The mandrake is extremely dangerous when not cultivated correctly." Our faces fall. "It is much safer to commit it to memory."

"Do you know it?" Reb says.

"Priestesses are instructed in its preparation," Tany says, offhand. "It's used in several of our rites."

"Can you help us prepare it?" Reb asks, and we hold our collective breath.

"I suppose I am not doing much else right now."

Tany takes in our eager expressions, pausing on Reb's, and shrugs. "Why not?"

Tany goes to gather the ingredients while Reb, Paser, and I remain in the scriptorium, organizing and putting away the scrolls we rifled through in our search for the finicky potion's recipe.

"It is a good thing Zina stayed at the oasis," I tease Reb, nodding at the hidden door through which Tany left. He flushes.

"Feelings are complicated, Sesha," he replies, with a pointed nod toward Paser's broad back. The tall scribe is reaching up to place a scroll on a high shelf.

I clear my throat, feeling my own cheeks flush. "I am aware."

"Speaking of complicated feelings" — Paser turns around, oblivious — "how long do you think until Yanassi notices that Pepi and Merat are in love?"

"That's all we need." Yet, a weight is lifting from my heart; Merat's relationship with Pepi frees something long tamped down inside me. Among other things, the princess's former affections for Paser have prevented me from fully admitting my own feelings for my friend. Telling myself this is not the time, I bend my head low to hide my emotions, and we continue working in silence. Something catches my eye and I utter a soft cry, unearthing a document from the pile.

"What is it, Sesha?" Paser asks as I closely examine the scroll I just picked up.

"This is in my father's hand." I look excitedly around the room. "He must have transcribed it when he worked here. Tany *said* he might have visited this place! Apparently, he and Pepi's mother knew each other well."

"Really?" Reb says slowly. "Now, that is something."

"What is?" I ask absent-mindedly, eyes devouring the script, spotting my father's distinctive but subtle embellishments here and there …

"Think on it, Sesha." My friends exchange looks, and I see that whatever occurs to Reb dawns on Paser, as well. "Tany said your father and Pepi's mother knew one another well?" Reb looks uncomfortable, but gamely presses on. "We spoke of feelings a moment ago. What if Ay and Kalali … once felt something for each other?"

"What are you saying?" Yet my body is tingling, recognizing the implication before my mind catches up.

"What if they were … involved?" Reb is warming to his theory. "Pepi has always reminded me of someone, and just now, when you mentioned your father and Kalali … well." He looks apologetic. "What if you are right, and Pepi *is* destined to rule?"

"What?" I repeat loudly, over the buzzing cicadas back in my brain.

"Perhaps it is he who is meant to maintain 'light and learning' through the land. After all," Reb reasons, "if Ay were Pepi's father, then he, too, would be one 'from the line of the physician' …" Reb's voice is drowned out by the noisy whirring.

Paser is looking concerned. "Sesha, perhaps you should sit —"

The humming increases, and for a second time this moon — always embarrassing for a physician — I faint.

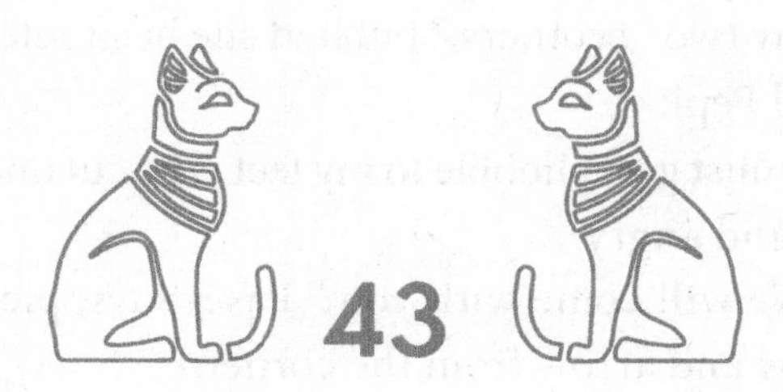

# 43

"I MUST SPEAK WITH MIN," I say. Paser fans a papyrus in front of my face.

"Easy, Sesha," Reb says, "it is only a theory."

But I have to admit it is a sound one. Pieces begin to slide into place, like the final bricks in a monument. Khyan's denial of fathering Pepi ... The fact that my father would've been in Avaris around the time Pepi was conceived ... Tany's odd reaction when she saw Ky on the royal ship — for the love of Isis, there *is* a resemblance there! One that has emerged as Ky has grown, the eyes, those angular cheeks ... My hand goes to my face, tracing the bones I inherited from Ay, Chief Physician to the Pharaoh of the Black Land. I see the former oracle Rahibe, starkly, against a navy, twinkling sky, pointing out the three stars in Osiris's crown. I thought she'd been referring to Paser and Reb, my two "brothers," but had she been referring to Ky and Pepi?

"I must go." I hobble to my feet. The cut on my foot is red and angry.

"We will come with you," Paser says, picking up his bow and arrow from the corner.

"It will be more obvious that way."

"That does not matter," Reb says stubbornly, picking up his own weapon.

I do not argue with them. "This way."

We find the wizened healer treating what looks like an advanced case of worms. Both doctor and patient look up, startled, at our approach.

"We must speak with you at once," I say firmly.

Min sighs. "I told you, I do not think preparing an infusion of mandrake is the way to —"

Paser cuts him off. "We need to ask you something. Privately."

Min wipes his hands and makes an apologetic motion at his patient. "One moment."

The man nods and lowers his skirt, scratching at his behind.

We walk a distance away to commune. "What is it?" Min asks, taking in our faces.

"You said you knew my father when he trained here at Avaris," I say, ignoring my throbbing foot. "Do you know if he … I mean, were my father and Pepi's mother ever … involved?"

"Romantically," Paser clarifies. I'm grateful he didn't say *in love* — it would feel like a betrayal of my mother, though it was before her time.

Min blinks, a guarded expression coming across his features. "I cannot say," he says slowly. "If they were, they were incredibly private about it."

"Did you attend Pepi's birth?" Reb demands.

"No, Kalali went to the priestesses' temple to have him," Min recounts, surprising us. "He lived among them for the first years of his life and was about four when his mother brought him to the court here at Avaris; male children must leave the sect at that age. Kalali's sister, Asru, had married Khyan by then. Pepi and Yanassi are only a few months apart."

"Was Yanassi's mother also a priestess?" Paser asks. I had not thought of that.

"She was." Min looks at us. "I thought you knew that. When Asru fell in love with Khyan, she left the sect to become his wife. When she died, Pepi's mother stepped in to fill the gaps her absence left in the kingdom."

"Back to Kalali and Sesha's father," Paser interjects. "Is there any chance Pepi could be Ay's son?"

Min considers this. "It is possible," he admits. "But it would only be conjecture."

I look at Paser and Reb. "We need proof."

"How?" Reb asks.

"Tany," I say. "I think she knows, or at least suspects the truth." Is this what she told the king in private?

"Let's go," Paser says.

"Wait!" Min nods at my foot. "Let me take care of that first. The demons will be at it in no time." I relent and he cleans the wound and stitches me up, with only a few curses and tears on my part, though in honesty, I barely feel it. My foot bandaged, we thank Min, who bids us be careful, and head off in search of the oracle.

"Sesha, have you thought about what else this might mean?" Paser asks as he and Reb walk — and I limp — toward the grove containing the mandrakes, after getting directions from a servant.

"I would have an older brother." Wonder is spreading through my body, replacing the shock. I've always felt oddly connected to the spy; now I know why.

"Not just that." Paser's expression is tense. "If Pepi *is* the one meant to rule in peace for forty years, then not only could it be Ky's line to erase the Hyksos, it could also be yours. If the Hyksos find out, your cover as Pepi's betrothed might no longer protect you, and that target on your back will grow bigger."

"As the only girl at temple and someone who has gone up against Queen Anat, a target on my back is nothing new." I wince as my injured foot comes down hard on a sharp stone. "Reb, you must be delighted."

"What do you mean?" He is puzzled.

"It appears I am not meant to rule a kingdom, after all," I say, as we approach the orchards. "How is that for tempering my pride?"

"But, if our theory proves true, you *were* correct in believing that Pepi is the one meant to rule," Reb reasons. "Which would justify all of our actions in trying to bring it about." He sends a grin my way. "You must feel so conflicted right now."

"How fortunate that that seems to be my natural state," I retort. Paser smiles, and despite everything, something inside me glows, like the sky at Ra's dawning. It seems there is one thing I am no longer conflicted about.

"Sesha!" I glance up at the shrill cry to see a small figure running toward us. "I've been looking everywhere for you. Ahmes and I *knew* you were in the city. You must come, Pharaoh and the queen are threatening to attack! The rest of their soldiers arrived and —"

"Bebi, Bebi," I say, as little Tabira's handmaiden flings herself at me. I quickly embrace and release her. "Slow down, what is happening?"

Her hands flutter in agitation as she flits from foot to foot, unable to stay in one spot too long, for fear of getting stuck. "It is the chieftain. He has taken Ky."

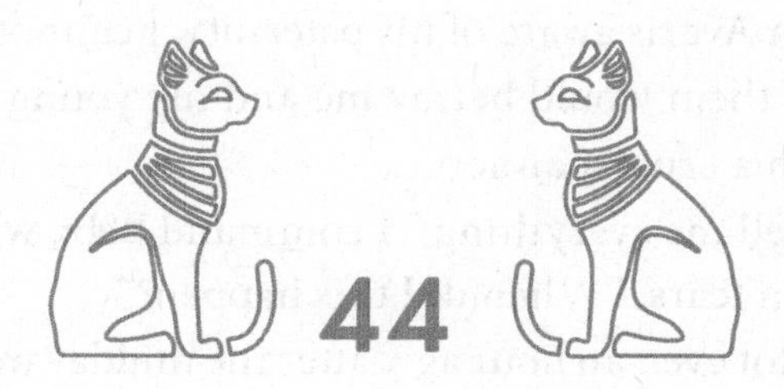

# 44

"WHAT?" BREATHING IS becoming difficult. "Why would Yanassi do such a thing?"

"I do not know." Bebi wrings her hands. "He offered to take the children for a ride in his chariot. When Ky's turn came, the pair did not come back. Pharaoh and Queen Anat are concerned, especially as these two" — she flicks her hand at Reb and Paser — "came to warn them something like this might happen. They bid me find you and bring you before them."

"Yanassi would only want your brother for one thing," Paser says in a low voice, voicing my deepest fear. "He has discovered who Ky's father is."

"How could he have found out?" Reb asks. Aside from the Theban visitors, whom the boys warned not to say anything, Pepi, Tany, and Merat are the only ones in Avaris aware of his paternity. I cannot believe any of them would betray me and my young brother in such a cruel manner …

"Tell me everything," I command Bebi, who is almost in tears. "When did this happen?"

"Not even an hour ago, after the midday meal. The children were enchanted by the Hyksos's chariots, and the chieftain offered to take them for a ride. Prince Tutan and little Tabira's lasted only a few moments, but then he took Ky —" she swallows "— and never came back."

"Perhaps they had trouble with the cart." Paser tries to soothe her. He looks at me. "It might only be coincidence, Sesha."

"And with Akin driving, the chieftain could not have fixed the cart alone," Reb adds, both of them grasping at spokes, the spokes of a broken wheel. "The lame soldier wouldn't have been able to assist …"

"Yanassi's driver was not lame," Bebi interrupts, cocking her head.

"He wasn't?" Paser and I look at each other.

"He was standing upright." Bebi squeezes her eyes shut, focusing. "By his dress and the style of sword he carried, he looked to be a Nubian."

My hand flies to my mouth. "Yanassi's mercenary," I whisper. But he left. Didn't he? Was it all a ruse? "He must've been following me." I turn to my friends. "He could have rowed out to Pharaoh's ship …"

"Where he pried the information from Crooked Nose," Paser finishes.

"I hope he also extracted a few of the mangy jackal's toes," Reb says darkly.

"Crooked Nose would not sacrifice any digits for our sake," I say. "He'd offer up the information to the Nubian in an instant." Which the mercenary would have immediately taken back to Yanassi.

"Where are Pepi and the princess?" Paser commands Bebi.

"Princess Merat is with her parents and Wujat." Bebi gulps. "She is reassuring them and trying to keep tensions calm."

"And Pepi?" Reb asks.

"He went after Yanassi. He promised Pharaoh and Queen Anat no harm would come to their son. But I fear they won't wait long to strike if Ky is not returned soon, unharmed." Bebi's face is full of dread. It must match mine.

"Hathor, help us, the whole city could erupt," I say. "Where could Yanassi have taken Ky?" My head swivels wildly in every direction, as if to catch a glimpse of the chieftain.

"I don't know," Reb responds. "But she might."

He points at Tany, who walks quickly toward us, satchels bulging on both sides of her body.

"What is it?" She senses the undercurrents of panic as she approaches. "Something is happening." It is not a question.

"We think Yanassi knows who Ky's father is," Paser says. "He's taken him, and Pharaoh and Queen Anat are threatening retaliation."

"Your brother has gone after them" — I try to be efficient with my words — "but we do not know where. Can you help?" I glance at the herbs in her satchel. Is there time to induce her into a trance?

Tany correctly interprets my expression. "I do not need my oracle powers to know where they went," she says. "Yanassi likely took Ky to the bluffs, where he and Pepi played as boys. I'd sometimes tag along, but it was remote and dangerous, so we were forbidden to go there. Which, of course, made them want to all the more." Her face is pale. "Your brother is there, I'm sure of it."

"Let's go," I say to Paser and Reb. "Will you come with us?" I ask Tany. There are other things we need to speak of.

But she shakes her head, patting her satchel. "After these events we will require a fair amount of love root to calm emotions." Tany grabs my hand and looks into my eyes. "Go."

She quickly gives us directions and, without wasting another breath, we race toward the brink of chaos.

"Why the bluffs?" I fret, limping hurriedly after Paser and Reb.

"Tany said it's remote; it would be easy to fake an accident there," Reb gives voice to my fears. "Presumably Yanassi would not outright murder Ky in Pharaoh and Queen Anat's faces."

I stumble, my cut screaming, and Paser puts out an arm to steady me. "You can't keep running like this." He nods at my foot.

"I'm fine," I repeat stubbornly.

Reb looks at Paser. "We need to move faster."

I step on another rock and cry out in pain and frustration.

"The horses," Paser says. "Sesha, wait here. We'll be right back."

I want to argue, to rebel against the thought of staying still. "Hurry," I beg instead, and they rush off in the direction of the stables. There's nothing for me to do but wait and torment myself with visions of what Yanassi might do to my brother. I imagine Ky trampled under wheels and hooves or being thrown from the cliffs … A rumbling sound interrupts my self-torture. I look up to see horses pulling a cart, barrelling toward me.

"Your chariot, Sesha," Paser calls, holding the bows and arrows. Reb has the reins.

"What …?" I splutter. "How did you …?"

"It was ready and waiting, it seemed, just for us," Reb says. "If the gods want to gift us with horses, I think we should not refuse them."

"Get in." Paser offers me his hand. His strong forearm bears my weight as he hefts me up into the chariot.

"Move!" Reb shouts, flicking the reins, and the animals charge forward.

The last time I spoke to my brother he persuaded Pharaoh to release Pepi and me, saving our lives. Now we race to save his.

*Mother, father, and all the gods who are listening, be at our side.*

# 45

THE RUGGED BLUFFS come into view.

"Look!" Reb nods at two chariots in the distance. Yanassi's and Pepi's. He pulls up beside them, bringing the horses to a halt. Jarred and shaken from the unaccustomed ride, not to mention Ky's abduction, I step unevenly down onto the grass.

"Here." Paser disembarks and throws Reb his bow. I reach down and grab my blade just as the Nubian walks out from behind a palm. He swings his deadly sword, fiendish grin in place.

Reb straightens. "A welcoming party."

"Lucky for us, it is only a party of one." Paser's bow is trained on the mercenary. "You did not fare so well during our last encounter," he calls to Yanassi's hired sword. "How is your leg?"

"Shut your face," the mercenary snarls. "My quarrel

with you was merely transactional, but now it is becoming personal."

"Let us keep to commerce," Reb says politely. "Whatever Yanassi is paying you, we can double it."

Paser and I exchange a look.

"You?" the mercenary scoffs. "You cannot afford my price."

"Not us," Reb says. "The pharaoh. All the riches he's sent to Avaris as tribute over the years? There are caverns more, treasures beyond your imagining. If you were to ensure the safety of the royal son, you'd be rewarded generously."

"I believe your queen wants you dead." The mercenary spits.

"She wants Ky alive more." I hope. "Here." I remove a precious jewel from my pocket, perhaps the same one I once offered to Tany. The mercenary's greedy eyes fall on the gemstone. It glows, radiating a rare yet tangible power. "This priestess stone has great magic." It must, to have gotten us this far. "Take it as an initial payment, only for allowing us to pass."

"And not following," Paser adds.

"Or I can just kill you and remove it from your corpses," he counters, swinging his sword again.

"You can try," Reb says, with a nod at the Nubian's thigh. "But you may not escape unscathed, and then there will be no additional treasure."

"The chieftain promises to compensate me well," he says, but his eyes stay on the glittering gem.

"He might," I reason. "But Yanassi cannot pay you if he is dead. And Pharaoh will surely see him killed if my brother is harmed."

"Kidnapping the son of his guest?" Paser shakes his head. "Bad form for a king, especially one who prides himself on honour."

"Just throw us your sword and take a few steps back," Reb coaxes. "Sesha will toss you the stone once you let us pass. Your employer need not know of this encounter."

"It is a very easy thing to do." Paser steps forward, bow trained on the mercenary. "I do not wish to kill you, if I don't have to."

"Let us pass." I hold the bewitching gem between two fingers and move it hypnotically from side to side, having had some experience with snakes. I take a step forward. Reb and Paser take one, as well. Then we take another. Another. And then I fling the gem as hard as I can into the brush. The mercenary's eyes are locked on the stone as it sails high through the air, landing silently in a large patch of grass.

"Go," I say, and then we are running, demons at our backs and in front. Sparing a quick peek over my shoulder, I see the mercenary hacking at large swathes of grass, hunting for the precious gem. Blood seeps into the bandage around my foot, but I ignore it as we reach more tall grass. We get low, pushing our way forward, straining for any sounds behind us, or noises ahead, hoping to identify our quarry's location.

"What is our plan?" Reb whispers. Paser gestures at his bow.

"Only as a last resort," I whisper back. If Paser kills Yanassi, Pepi might be forced to execute my friend, should word get back to the citizens of Avaris. Pharaoh and Queen Anat would feel his life fair compensation. I will not lose Ky *or* Paser.

"This way." Paser nods in the direction of voices, and we follow him through the tickling grasses, keeping a sharp eye out for vipers, of both the animal and human varieties. The voices grow louder as we approach, and I recognize the sound of Yanassi and Pepi arguing, having heard it often enough. Paser puts a hand up and we stop, hearts thudding. Peering through the grass, we see the chieftain and the Hyksos spy standing on the bluffs. Pepi appears to be entreating his co-regent.

Where is Ky? Desperately, I scan for my brother. By the gods, are we too late?

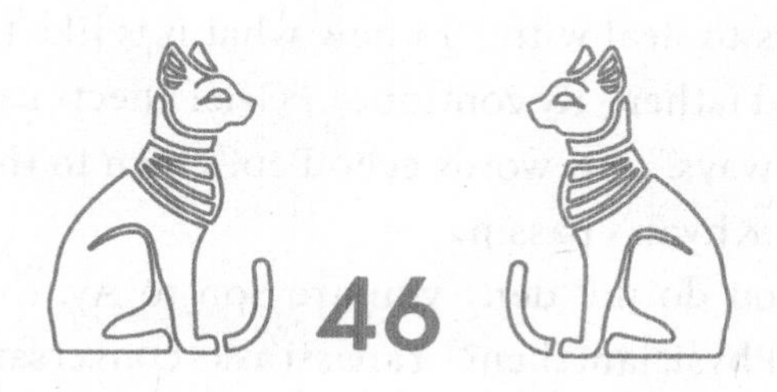

# 46

"THERE, SESHA," Paser whispers at my ear, and I almost faint again. I stamp my foot down hard, and the pain brings my vision back into sharp focus. Ky is sitting on a rock, hands bound, though his feet are free. His face is pale, but he is not crying.

"... It's not too late, Cousin," Pepi urges the chieftain as we creep closer. "We can say your chariot suffered an accident. Pharaoh and the queen do not have to hear of this."

"If you release me, I will say nothing," Ky calls out, voice cracking, whether from fear or his maturing, I do not know. My brother has grown in more than height. There is an assuredness in his manner, despite his bindings, that is even more pronounced than when I last saw him in Thebes. Watching him and Pepi work together to sway the chieftain, I see both their resemblance to my father, and to myself — though neither recognize it in the other yet, having more pressing matters to deal with. "I know what it is like to lose a beloved father," Ky continues. "Grief affects us in profound ways." His words echo Pepi's own to the chieftain at Khyan's passing.

"You do not deny you are Son to Ay, the Great Royal Physician, then?" Yanassi asks conversationally. He seems remarkably calm. Eerily calm.

"I do not deny it," Ky says, a slight tremble to his lifted chin but still no tears. "I am proud of it." My heart breaks at his courage and at his next words. "Though Pharaoh and the queen are my family now."

"I hope you have not forgotten you also have a sister." I step out of the bush. Paser and Reb step out behind me, both bows trained on Yanassi.

"Sesha!" Ky shouts.

"What is this?" Yanassi rounds on Pepi, gripping his ax in his left hand. "You mean to ambush me, Cousin?"

"I am as surprised by their presence as you, Cousin," Pepi says, cheeks hollowed by grief and stress. He is unarmed and holds his hands out peaceably. "Considering there was no time to send for our Theban friends, here."

"Let him go, Yanassi," I say. "It is four on one, and we do not want to hurt you."

Ky stands. "Five."

Yanassi looks at Pepi, amazed. "You would help these Theban whelps over your own flesh and blood?" He takes a step toward his cousin. "The prophecy states one of the physician's line will wipe our people from the land. You would let them doom your countrymen and kingdom?"

Pepi hesitates and Yanassi continues. "We grew up together, our mothers were sisters. Do not forsake your family."

"Pepi is our family, too," I shout. I have no choice. Pepi is wavering.

"I'm talking of blood, scribe," Yanassi snarls.

"So am I."

The chieftain rounds on me. "What poison spouts from your mouth?"

"Pepi is our brother," I say, motioning at Ky and myself. "He is the son of Kalali and Ay!"

I do not know who looks more shocked: Ky, the chieftain, or Pepi.

Pepi shakes his head, unwilling to part with his long-held reality. "I am Khyan's son."

"You dream!" Yanassi roars. Paser and Reb, who had let their arrows down, raise them again.

"Where is the evidence of this?" Pepi demands. "Did Tany tell you?"

It would be easy to lie, but I cannot. "There was no time to ask," I say. "But if you look at my brother, you might see the truth in his face." Pepi turns to stare at Ky, who sports a matching dazed expression. "The timing, the resemblance, it fits. They kept in touch. Tany did say she believed our father was Kalali's source."

"Why would my mother lie to me?" Pepi demands.

"I cannot speak for her, but maybe she knew you were destined to rule and thought it best if you grew up in court, a member of the royal family at Avaris. If you believed yourself the son of a great king, you'd become one yourself." I nod at Ky, heart pounding. "May I untie my brother?"

"Take a step toward him and I'll cleave his head in two," Yanassi thunders, striding over to my brother. Pepi deftly inserts himself between Ky and the chieftain, who lifts his brutal ax high as I scream. "Out of my way, Cousin!"

Pepi catches Yanassi's arm before he can bring his weapon down. He looks between the chieftain, the man he believed all his life to be his brother, and Ky, who I'm certain is his actual brother, as well as being the young son to the pharaoh and potential eradicator of the Hyksos line.

He makes up his mind.

"You cannot kill this child," Pepi shouts at his cousin, still restraining him. "Whatever the prophecy, he is an innocent."

"Fine. I will kill you first, then him." Yanassi rips his arm from Pepi's grasp and lifts his ax high again. "Give my regards to your mother."

There is a *whir* followed by a dull *thunk*.

The chieftain looks down at the arrow now lodged in his armpit. Grunting, he yanks the shaft from his side as Paser reaches for another. Blood spurts from the wound.

"Stop," Pepi shouts, holding a hand up to Reb, who is sighting his own arrow. "Enough."

"Even the Thebans can see it is me or them, Cousin." Yanassi swings his ax again, but his injured side affects his aim. Pepi ducks, grappling for Yanassi's ax. The pair wrestle over the weapon, stumbling back toward the bluff's edge. Paser and Reb walk forward, bows at the ready but not wanting to fire, in case of hitting Pepi. I run to Ky and use our father's blade to cut his bindings.

"Sesha," he sobs, as I finally get them off, and he turns to embrace me. I breathe in his familiar scent, holding him tightly to my chest. His tears come then, soaking my clothes, and I feel my own as we turn to face the fight. Yanassi, the larger of the two, has the upper hand, but Pepi clings to the ax like a monkey; the chieftain cannot draw it back to strike him.

Yanassi forces Pepi toward the ledge and the spy stumbles, his burly cousin landing on top of him. We run over to the fray; Paser and Reb drop their bows and throw themselves on top of the chieftain, trying to tear him off Pepi.

With the strength of six men, Yanassi struggles to his feet, hauling Pepi up, as well, ignoring the blows Paser and Reb land on him. His ax — dropped to wrap both hands around Pepi's throat — glints on the ground. The spy is turning purple as he gasps for air that does not come.

"Sesha," Paser cries, "*defang the snake*!"

I leave Ky with my blade and run to Yanassi's ax, picking up the heavy weapon, then race to the scuffle, where the chieftain is in the midst of expressing his extreme dissatisfaction with his co-regent. So ingrained are my healer's instincts, I hesitate, only a fraction of a breath, my limbs refusing to lift the ax to commit such willful, irreparable harm to a body.

Ky has no such hesitations.

In the mere seconds it takes to consider my options, my brother is at my side and has snatched the chieftain's hefty weapon from my grasp. "If one of my line is to wipe the Hyksos from the land, I will start with you!" Ky brings the ax down with all his might toward Yanassi's hands, which are still encircling Pepi's neck in a strangling death grip. The duck-billed ax slices cleanly through the chieftain's left wrist, severing it from his body.

I scream again as the chieftain lifts his spurting stump and stares at it in disbelief. The sound of shouts in the distance makes us all look up. Armed Theban soldiers led by the pharaoh bear down on us. Bebi must have relayed our location.

Yanassi sways, looking at his mangled arm, and takes a step back toward the cliffs. "So be it, Cousin," he says softly, knowing he is only minutes from being ripped to pieces. "May the blood of our people be on your head."

"Yanassi, no!" Pepi shouts.

"Tell my story, scribes!" he shouts, then turns and launches himself from the bluffs. The rest of us race to the ledge and stare down at Yanassi's motionless form on the rocks below, the king's son gone to follow his father into the afterlife.

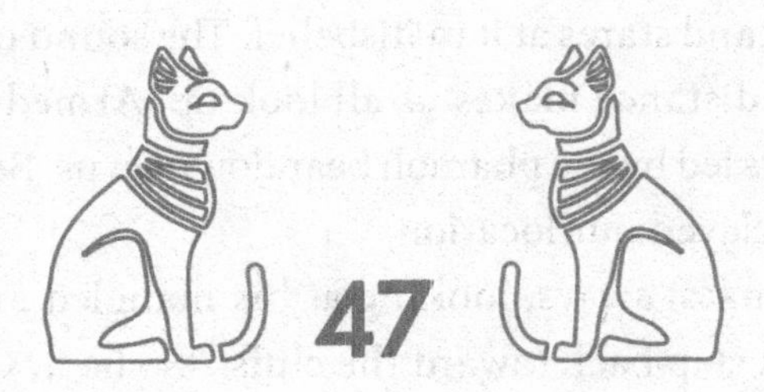

# 47

BACK AT THE PALACE, the afternoon's uproar is slowly subsiding.

Pharaoh, Queen Anat, and the rest of Avaris have been given an electrum-coated version of the truth: driven by grief, Yanassi ended his own life, and his body has conveniently been taken by the tides. By the time it is retrieved, the fish will have done their work in disguising his injuries. Ky has agreed to adhere to this minor alteration, which is not much of a stretch, really, in order to prevent any further aggression on the Theban royals' part.

I have spent the last several hours in my brother's company. He is with me now, under Min's care. The healer shakes his head at the state of my foot but does not lecture me. Instead, he cleans and re-binds the wound while I grit my teeth, gripping my brother's hand tightly. Pepi and Merat are with Pharaoh and the queen, while Paser and Reb are with Tany in the scriptorium; we do not want the royals getting wind that the oracle is here.

"Stay off that foot, Sesha." Min is stern as he passes me a suitable length of wood to use as a crutch. The doctor was shocked to hear of Yanassi's passing. I think he knows there's more to the story, but the people of Avaris do not need any more drama at the moment.

What they need is a strong leader. With all the recent upheavals, the council and other prominent Hyksos have lent their full support to Pepi as he attempts to placate the princess's parents and calm the city.

"You really believe the Hyksos spy is our brother?" Ky's brown eyes, so like my father's and Pepi's, are wide. He seems stunned by his own actions in the day's events but is soothed by a small portion of the mandrake concoction Tany brewed in our absence. Kazir took a large batch to the other palace, where the rulers of the Hyksos and Theban dynasties are attempting to repair their damaged relations. With luck, the love root will have a calming effect on all involved.

"I believe he is." I do not go into the details of the third prophecy, not wanting to further increase the guilt my brother may feel at being a potential threat to thousands. He's been through enough for one day.

"Ky." It is Ahmes. The shaved healer approaches, hands clasped behind his back. "Pharaoh and Queen Anat are leaving the capital. Your presence is required at once."

"Greetings, Ahmes," I say to the physician, my former teacher and my father's protege.

"Hello, Sesha," he says, cautious. I introduce the two healers, who regard each other with professional curiosity. "You are well, then, among the Hyksos?"

"I am, thank you." I hesitate. "How are things with Pharaoh and the queen?"

"The princess is working her magic. Now that their son is returned" — he nods at Ky, whose life he once saved with the scroll's help, performing a delicate surgery to drain the excess fluid from his skull — "they are slowly calming. I think the restorative tonic brought by the other healer is working." His mouth twitches. "Though Queen Anat is still calling for heads over the abduction of the young prince."

"I am glad the royal family feels such strong affection for my brother." I am careful to keep any resentment from my voice.

"He is important to them." Ahmes hesitates. "Ky is a future heir to the Black Land."

The way he says the last statement makes the hairs on my arms ripple. In that instant, I wonder if Queen Anat is aware of the prophecies. *But how?* An image of the cooing priestess doves comes to mind; is it possible she intercepted one? Perhaps a little bird told her. Uncertainly, I look at my brother. His colour is better, and is it my imagination, or is there a faint whiff of satisfaction in his manner?

"With Pepi on the throne, it is time for peace," I say firmly to both of them. Though there will be no immediate wedding, I know Merat will choose to stay in Avaris. She and Pepi will likely marry, and the nations will be restored to harmony. For forty years, at least.

Ahmes nods. "May it be so."

"Ky." I turn to my brother, wishing I could keep him by my side but knowing the royals would never allow it. "I love you. Be well and take care. We will see each other again."

The sweet child I once knew embraces me, now a young man, destined for great things. "Be well, Sesha."

We stand on the banks, watching Pharaoh's massive ship sail into the sun. Pepi declares that Khyan's palace be filled in the next few days, in honour of both the king's and Yanassi's passing. He, Merat, and everyone at the old palace will move into the new one vacated by Pharaoh's family.

The Theban dynasty stands erect on the ship. I wave to my brother, praying the brutality he's witnessed does not damage him. He waves back, making no promises. My eyes meet Queen Anat's, which hold a faint gleam of triumph. If I had to guess, I'd say she still has the original scroll. And of course, she has my brother. Crooked Nose, slightly the worse for wear, stands sulking behind them. Beside him is the Nubian mercenary, who was rewarded as promised and has found new employment. I wonder if he ever located the gemstone. Paser, Reb, and I have decided to remain in Avaris, to work as healers and as ambassadors between the kingdoms. Pepi's asked us to transcribe his collection of scrolls, ensuring they will be around for future generations. He is building a bigger scriptorium, off the new medical wing. I am to oversee it, working alongside Paser, Reb, and Tany, who also decided to remain in Avaris for a time, instead of returning immediately to the priestesses. Reb may have something to do with that.

The ship passes boats on their way into port — more wedding attendees who will be sandblasted to hear all that has taken place — before it finally glides from sight. Despite already missing my brother fiercely, I know that though our lives are on different paths, they will intertwine again one day.

With any luck, it will not be on a battlefield.

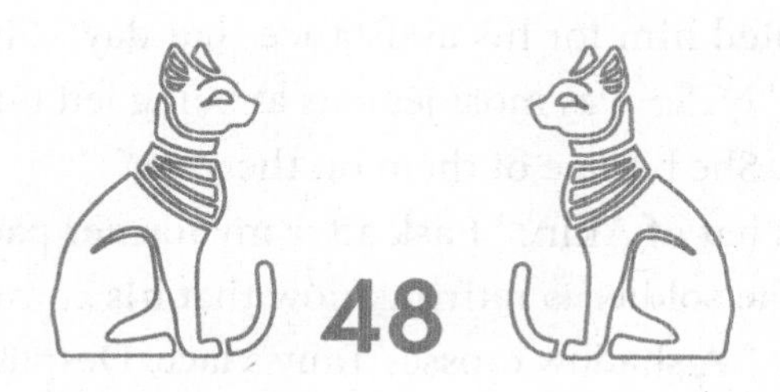

# 48

A DECAN LATER, AFTER the mourning period and Pepi's official induction ceremony, Paser, Reb, Tany, and I carefully pack up the remaining scrolls, sifting through the events of that fateful day.

"I am still unclear on how the chariot was suited and waiting for us," Reb says.

"Oh," Tany says, with a modest smile. "That was me."

"You?" Reb gapes at her. "How did you know — never mind." He shakes his head.

"I thought you were brewing the potion." Paser drapes a linen over a basket of scrolls to protect them during their transfer. "When did you have time to ready the horses?"

"I asked one of the soldiers for help," she says. "Your cousin, Son of Ramose, affixed the animals to the chariot with a few of his companions. Pepi has promoted him for his assistance that day." She grins again. "Nefer was most jealous at being left out of the action. She bit one of them on the arm."

"What of Akin?" I ask after my former patient.

"The soldier is retiring, now that his commander is gone." A shadow crosses Tany's face. Despite everything, Yanassi was still her cousin. I know Pepi mourns him, as well. They both grew up with the chieftain. "Pepi asked him to stay on and train others how to ride. Akin knows his horses."

I think of the soldier's wife, Amara, and her sister, Alit, and make a note to visit them next week, once the move to the palace is complete. I will also see if Alit will loan me her cat to help keep the new scriptorium pest-free. I'm not sure what I will have to give up for Temit. Alit strikes me as a shrewd bargainer.

Pepi sticks his head in, Merat behind him. "How are things?" he asks.

"Very well … Brother." I send him a warm smile, which he returns. The endearment gives me a strange bittersweet feeling. Though no one can replace Ky, Pepi gives me joy, not only in and of himself, but in a way that also brings my father's spirit close.

Just yesterday, Pepi and I'd moved aside one of the heavy woven baskets filled with scrolls blocking the secret exit of the scriptorium. There, carved into the stone, were the names *Ay* and *Kalali*, encircled by the *shen*, the symbol for eternity, confirming any lingering doubts.

I do not bear my father a grudge for his first love. I look at Merat — shining with happiness at finding it at last with someone who returns it in equal amounts. This life is too short to pine too long for one who does not return your affections the way you want them to. I know that now.

I also know my father loved my mother fiercely; he chose to make his life, and have my brother and me, with her. But he also created Pepi with Kalali, and even though Kalali never informed him of his son's existence, one should not be sad about having another family member to love.

Paser comes behind me and leans over my shoulder. "Seeing as how we finally have some time in which we are not racing around unearthing precious documents and unraveling earth-shattering prophecies, I was wondering if you'd care to teach me your famous recipe for bowel bind this evening?" he whispers. A warm glow spreads through my body, and I wonder if I sparkle as brilliantly as the priestess stones, under the face of my sun.

"I can think of nothing I'd like better," I say. Reb and Tany laugh at something Merat says. The princess catches my eye, and we smile at one another; we will be in each other's lives always.

"Here, Sesha." Pepi reaches into his robes and pulls out our copy of Imhotep's scroll. "I would like this one transcribed first, please."

I take the precious papyrus in my hand, and Tany suddenly gets a blank look on her face, the same one that appears when she's about to say something … prophetic.

"Edwin Smith" pops out of her mouth.

"What is that?" Reb asks, confused. "An incantation?"

"I don't know," she says, looking equally flummoxed. "It just came to me."

"What strange words," Merat murmurs.

I look down at the document in my hand. "This has certainly caused a lot of fuss."

"Ah, but words are important," Pepi reminds me. "They are the most powerful tool on earth."

"Which is why we should be mindful of their use," Reb agrees, looking at Tany, "both spoken and written ones."

"Said like a true scribe," Paser laughs. He picks up the basket of scrolls to carry over to the new palace and is followed out by Reb, who carries his own basket. Tany and Merat chat as they leave the scriptorium behind them. Tany has been regaling the princess with tales of her time with the priestesses; Merat seems fascinated by the sect. The oracle has sent them a reassuring word with a promise to return in three moons. She hopes the priestesses will not be overly displeased by her decision.

Pepi and I are left standing there, alone, and the former spy, now Hyksos king, faces me.

"I know why you did not want the prophecy to concern you," he says quietly. "Being responsible for a kingdom and the peace of its people is an enormous weight to carry."

"You do not bear it alone," I say, with a nod at our friends, our family, whose departures magnify the echo of the emptied scriptorium.

"I am grateful for that." Pepi's eyes wander to the hidden passageway, where our parents' names are inscribed. "Often these past months, I believed I had no one." I know he is thinking of his mother, of Tany's assumed death, of his dark nights in a pit. "When my uncle denied my parentage, I was devasted. It felt like he did not think me worthy of being his son."

"He loved you," I remind him gently. "It was not a rejection, only his truth. He made you co-regent. He knew your worth."

"I know."

Tany has admitted that during those moments she had alone with the king, he shared with her the prophecies that the previous oracle had made of his own future. She had foretold of the circumstances around his successorship, saying he would have to make a pivotal choice among contenders.

"And though Khyan did not sire you, my brother, there is another great man who did." I wave the scroll in my hands, our father's and my transcription, breathing in the scent of my trade, our legacy to the world. "Come," I say, holding the papyrus and my other hand out to Pepi. "I will tell you of him."

After all, to an Egyptian, there is nothing more important than being remembered.

# Author's Note

SECRETS OF THE SANDS began with Sesha's scroll, the Edwin Smith Medical Papyrus, and imagining who could've authored this real-life ancient artifact. This fascinating document led me to the discovery of the Hyksos people, as well as their place in one of Ancient Egypt's most mysterious pockets of time, the Second Intermediate Period. While this is a work of fiction, the central Hyksos figures in it are loosely based on real people from this era and the little we know about them. In particular, this novel is a reimagining of how the Hyksos king Apepi came to power and is a creative snapshot of his and his people's story.

As with any historical fiction, I strived to be meticulous in my research while being mindful of my own lens with which I view the world and recognizing that this story is set approximately 3,500 years in the past. There will always be conflicting theories on events so long ago, particularly as we undertake further research — who knows what we have yet to uncover!

I believe that experiencing the past in such a visceral way allows us an enhanced perspective of our present. It gives us an appreciation and empathy for those who came before us and connects all of us going through life, at this particular moment in time, together. Thank you for joining me on this adventure; it is both an honour and a privilege to bring the past alive for readers and, as a modern-day scribe, one I undertake with the utmost respect, passion, and love.

Alisha Sevigny

# Acknowledgements

THIS SCRIBE GRATEFULLY acknowledges the people who helped make this series possible and is likely forgetting someone from the following list.

To Jess Shulman and Shari Rutherford, for their superior editing skills, and Jenny McWha, for managing the book writing process (and being flexible with deadlines). To my fabulous art director, Laura Boyle, and amazing illustrator, Queenie Chan, for another exceptionally stunning cover. To everyone at Dundurn and to Kristina Jagger, for being my cheerful go-to for all things.

To my fellow scribes who urge me onward when it all becomes a bit much, particularly the wildly talented Meaghan McIsaac and Angela Misri.

To my Ancient Civilizations teacher, Mrs. Fulsom, who was delighted by the intensity with which I devoured all things Ancient Egyptian, and who bestowed upon teenage me the Comparative Civilizations award. To all the librarians and teachers who work tirelessly to get books into the hands of young readers, who create safe spaces and who water our future seedlings of creative and literary geniuses — thank you for all you do.

To the doctors, nurses, support workers, and healers who have cared for others with unwavering dedication and tireless efforts since the beginning of time — you are most appreciated.

To my junior readers Ariana Arruda Starzenska, Lucy McGeachie, Aira Unterman, and Charlotte Finlayson. Thank you for your thoughtful feedback and continued harassment as to when the next book was coming out, thus encouraging me to keep writing it.

To the friends, family and readers who support me — I couldn't do this without you.

To my incredible husband, Aaron, and cherished children, Aira and Nolan, you three are my inspiration and heart — thank you for your patience when the words call me away. I write them for you.

This book is dedicated to all of the above and to my father-in-law, Paul, and my dear friend Natalie, who both passed away during its writing, leaving those of us who knew them "to mourn and remember them, which it is our utmost privilege to do." To Natalie's children, Madalena and Patrick: your mother loved you with the ferocity of a thousand lionesses.

To the rest of you dreamers, explorers, and adventurers: may you live your journey to the fullest, with good friends at your side, your hearts lighter than Ma'at's feather of truth.

Xoxo, Alisha

# About the Author

ALISHA SEVIGNY is the author of the YA contemporary romances *Summer Constellations* and *Kissing Frogs*, as well as a baby board book, *Give Me A Snickle!* She is a film school graduate, actor, former literary agent, and a freelance editor who enjoys mentoring new writers. Alisha has also taught English and yoga, and is a certified reiki healer and professional tarot card reader. She was born and raised in Kitimat, British Columbia, and is an avid traveller, nature enthusiast, and lover of ancient civilizations.